JUST ONE MORE

BOOK 2

LaQuarn Michaels

JUST ONE MORE 2

Copyright © 2011 by LaQuarn Michaels

ISBN 978-0-9801585-4-0

Library of Congress Control Number: 2012931598

Printed and bound in the Unites States of America.

First paperback edition, January 2012.

This is a work of fiction. Names, characters, places and incidents either are the product of the author's imagination or are used fictitiously. Any resemblance to actual persons, living or dead, events, business establishments or locals is entirely coincidental.

Published by:

Transcending Works, LLC
P.O. Box 647
Lovejoy, Georgia 30250

For K.C.A II
Love You Always

Also by LaQuarn Michaels

The Last One

Just One More

Just One More 2

CHAPTER 21

D r. Milton leaned one arm against the wall, cornering Lou-Lou's movements.

"Who would have thought huh?"

Her eyes roamed his face clandestinely. "Small world," she said grabbing for her mink, ducking beneath his armpit, and sidestepping her way towards the door. He helped drape her fur over her shoulders, raking his fingers through her hair.

"Impressive. Your hair is trackless."

"Black doesn't always equal track."

"I didn't mean to insinuate that it did." He pointed over his shoulder. "Bunny's a proud advocate of the track." Lou-Lou couldn't help but laugh, for she could only imagine what else was fake on that woman.

"You should stay. Have another cocktail."

"I don't think so. You should get back to your friends."

"They'll be fine. Rose is obsessing about the 60's when burning your bra and bridges was a sign of liberation and women freedom."

"How entertaining." Lou-Lou finger waved goodbye to a few guest who stumbled their way into the hall.

"Party inside guys," he said, holding the door for them to re-enter. She moved swiftly towards the elevators, with Dr. Milton hot on her heels. "What's the rush love?"

"Look, Bradley and I haven't exactly been on the same page."

He smirked. "Really, I hadn't noticed."

"You're funny."

"He's in the bathroom. Might be there for a while since he'd downed the whole bottle of Crown."

"My point exactly. He's a nasty drunk. Things will turn ugly if I don't leave."

He took a peek at her shoes. Bunny had been talking non-stop about how cute they were. "Six inches of pain. Sexy though," he complimented.

"Beauty hurts," she said leaning in, mashed the button for the next ride down.

"So you're the one who got away. My brother talked about you all the time, but with my practice and other obligations, I never had the chance to fly out to New York and meet you. Sorry I missed the engagement party."

"Don't explain. Bradley wasn't exactly the one with an hour or two to spare for family gatherings. Unless of course it was over liquor and Black Jack, in Vegas."

He chuckled. "Vegas. His poison."

The elevator doors opened. She stepped onto the lift. He followed. She mashed the *Lobby* button and then backed herself into a corner.

"Father warned him about Sin City. But you know Bradley, big talk, always showing off, putting his wallet where his mouth is. He finally wrote a check his ass couldn't cash." He laughed.

She glanced at him, not exactly seeing the humor in it all.

"Father said it would happen. You know the old man prophesized that Bradley would come back begging on his hands and knees before he reached thirty five."

"Begging?"

"Bradley was always a self starter, self motivated, *I can do it on my own* kind of a person. Self sufficient pretentious bastard if you ask me."

He laughed wickedly. "They've bumped heads from the time he could talk. His first word was *Mama*. His next, *money*."

"Is that right?"

"Bradley never compromised for father. Did you know he started his first business at ten?"

"No, wasn't aware of that."

"It was successful too."

"Let me guess, a lemonade stand on wheels," she said, jokingly.

"*Au contrair mon frere'*... he did indeed turned lemons into lemonade. He advised gramps on how to maneuver a couple of million. The old man made a sizable profit listening to the boy genius."

"A couple of million is hardly lemons," she said.

"Bradley earned every last cent of his inheritance by the time he was out of middle school. In high school, Father wanted him to play Lacrosse, but Bradley did wonders with the rock in his hands. He knew how to shuck and jive like Magic, and Jordan. Father said basketball was dominated by the blacks and that he would never make it off the bench."

"Did he make it off the bench?"

"Every game. Got a four year ride off the hoop and ball. That killed father."

"Why?"

"Well, because father wanted to cut the check. Send his first born off in style. Scholarships were for the under privileged. Father's wallet gave him respect. Slapping a check down for Bradley's education would have been an honor. His father did it for him. He wanted to do the same for his sons."

"Weird."

"What?"

"Nothing." She kept her comments to herself.

"Eventually they got past it, started to repair their relationship until..."

The elevator doors opened, he allowed her to step out first. They walked slowly through the empty lobby.

"The next big blow up damaged them for good. Father wanted him to take up *Law*, and follow in his footsteps at the Firm. Bradley considered, but at the end of the day, he loved numbers. He jumped both feet into the financial realm of things. Father was pissed. He practically disowned him for being disobedient."

"Damn. That's extreme."

"You don't know the half. Father cut him out the will. For years he wanted my grandfather to do the same but he refused. Gramps and Bradley were like this." He twisted his fingers.

"When gramps got sick, my father took over. With Power of Attorney our father made some adjustments. As gramps became more senile and every bit of child like, father gained total power over the family dynasty. Bradley's inheritance is no longer a topic of discussion."

"But you said yourself, he earned it."

"Gramps never put that in writing. Had he made it a contract, work for hire, there wouldn't have been a damn thing father could do."

"And your father knew this because he's a dirty ass lawyer."

He paused his stroll.

Embarrassment covered her face. "Forgive me."

"Don't apologize. My family is complicated."

"Well at least Bradley was successful. He did well for himself. It's just that the economy set him back," she defended.

"Gambling set him back. You said so yourself."

He touched the side of her face, she brushed his hand away.

I'm sooo not feeling you right now.

"You okay?" he asked.

"Oh, I'm good," she said with certainty.

"You seem upset?"

"I said I'm good."

She checked her watch. The only gift from Bradley she hadn't given away to the greasy pond man. She handed her ticket to the Valet Attendant and watched as he scurried off to get her car. Moments later her *Gerber* baby came whirling around the corner. Rims and paint sparkling.

"So, same time next week?" he asked.

She slipped in behind the wheel. "Anything for you, just call and confirm the date, time, place. I'll make sure I have everything you need."

He leaned in for a kiss. She gave him a peck on the cheek. Coldness registered across her face. He felt her chill. She couldn't help but think of Bradley, and how unfairly he'd been treated. His own father treated him like shit, and she'd only added insult to injury.

He backed away as she shifted her gear to **D**. Just as she was about to pull away, and head back to her hotel room, she caught a glimpse of the poor bastard staggering off the elevator. Tilted hat, leather coat half on-half off, drink still in hand, sipping.

"See what I mean. Father said he would fall off his high horse."

She shifted the gear back to **P**, opened the door, knocking the doctor in the groin. She quickly moved towards Bradley, stopping inches from his face. Dilated pupils, funk-box breath, flushed skin. She adjusted his coat, ran her fingers through his messy hair and smacked his face.

"Hey, whatchu do that for?"

"Shut up and walk."

His wobbly legs barely kept the course, as she yanked him by the arm.

"Bryan, that you?"

Dr. Milton backed away, clearly scared of what Bradley might do in his drunken state. Instead of leaving well enough alone, he decided to mention the one person that made his brothers blood boil. "Father will be thrilled to know that you're still hitting the bottle."

Bradley threw a punch, knocking his smug crooked.

"*Ahhhh.*"

"I've got more for the old man. Go run and tell that," Bradley spat.

"Get in the car," Lou-Lou demanded, shoving Bradley head first into the front seat.

Eight and a half blocks away, they pulled into the parking lot of the Embassy.

Bradley was in a comatose state, snoring like he'd swallowed a tractor trailer. One hundred eighty pounds lay slumped over the dashboard, reeking to high heavens. Lifting him by herself wasn't an option, and leaving him there until he sobered would prove to be catastrophic.

"If you hurl, that's your ass."

Lou-Lou did the only logical thing known to a woman in distress. She dipped into her purse and paid hotel Security a crisp hundred to load Bradley's drunken ass onto the brass luggage carrier. She paid an extra hundred to have him lifted and tossed into the tub, clothes and all.

5

Hours later she felt his arms wrapped around her waist. Hard organ pressed against her backside. She wiped the crust from her eyes, looked up and noticed that he'd ordered breakfast. French toast, link sausages and scrambled eggs, lightly drizzled in hot maple syrup.

"Coffee?"

She groaned. "Yes, please."

He rolled out of bed, family jewels dancing with each step towards the bar. She watched as he tore open two packs of Splenda, added two mini-moos and stirred. Just the way she liked it.

"Because of you, I'm like brand new." He took slow movements back towards the bed.

"Be careful. It's hot," he cautioned.

She sat up, positioned her back firmly against the leathered headboard.

"Thanks."

He scratched his five o'clock shadow, and shot her a wry smile. "Awkward night huh?"

She shrugged as if their three-way didn't mean a thing.

"Thanks for, you know, rescuing me."

She shrugged again, placing the hot cup onto the nightstand.

"Smells good," she pointed, wanting him to fetch her food.

He watched her go to town. Metal to glass. Clink to clank. A long disgusting belch added to her symphony entitled *"Hunger"*. She swallowed more coffee, and belched again. "Ribs were touching my back. Food last night was for the birds." She kicked her long legs over the side, and skipped towards the bathroom. He busied himself with the tray, sipping what was left of the coffee.

"Damn."

"What happened?" she called.

"*Ah*, nothing." Hot liquid splattered the marbled faced stand. He grabbed a towel. Sponging away until the surface was dry. He patted his hand against the top. *Sticky.*

The shower came on. So did the shower radio. Words from a song he'd heard just recently echoed from the ceramic walls. Urban music wasn't exactly his forte. His exposure to the culture of hip-hop came by living with Lou-Lou. The woman behind that bathroom door kept him up to speed on the latest. He imagined her swaying her hips, and popping her ass to a tune created by people who looked just like her.

Steam bellowed out as the bathroom door swung opened.

"What you grinning about?"

"Was I grinning?" He slapped his own face.

Towel wrapped her hips, girls sitting properly, hair tied up in a scrunchy. She snatched her purse from inside the armoire, checked her phone. There was a missed call from Roy.

"It rang while you were in the shower. Who's Roy?"

"Stay out my things please."

She hit the pump several times, squirting a considerable amount of lotion into her palm. As she lathered in agave and Jojoba oil he focused in on her navel. His eyes scanned her full frontal then landed at her toes.

"Roy your new man?"

He stood, pumped a few squirts into his own hand. He rubbed her back, up and down, slowly massaging the cream into her skin. He kissed her neck. She stopped him.

"Don't take this the wrong way, but I'm not looking to start nothing."

"But last night..."

"Business. Nothing more, nothing less."

He took two steps back. "Business huh? Just what kind of business you into these days?"

"Things that are known shall not be explained." She winked.

Thong covered her *Va-Jay-Jay*. Long sleeve thermal slipped over her bra-less chest. Jeans, socks, trainers covered her feet.

"Comfortable?" he asked.

"Very."

She grabbed a nip from the bar. Swallowed. Grabbed another. Swallowed. Fire oozed down her throat, opening her chest. She chased it down with a sip of Sprite.

"How'd you meet Bryan?"

"Through a friend."

"Let me guess, Caroline?"

She looked surprised.

"Did she not mention we were *brothers* when she set you two up?"

"No, her ass didn't mention it. I wish she would have."

Hearing Caroline's name made her wonder exactly how Africa was treating her friend. *I've got the Global Phone. I'm still reachable.* Lou-Lou couldn't imagine escaping the tabloids for the sake of the church. As far as she was concerned, the church could kiss her ass. Baby or no baby, there was no way she would veil her face, or in Caroline's case, her body.

"You're dealing now?"

"More like supplying a demand. It's a temporary gig."

"Aren't you scared of getting busted?"

"Scared money-don't make money."

He lifted the digital camera off the bed and scanned the photos. "I'm assuming it pays well." She unloaded some shopping bags. Macy's, Vickie Secret, Bloomingdales items covered the foot of the bed. She grabbed the matching cashmere hat and scarf set she'd been looking for.

"I do alright."

"This blue coup says you're doing better than alright."

She snatched the camera, placing it inside the suitcase with the rest of her valuables. It made no sense to unpack for fear she might need to book out at any given moment. She stuffed her purchases back into her suitcase.

"Nothing wrong with upgrading," she defended.

"The insurance company still has yet to find the Benz. You cost me a lot."

"I cost you nothing," she snapped.

"I drove pass the house a few times, mostly after midnight to avoid small talk," he confessed. She turned to face him. She loved that house. So did he.

"Really?"

"The bank has scheduled a public auction. It's predicted to sell for a third less than what I originally paid for it. Fucking-fucked up economy got me fucked up, broke. *Shit.*"

She snickered. Feeling her nip.

"Oh it's funny?"

"Not even. Just laughing because…"

There was a knock at the door. They looked at each other.

"Expecting company?" he asked.

"No. Check." Her voice low, barely audible.

Bradley inched his eye over the peep-hole. He twisted back, looked at her.

"You dry cleaned my suit?"

She nodded, grabbed two twenties from her purse, and tipped the poor bastard responsible for cleaning the barf.

"Get dressed."

"Just like that, huh?"

"What else is there to discuss?"

He slammed the plastic covered suit down on the bed. "You have a lot of explaining to do. What business do you have with my kid brother?"

"Oh baby, he's no kid." She wet her lips.

She fastened the clasp on her watch, tightened her diamond studs. Next she grabbed the big metal prong brush with the plastic tips, and styled her hair into a neat pony tail.

"How long you been fucking him?"

She paused. Sat the brush down, and placed a concerned hand onto his shoulder.

"Have a seat."

He did.

"Who are you?"

"Lou-Ann Dobbs."

He shook his head. "Try again."

Sympathetic eyes roamed his face.

"You're dealing drugs, driving around in expensive cars, who the hell are you?"

"Don't hurt your brain. I'm Lou-Ann Dobbs. I do what it takes to stay on top."

He hissed. "Obviously."

"Listen. I know all about your pops. Dr. Mil… I mean Bryan told me."

He stood. "Told you what?"

"Your father is a smug son-a-bitch who can't stand to see you make it."

He yanked his suit off the hanger. Angry jerks and tugs cause him to work up a sweat.

"I understand why you refused to ask him for help, and I admire you for that."

He stopped. Sat down. Shirt undone. Pants undone. Life undone. Holding on by threads. Sanity, slipping by the day. Childhood issues breaking him down. He cried into an open hand. After his meltdown, he stood. Wiped his blood shot face, and continued to dress. She tossed him a nip. He tossed it back.

"Pour me a grown man drink. No ice."

Hard rock glass.

Five nips.

He downed his poison in on gulp.

She leaned her butt against the dresser, legs crossed, arms folded. He pointed towards the armoire. "You sure you know how to handle that thing."

"What thing?"

She sprung up, moved quickly across the room, stopped in front of the armoire. Her gat was where she left it. She ran back in the opposite direction, yanked opened the end table, wiped her forehead. She closed the drawer. Everything was in place.

"After all these years you don't trust me?"

She lifted one shoulder. "Has nothing to do with trust. Circumstances changed, therefore changing people."

He held out both hands, expecting to receive. "May I see the gun?"

"Never that."

"*Ah*, c'mon, let me hold it."

"No."

"Make me another drink."

"No."

"Don't be such a bitch about it."

She gave him a look.

"Just one more. Please."

She tossed him one nip. This time he took what he could get.

"I'm checking into the Betty Ford center next week. My father is paying the bill. It's the least he could do after stealing my inheritance," he said, sipping his nip, liquor barely wetting his tongue.

"California?"

He nodded, rubbing an open hand over his head. *Stressed.*

"Went to that fuck-face for a loan. I actually humbled myself and asked my damn father for help. Two hundred grand. Seed money. A couple of nickels by his standards."

"And?"

"He laughed, told me I was a loser, and that he was embarrassed to call me son. Then fuck-face hung up on me."

"Damn. That's harsh."

"Bryan convinced him to help me get my life back on track. He fed him some bull about our mother turning in her grave, and how it was his duty as a father to make sure I was okay. He refused to cut me a check, but did agree to pay for treatment."

"You do need help."

He looked up at her. "You don't think I know that?" He stood, walked towards the bar, and grabbed another rock glass, a handful of nips. He sat back down, poured, and stirred his concoction. "I lost my job, my house, my cars, my money, *you.*"

Tears slipped from his red rimmed eyes. "The bottle helps. The bottle hurts," he lifted his glass. *Bottoms up.*

"Bryan is forbid to loan me anything. Fuck-face threatened to erase his name from the will too if he does. Bunny used her credit card to book me a flight to Atlanta for the party. She even bought me this suit, and those shoes. Bryan's help is untraceable."

She shook her head. Bradley had quickly become a case of *Hosea Feeds the Hungry.* "What you need with two hundred grand?"

He smiled. Wiggled his toes. Got happy.

"What's up with the stupid grin?"

"Since I can't get to Vegas, I was thinking of bringing Vegas to me."

She sucked her teeth. "Here we go again."

He hopped up, swallowed what was left of his drink. He patted his pants pockets.

"Where are my cigarettes?"

Lou-Lou opened the top drawer to the dresser, tossed him his smokes, his wallet, and his cell phone. The small bag of coke stayed.

"Matches?"

She pointed towards the bar. Fire sparked the tip. He closed his eyes, and inhaled.

"Where was I?"

"Two hundred thousand. Bringing Vegas to Atlanta. You gambling *again.*"

"Not just gambling, but hosting a party. I'm talking about inviting some of my high roller friends down to my estate for some gaming."

She couldn't help but crack up. "High roller friends... Estate... *Betty Ford Center here we come.*"

"*Ha. Ha. Ha...* laugh all you want but I'm still connected."

She twisted her lip, "Connected how?"

"Don't worry how, just know that I am. I just need seed money. Show money. Enough money to see my plan to the end." He bit down on his bottom lip, million dollar thoughts flooding him all at once.

Lou-Lou had thoughts of her own. Vegas style gambling, Estate partying, big wigs with million dollar hands, in one room, at one time.

Cha-Ching!

"Two hundred thou- Is that all?"

He snapped back into the now, looked at her. *"Is that all?"* he mocked, "As if you got that kind of dough."

"What if I do?"

A flutter of excitement went through him. He stood, sparked another cigarette, and started to pace back and forth. Chain smoking calmed his nerves.

"Fuck Lou-Lou, if you got your hands on that kind of cash, and you're willing to invest..."

"If you're connected like you say you are, and your plan is air tight, I'm willing."

"Oh, baby they still know my name. Numbers is my game," he said in his cocky *I'm the man* tone.

"My plan will go off without a hitch."

"You sure, I mean this is a lot of dough I'm fronting you."

"Don't worry doll. You'll see that back and then some. I'm connected to the cards baby. Came out the womb holding the deck. I play to win."

The Bradley she'd grown to love was stripped of his titles, his possessions, his money, his arrogance, and was now hungry. *Pressure bust pipes.*

"My good friend Rose will rent me her place."

"You mean crazy Rose from last night?"

He nodded. "She has an estate home in Windward she hardly ever stays at. She spends most of her time in her midtown loft. We can rent it for a couple thousand, which is really cheap."

"*Windward*, never heard of it."

"Up north, Alpharetta, down 400. Her home is not too far from Lake Lanier."

"Nice."

"Oh, better than nice. It's the *crème de la crème*. Her digs are *totally* posh. Elegance radiate from the time you whip onto the acreage property. It's *totally* private, and *totally* perfect to host a party there."

"Okay, I'm *totally* excited," she teased.

He was turning her on. His big money talk had her wanting to give him some of her kitty. Daddy Warbucks had his mojo back. She finally had him exactly where she needed him.

Cha-Motherfucking-Ching!

CHAPTER 22

The minority report was on cable. Tom cruise was in the year 2054 intercepting murders, and arresting would-be killers. Genetically altered humans with special powers could foresee future crimes, therefore changing the destiny of the victim before they caught it in the noodle.

Roy settled in the recliner, left hand down his boxer shorts, playing with his pubes. Sci-Fi flicks made him think. Paranormal events, the far and beyond, the possibilities of life outside the realm of planet earth always intrigued him.

"It's all bullshit," Kema spat.

She stood in the window, wearing an oversized Hawks jersey. Her hip poked out, puffing a blunt, watching the girls play Double Dutch across the street, beneath the big oak tree with no leaves.

"Remember the guy from the beginning of the movie?" she asked.

Roy grabbed the remote, turned up the volume a notch.

"The poor bastard came home to find his wife fucking some other man."

She tapped her forehead theatrically. "In his mind, he knew he would kill them both. Yes, that tiny voice said, *kill that bitch and her man.*"

"*Shush,*" Roy said, without looking back at her.

"It was only a thought. I've had plenty of thoughts like that, plenty of times before." She took a tote, coughed. Lungs burned, eyes watered, saliva dripped from her agape mouth. She bought her burning bush eye level, trying to remember if she'd rolled the *Kush*, or was it the *Purp*?

"Tom and his vigilante ass came busting through the door, sparing that bitch life," she said angrily. "I mean who the fuck is he, God?"

"Shush."

She looked over her shoulder; saw that Roy hadn't moved an inch. His eyes glued to the flat screen that mounted the small fire place. She flipped him the bird.

The girls across the street were getting it in. Legs moving, arms wailing, back arched forward, face-facing the ground, pounding the pavement with their tennis shoes. Two of her trusted buddies on each end, whipping the telephone wire to her rhythm. The faster she went the faster they turned.

"He hadn't touched a single hair on her blonde head, but he gets thrown in the slammer."

Roy whipped his neck in her direction. "Put that shit out," he barked.

"I'm stressed."

"I'm trying to watch my movie. Put that shit out."

"How many times are you going to watch this stupid movie? You've seen it a gazillion times."

"Don't worry about all that."

"Okay, fine. Watch your stupid movie."

He turned back, faced the tube.

"Aren't you going to ask why I'm stressing?"

"Nope."

"That's fucked up Roy."

He gave her a look, and then settled back into his comfy position. Hand shoved down his pants, rolling his own dice.

Fuck that, I'm smoking.

Kema pulled on her desire again, flicking ashes into the glass tray on the window ledge. The group of girls out front doubled in size. The crew from up the street made their way onto the block. A friendly competition was underway.

"I remember when I used to jump. Back in the day..."

She took one last pull; outted her smoke, pulling the drapes closed.

"... I was the Queen. None of those chicks could mess with me. My movements were precise." She demonstrated by jumping sideways into the invisible rope, legs charged up, running in place, turning, dipping down to touch the floor, whipping back, then forth, then back.

She stood on that same block, right across the street, underneath that same big oak tree, just five summers ago. Competitions weren't so friendly during that time. The losing team usually didn't take the *L* so gracefully. It never failed, somebody usually got to talking greasy and before you knew it, blows were exchanged.

Kema stopped, caught her breath. The scar above her left brow reminded her of one incident in particular. Charity, her childhood nemesis had gotten beaten fair and square. However, according to Charity her turners weren't playing by the rules. It was her theory that one of the girls sabotaged her jump by turning off key. Loud talk escalated into pushing and shoving. A good old fashion fight broke out, and Kema's crew was wrecking shop. Dog walking Charity big ass was a pleasure. All was in Kema's favor up until she tripped off the sidewalk. Head clipped the bumper of a 1981 Buick Skylark, knocking her out cold.

The buzz from her cell phone invaded her thoughts. It was her brother Ace calling. She winced. *I forgot to call him back.* She opened the flip. "Before you say anything..."

Ace cut into her words. "You don't love me no more?"

A smile big as the sun surfaced. "You know you still my number one. I've been meaning to call you."

Roy looked up at her. She couldn't tell if he was feeling a bit green, or if he was just annoyed. He was unreadable like that.

"Thought you were coming to the wedding, what happened?" Ace asked.

"Something came up. How was it?"

"A hot ghetto mess, but it was all love. Saw some of my peoples from back in the day. Remember that fool Vick?"

"Yeah, what up with that fool?"

"Fat as shit. I'm talking five stomachs. He gotta weigh about four hunnit easy."

"Shut up. Not fine ass Vick."

Roy shot her an evil glance. She blew air kisses at him, and mouthed *It's my brother*. He shrugged, pointed towards the tube. She took huge steps towards the tiny kitchen. Crown molding split the wall horizontally. Pink and yellow flowery wall paper at the top, creamy beige glossy paint at the bottom. Salmon colored laminate flooring had hints of gray in it.

"I hate this kitchen," she said, surveying the ugliness. The décor was dreadful.

"Told you, you would. Don't know what possessed you to move in that match box."

"It's grandma's house," she said sympathetically.

"It's old and creepy."

"It's been in the family almost fifty years."

"Fifty two to be exact, but still it's old and creepy."

"You think she killed him?"

"I don't want to talk about that," he said quickly.

Her brother Ace hated coming to stay with their grandma for the summer. He was scared of the spirit stories their big momma used to tell about their grandfather Big Bo. Rumor had it their grandma killed their grandfather with rat poison. Big momma told an entirely different story.

As far as they knew, Big Bo drowned in his own salvia, right there at the kitchen table. Big Momma said Big Bo staggered in from the juke joint one night, talking crazy and making threats. She left him at the table, and found him the morning after, blue in the face. No one really knows.

"The house has potential. Just need to get around to doing some work on it." She stared up at the water stain that was masked with many layers of paint. Brown water still forced its way through, reminding her that the roof needed replacing. She pulled the curtain, looked out onto the backyard space. She recalled many days playing out back, doing flips and sliding down the old dirt hill. She was a true *tom-boy* at heart.

"Still, I don't know how you do it."

A two seater oval shaped glass table was just the right size to squeeze into the breakfast nook. The kitchen was straight out the 80's era. New stainless steel appliances added a touch of modern day love.

"It's paid for, besides I love the neighborhood. We had some great times in this house." She let the curtain fall.

"Really, you love the neighborhood?"

"Shut up, don't wanna hear it."

"Your *neighborhood* has been on the news about four times this year alone."

"It's not that bad."

"Homicide, house fire, home invasion, hooker raid, need I continue?"

"I'm comfortable here."

"In the hood?"

"It's not the hood."

She opened the fridge, looked in, grabbed some deli sliced honey turkey, cheese, and squeeze bottled mayo.

"Spoke to the doctor today."

She placed the contents of her tasty sandwich on the table, took a seat. She'd been kicking herself for not having the time to stop in and check on her mother. Truth was, she couldn't stomach seeing her so frail and helpless. The same thing that took Big Momma out was now knocking at her own mother's door. She wondered if it would eventually come to claim her.

"What the doctors say?" she asked, bracing herself for the worse.

"Mommy not doing too well. They recommended this new treatment, but..."

"But what?"

"Her insurance will only cover eighty percent."

She shoved her once delectable meal away, placing an open hand against her head. "How much?"

"Like fifty."

"Thousand?"

"That's just an initial payment to jump start treatment. There's a total of three phases, each costing like fifty, total looking to be about one hunnit and fifty. Then there's..." He paused. "Are you crying?"

"No," she lied.

He continued, "Then there's her medication which insurance will cover, but the co-pays will add up and..."

She sniffled.

"You are crying."

"Boy, I'm good. Coming down with a cold," she grabbed a napkin, blew her nose.

"Doc said there's a fifty-fifty chance that the treatment will make her better, but he can't be certain."

"A hundred and fifty thousand still can't buy you certainty."

"I know."

She blew out air. "I'll get you the first fifty today."

"You got that kind of cheese?"

"*Hum*, not on hand, but I can go to the bank and withdraw it."

"Kema, what the hell are you into?"

"What do you mean?"

"Well..." he paused. "I've been watching the way you spend, and you're living in that fucked up bungalow in the most crudest part of town possible... talking about renovating... driving a Lexus, just bought me a brand new Tahoe... got momma living her last days looking off the lake... and on top of all that you about to drop fifty large to extend her expiration date."

He paused and took a deep breath.

Her eyes watered again.

"Let's not forget the help you extended when I was, you know diagnosed with post traumatic stress disorder."

She sat back in her seat, shook her head. Her brother was in fact a loon. He was crazy as a betsy bug. He slipped in and out of some traumatic place, often reliving some horrific time from when he was at war.

Ace had yet to tell her all that transpired while in Afghanistan. He spoke bits and pieces, and for him that was too much. His world had become some top secret mission. He was closed shut, a sealed envelope, an encrypted disk, with the word confidential stamped across his life. The *United States Military*, his puppet master.

"Those dreams, they starting up again," he admitted painfully.

"Are you taking your medication?"

"*Y*-yes, taking it, but I'm getting that itch again. Feeling like I wanna put a whole in something. Wanna blow shit up. I'm seeing blood all the time."

"Maybe you need to up the dosage. You should speak to your doctor about it."

"Maybe."

He was talking. This was good. He usually never talked about *it*. Solitude was his pleasure, seclusion, his best friend. Her brother kept things bottled, cork screwed and buried. He was the type to laugh, joke, shoot the breeze about everything beneath the sun, but when it was time to talk about Ace, he clammed up.

"Who was the chick you had over last night?"

"Bumped into an old friend from back in the day while out with the boys. Saw her at the restaurant, one thing led to another and she came back to my apartment."

"And."

"Things jumped off. Do I need to be specific?"

"Hellz no."

"She said I raped her."

Kema dropped the phone, picked it up. "Rape?" she whispered.

"Can you believe that?" A nervous chuckle escaped him.

"Are you sure nothing happened that would make her feel, you know, uncomfortable?"

"*Maybe* I was a little rough, cause' I did spank that ass, but rape? That's not even how I roll. Can't stand dudes who violate sisters, *women* period," he said, feeling relieved having told her.

"You explained this to her?"

"Of course, told her everything."

"Everything as in, *everything?*"

"Don't sound so surprised."

"She must be something special because you never talk about *it*."

"Guess I'm finally beginning to heal."

"You should call in sick today. We can meet up, have dinner, and do some shopping. Kick it like old times," she suggested.

"Can't."

"*Ah*, c'mon it'll be fun," she insisted.

"Don't you have company?" he said with a bit of a snarl.

"What makes you think that?" she quizzed.

"Took a wild guess."

She was invisible to Roy. He saw nothing but Tom's gay ass on the tube. And when that was over, he'd be sure to find something else to hold his attention.

"I'm sure he won't mind me slipping away for a few hours to be with my big bro."

"Who the hell is this cat? What kind of man doesn't want to meet his girl's family?"

She cleared her throat.

"Am I asking too many questions?"

"Sort of, kind of, I mean you haven't exactly dropped a name on your slut-bucket friend you picked up at the restaurant last night."

He laughed. "True. And she's no slut. In fact I was hoping you two meet before she heads back to New York. I'm thinking we link up at Houston's. You both can chitchat over spinach dip and cocktails while me and yah boy get more acquainted."

"The offer is cute, but...I don't know."

"Just think about it."

She promised that she'll give it some thought. "Wait, she's an up north chic? Oh, it'll never work."

"And why not, Miss I have all the answers?"

"Whatever. Trust your baby sis. It'll never work. I bet that chic high maintenance. And if you haven't noticed Bro, you ain't no baller."

He laughed. "Yeah, well I'll have you know my financial situation is about to change for the good."

She smiled. "Somebody's getting a raise?"

"You can call it that. And when I do, I'm treating you some place nice."

"*Ah* shucks now. I'm holding you to it."

"Do that."

"My *man* just walked in. Can I call you back?" she whispered.

"You mean that coward who refuses to meet me face to face?"

"Don't take it personal. He's not a people person."

"People person or not, you've been seeing scrams for a hot minute. Don't you think its only right I set eyes on him?"

Roy stood with the fridge door opened, his hand still shoved inside his shorts.

"You hungry baby?"

"What it look like?" Roy said, bending further to view his selection of edibles. Kema wasn't exactly Susie Homemaker, but she could make a decent grilled tuna-melt. Roy pulled back the lid on the tuna, made a face. "This shit stink."

"When the time is right, you'll meet him," she whispered into the receiver.

"Whatever. Tell scrams we need to have a sit-down. Man to man."

"I'll bring the money to you tonight," she said, refusing to relay his message.

"I'm working tonight."

"Tomorrow then."

"Why don't you go to the facility, speak with the doctors? Hear first hand what's required before you cough over that kind of money."

"*Hum*, well, I'll see if I can swing that way."

"Go see Mommy."

"Okay."

"I'm serious."

"Gotta run. Love you much."

She quickly hung up before he could say it back. She sat there, in her own world, thinking. Roy made a grunt noise. She narrowed her eyes in on him.

"My brother wants to meet you."

Roy gave her the evil eye. "What for?"

"He's curious to know who's got his baby sisters heart."

"Not interested."

"Why not?"

He hissed, "You fixing me some food or what?"

"Yes. I got you."

She pulled at the loaf of bread and began preparing Roy a *hungry-man* turkey and cheese. She carefully layered each slice neatly against the loaf.

"Remember that bad ass watch I bought the other day?"

He shrugged. "What about it?"

"Can't seem to find it. Have you seen it?"

"Wait, you drop ten stacks on a watch and can't find it?" He laughed.

As usual, he made her feel dumb. She prepared the rest of his meal in silence. "Damn, no thank you's?"

He bit into the sandwich, mouth filled to capacity, chewed and swallowed "You could have added a touch more of Mayo, but thanks."

I'll give you a touch of Mayo alright. "My bad, I'll make it better the next time."

"Let me catch the rest of this movie. Grab me a beer and some salt & vinegar chips."

If you stop grabbing at your dick long enough, maybe you could grab your own beer and chips, she thought, with a smile of course. It was the wrong time to irritate Roy, for she needed him more than he actually knew. Her mother needed treatment, and Roy was her money tree. With an icy cold beer in hand, she headed back into the living room. Tom Cruise still on the screen, locking folks up for "thinking" shit.

"Here you go baby."

"Good looking."

He handed her the plate. Every crumb devoured except for the ends, which Roy had the habit of pulling away like a two year old. "What?" he asked, noticing she hadn't budged from his side.

"*Hum...*" She stood there waiting to say something, but lost her train of thought.

"*Damn.* I hate when that happens. Too much weed," she joked.

He stood, slammed the remote into the seat of the recliner.

"I'm out."

"No wait, don't go."

"*Yo.* Let go of my arm."

She released him, followed him into the back room. Roy slipped on a sweat suit, stuck his feet inside his boots, and grabbed his fitted cap.

"Where my keys at?"

She shrugged. Smirked. Giggled just a little. "Let me think."

"Bitch, I will bust your fucking head."

Startled by his obvious threat, she pointed towards the nightstand. She'd hidden the keys inside the hollow space of the lamp. Roy wasn't the one to be playing *hide-the-key* with. He wasn't the one for the drama. Busting her head would be something he wouldn't think twice about doing. He lifted the lamp. The space was empty.

She backed away. "It was there this morning. I promise."

"Oh, you think it's a game?"

She backed away some more, fell into the closet door, which collapsed.

"*Wait.* Let me think."

Weed smoke clouded her judgment, made her forgetful. Most of the time, it made her stupid. Kema circled the room, mentally retracing her steps. *Keys, where the hell are you?* She rummaged through the nightstand. A roll of magnums fell. She picked them up, tossed them back inside. Loose change, pens, hair clips, weave tracks, important documents filled the space. Her hands glided across an envelope which contained Big Momma, and Big Bo's death certificates. A familiar chill crept across her frame. She quivered.

"Here they are. See, told you they were here." She turned and noticed the eerie look on Roy's face.

"You felt that?" he asked.

"Felt what?"

He stood motionless. Large eyes roamed the immediate area as if something was out there, with them. Paranormal instincts kicked in, but instead of exploring, he ignored the feeling. Roy adjusted his cap, pulling it down over his dark eyes.

"I'm out."

Kema sat amongst her grandparents spirits. At the edge of the bed, she sat there feeling their presence. Maybe Ace was right. Maybe the old house was haunted, but she didn't care. It would take more than a few shivers and quivers to scare her off.

***

Her nose round and pudgy, her eyes football shaped and pretty, her forehead was more like a five-head, high and wide, just like Big Momma's. Her lips were all Big Bo's. Full with the indentions at the top. Her hair used to be long, thick, and natural. All that was left was a beautiful bald head, which she wore magnificently.

Kema couldn't recall how long she'd been standing, holding the floral arrangement, at the back of the room. Her mother sat in a wheel chair, facing the open bay window, overlooking the lake.

"Do you need me to go with you?" a nurse asked compassionately.

"No ma'am. I'm just..."

"She's been expecting you."

After a long while, Kema took baby steps towards the woman who gave her life. Shaking like a leaf, she leaned in and pecked her mother's cheek.

"Hi Mommy."

"Well... it's.... about... time."

Kema sat with her mother for hours, chatting about her new boyfriend Roy, and his make-believe job as a lawyer, and her supposedly thriving career in IT. She'd told her that Big Momma's house was under construction, receiving its well needed face-lift. She lied about her potential engagement to the man of her dreams. She lied about wanting to start a family, with hopes of one day soon giving her a grandchild.

She lied...

and lied...

and lied...

and lied until darkness fell upon them.

CHAPTER 23

At the corner of Rock Quarry Road, in Stockbridge, Roy stopped at the Texaco to clean out his truck. It was imperative that he rid all evidence of Kema, or any other female for that matter. He was going home. A place he'd been missing from for almost two weeks now.

He snatched a plastic bag from the second row. He looked in; saw color coded hair. 1B-100% human-wet & wavy-14 inch-track weave, a curvy needle, thread, detangling hair spray, stainless steel shears, hideous neon yellow nail polish, mink eye lashes, emery board, lavender body spray, flat iron, and Kema's expensive watch.

He tossed the bag with all its contents into the trash. All except the watch and lavender spray. A universal scent accepted by all women.

He lifted the retractable seats, dug his hand between the cracks, pulled out a lonely hoop earring, single acrylic nail, and a used condom. The soiled plastic went up and over his shoulder, landing slam dunk into the round plastic receptacle. He climbed in, stuck his head into the third row, and noticed another bag. He looked in, smiled. Sexy undies with the matching bra. He trashed the intimate wear, cleaned the ashtrays, wiped away traces of hair, and smudges of lipstick. After one last look over, he ran his truck through the washer.

He circled the block twice. The lights were out, drapes closed shut, cozy house deserted. On the third go-around, he spotted her red and white mini cooper speeding down the block. The tiny car whipped into the driveway, and backed into the garage.

Speed demon, he thought as he watched the garage door close shut.

He gave her a moment to shit, shower, and slip into something a bit more comfortable. He thought of calling her first, but changed his mind. Calling, instead of showing up, face to face would leave a bad taste in her mouth. Although, she was unusually cool about the hours, days, sometimes weeks he kept away from home, calling would insult her intelligence, make her feel like them *other* chicks. So, he waited, gave her a solid hour to cleanse her body of the days stress.

He whipped into the driveway, and parked. The sensor light beamed as it picked up his movements towards the front door. His lady lived a modest lifestyle. Single family, detached brick home, ranch style sitting on a basement. Paid for with the help of drug money. He loved her like that. Loved her enough to satisfy her balance, wiping her debt clean.

His key, it worked. Not that he had any thoughts about it not working, but you never know. Shorty could have had a change of heart. Every woman had a limit. With one swift twist of the wrist, he entered.

There she was, his lovely, his queen, enjoying *Baduizm*, sipping a glass of Riesling, going over reports. *Next lifetime*, her favorite cut off the album, was the sound track to their situation.

He closed the door behind him, activated the security code on the keypad. Three beeps indicated they were monitored. *Alone.* The file she examined slipped from her finger tips. She stood, took sophisticated steps to meet in him the foyer. Her face, just inches away from his. Her eyes closed, breathing in his energy. It was her way of checking to see if she needed to burn an incense to rid whatever mood he was in. Her fingers traced the line of his brow, moved slowly down the bridge of his nose, the curve in his lips parted, pulling her finger in.

"You miss me?"

No words could describe just how much she'd missed him. She'd been worried sick about him. Tossing and turning most nights, thinking of her man. Expressing her worries just wasn't her style. Becoming one of those females who nagged, complained, and fussed their point just wasn't her way of doing things. She signed up for that assignment which was why she dispensed all forms of inconvenience when he was around. Now that they stood close as siamese twins, her mind began the process of relaxation.

He tipped her chin. "I asked you a question."

Her tongue did the talking.

"Damn baby, I miss you too."

She stepped back, took him in, and made sure he was in one piece, healthy.

"Are you hurt?"

"No. I'm good."

She opened his coat, lifted his sweater, startled by the tool in his waist. Her fingers bypassed the steel, made their way up and down his beautiful skin. No bruises, no gunshot wounds. The last time he showed up at her doorstep, he was stabbed, leaking blood from his bicep.

"*Hmm*, your hands feel so good."

He halted her search, grabbed her face, and kissed her lips. She threw her arms helplessly around his neck. Thick legs wrapped around his waist. He held her there, posture straight as a board, bouncing her up and down as if she didn't weigh more than he.

She was a big girl.

Plus sized beauty.

Thick and juicy.

A new look for him.

Roy wasn't your typical chubby chaser. Not that he discriminated, but like most people he had a preference. He'd met some beautiful big girls in his day, but none struck a chord like she did. From day one, her style, her presence, every inch of that woman was a blessing. She had a way of keeping him in tune with the softer side of himself, something no female has ever been able to do.

***

Their chance meeting came the day he rescued her. Roy was no hero. He usually turned the other cheek, and kept his mind on himself. That day, he spotted her, in distress, stranded off I-20 facing east. It was the devil's kitchen outside. Heat rose from the asphalt. Scorched tires gave off an intense rubbery smell. Her tire blew, leaving her Mini Cooper sitting on rim.

"Oh my God, thank you so much for stopping. I've been sitting here for over an hour, can't get no damn reception in this area. I've been practically begging people to stop, can't get no damn help in this part of town. I'm hot, tired, stranded, hot…. Did I say hot?"

He handed her a bottled water he'd just purchased from the BP, off Panola Rd. Roy had just left his shorty's house, and was on his way to Lithonia to pick up some cheese from Kema.

She guzzled, wiped her mouth. "Thank you, thank you, thank you."

"What's the problem?"

"Tire blew out, been needing new tires for some time now, but just couldn't afford them. Those bad boys run a buck and quarter a piece. The man at the shop said he would wave installation, taxes, and charge me a flat rate of a buck per tire, but four hundred is more than I can afford right now."

She wiped the sweat from her forehead, smoothing the edges of her auburn puff. Beads of water glistened in her natural coil. He was feeling her Jill Scott vibe. Sensual, sexy, erotic, and well dressed. Tight waist, Aqua blue baby doll top, flowed well past her booty, showing off just enough leg. Cream knee length spandex, open toe platforms with the single strap, caressed her ankle. Her lock down finger, *bare*.

Roy squatted, took a closer look, at the tire. "You're lucky."

"That bad huh?"

He stood, and went to check the other tires. "Your thread is gone."

She looked away, embarrassed. "Dangerous huh?"

"Severely."

***

Hands gripping her *Badunkadunk*, squeezing her Charmin's-extra soft ass, their tongues twirling and swirling. He placed her back against the wall, undid her top. Firm honey coated melons held in a lacy restraint. His head delve into her bosom in search of a nipple. Finally, he came up for air.

She slid her legs to the floor, chest still pressed against his.

He looked into her eyes and said, "You're so beautiful."

She smiled. "Let me take your coat. Are you hungry?"

Thinking of Kema's sorry ass turkey and cheese sandwich made the back of his throat dry. "I'm starving."

Just as she was about to step away, she turned back. "What's in the bag?"

"A little something for my baby," he teased.

"Give it here." She snatched the plastic, looked in.

"I didn't have a chance to wrap it."

"Oh my God." She let the body spray fall with the bag. She squealed at the sight of the watch. The serpent style, bracelet watch combo was cased in eighteen karat gold. Round brilliant cut diamonds outlined the face. "BVLGARI. This must have cost a fortune."

He wet his lips, smiled handsomely. "So you like it?"

"Are you kidding me?"

He watched as she tried it on. She tested its versatility, trying it many ways, expanding the length of the bracelet to spiral her arm, and then enclosing it to elegantly wrap her wrist.

"There's body spray in the bag."

"*Oh*, I'm sorry baby." She picked the deflated bag off the floor, looked inside.

"*Hmm*, lavender, my favorite." She spritzed a tiny bit on her collar-bone.

"Glad you like it, now how about that meal?"

She rushed towards the sofa, stacking her files, shutting down her laptop, stuffing her day's work into one pile on the coffee table. She lit a candle. He removed his fitted hat, and boots.

"Have a seat baby while I cook."

"You rearranged the furniture."

"I did. The energy was all wrong."

He smiled; loving her energy. Her need to have it flow positively through her life was a plus. She hit #4 on the CD changer. Jill's voice flowed through the surround sound hook-up. "Baby you missed one *helluva* concert."

He followed her into the kitchen, hopped on the swivel chair and placed both elbows against the raised counter. He sat quietly as she prepped for their meal. Red non-stick pots and pans hung above the island. She grabbed the skillet, and the sauce pan. She turned squatted down low for the small Pyrex dish.

"When I tell you my girl Jill rocked it." She whistled.

"This song right here..." she opened the drawer, grabbed a wooden spoon, and pointed it in the air. Her big hips swiveled slowly; her chest bucked to the beat, on queue she made love to the music. It was no doubt she could move with the best of them. Her mother was a professional ballet dancer, her daddy a jazz musician. In her spare time she wrote ballots.

"Oh, baby, the crowd went bananas."

She grabbed four pieces of tilapia, one whole onion, green, yellow, red peppers, lemon, and cooking spray.

"Sounds like you enjoyed yourself."

"*Oh*, baby I did. I've wanted to see Jill live since she came on the scene. The fabulous Fox Theater was packed. I mean everybody and their momma was there. I even sat in the same row as the Atlanta housewives," she said with much excitement in her voice.

"Is that right?"

"Those ladies looked absolutely fabulous."

That was his girl, always finding something nice to say about everyone. For the little time he'd known her, she'd never uttered a single solitary bad thing about her ex-husband. Her shotgun wedding ended the night it started. From what she told him, they were on two different planets. Luckily for Roy, her ex-moved back to Connecticut, Hartford to be exact. It was her hometown.

***

That day off the expressway, he waited with her until AAA came to tow her vehicle. Completely comfortable with him, she trusted her gut, climbed into the passenger's seat of his truck and found relief. Cool air dried her sweaty body.

"I feel like I stink," she confessed, just in case he was thinking it.

"You don't."

"Really, you can be honest. I'm a big girl, and I've been standing in the dead heat for an hour before you stopped. My thighs are sweating profusely."

She was so honest.

He leaned over, took a whiff of her. "You smell good. What scent is that?"

She blushed. "Oh, I never pay attention to the bottle. I grab, point, and hit the nozzle." She looked around, "This is a really nice truck. Big as ever, but nice. You probably spend a bill just filling this bad boy up."

"A bill? Where you from?"

"I'm repping the *CT* baby. Hartford in the house."

"Wow. That's funny."

"Why do I always get that reaction from people?"

He twisted his lips, looked at her. They both laughed.

"Thanks for the compliment. It runs me close to a bill each trip to the pump."

"Guess you're wondering why a girl my size is driving a mini cooper huh?"

"Nope, didn't wonder at all."

She searched for the lie in him. However, she couldn't place anything against the man, couldn't find a reason not to like him. Even when she brought up her weight, she looked for a wince, smirk, word or phrase to dead her feelings.

Roy looked through the rearview, saw the tow truck approaching. "Stay here."

"Oh, that's okay. I'm good now. AAA will make sure I get home. Thanks for stopping."

"Please, allow me to..."

She hopped out the front seat before he could finish his sentence. He watched her strut towards *Dirty Red*. Roy noticed the truck didn't have the standard AAA logo branded on the side of the door.

"Hold on, what's your name sweet heart?"

She looked back at him, smiled. *Dirty Red* already hooked the cooper, and was waiting for I.D., signature, and a location.

"Sonny."

"Can I take you home?"

She looked back at the trucker who looked hot, sweaty, and from the scrawl on his face was obviously having a bad day.

"I don't know you."

"You don't know him either. Take your pick."

***

She stirred brown rice, added a touch of olive oil, and tapped the wooden spoon against the rim. The telephone rang. She wiped her hands against a dry towel, picked it up, and hung up.

"Who was that?"

"Telemarketers." She adjusted the fire beneath the rice.

"Wish I could have been there," he said, eyeing the cordless phone. *She's lying.*

"I can't thank you enough for the tickets."

"Who did you decide to take?"

For weeks she'd been undecided. Since Roy wasn't available to attend, it was a toss-up between her two best girlfriends. Shauna was her buddy from college, roommates for four years to be exact. They did everything together. Chrissy was her buddy from Church. She praised the lord with her every Sunday, and occasionally hung out at Barnes and Nobles for coffee and a quick chat.

She pulled the bottle of Riesling from the fridge, placed two long stem wine glasses down on the counter. She poured a respectable amount.

"You know I love my girl Shauna, but ever since she lost her weight she's been bugging me about mine. I mean she's constantly telling me how big I am, and how much healthier I would be if I worked out sometime."

She took a sip. "Last week, when I was shopping for my dress to wear to the concert, she hurt my feelings."

"What that bitch say?"

She looked at him.

"I'm sorry. What she say?"

"She said, *girl you know that dress would look even better if it were a size eight.*"

"Did you snatch that bitch by her..."

She stopped his tirade by kissing his lips. "I snatched the dress off my butt and purchased it anyway."

"I can't stand her. She always trying to put you down. Wig wearing hooker."

She laughed. "Be nice."

"So is it safe to say you chose Chrissy?"

She rolled her eyes towards the ceiling, took another sip.

"Well, not exactly. I invited her, she accepted, and then the day of the concert she calls me saying how God told her she was above the ruckus. So, I say, *what ruckus?*"

She shook her head, laughed. "The child told me, that God said, she's no longer permitted to indulge in secular music. How Jill's lyrics are explicit and how talking about the human anatomy in songs is the work of the devil. She even went as far as telling me that the devil was a fallen angel, who was in charge of music, which basically explains why our music is so perverted, twisted, toxic, and how we are so influenced by the wicked art, and..."

Roy laughed. "This chick made it sound like you asked her to a 50 Cent concert. I mean damn, it's Jill."

She shrugged. "So, Shauna accepted at the last minute, and boy did we have a good time."

"Glad you enjoyed yourself babe. For real, you deserve it, even if you had to take that wig wearing hooker."

She popped him with the spoon.

"Ouch."

She sat her glass down, went to check the rice. The fish was baking nicely. She pulled a bag of carrots from the fridge and proceeded to slice them julienne style.

"Damn girl, its smelling good up in here."

"Thanks. I've been staying away from the beef. I haven't had a burger in two weeks."

He walked up behind her grabbed her hand, made her drop the spoon. "It shows. You've trimmed down around the waist." She leaned her head back, he kissed her neck.

"You know, you don't have to lose an inch for me. If you do, do it because you want to. Not for me, that hooker Shauna, nobody. You hear me?"

She turned to face him. "Can you watch the food while I run to the store?"

"Now, I mean... right now?"

"I'll be right back. Need to get more wine for later, plus we're out of Trojans, *remember*?"

She winked. He smiled.

"Okay, hurry up back though."

She slipped away from his grip, pulled on a pair red galoshes, grabbed a matching sweater coat, slipped her chain-linked hand bag over her wrist and stopped at the door. She looked back.

"You forget something babe?" he asked, pulling two dinner plates from the cabinet, and placing them on the table.

"Can I drive the truck?"

"Of course," he said, tossing her the keys.

"Something wrong with Ms. Cooper?"

"Ms. Cooper is running like a champ. I'm on *E*, and don't wanna waste time stopping for gas."

"Okay, hurry back. I'm hungry, horny and missing your pretty ass already."

"Be sure to stir the rice every few minutes, cut the fish off in five, and mind the carrots." She squealed on her way out the door.

He watched her back the truck out the driveway, and sped down the residential block. She was predictable. Asking to drive his truck, instead of Ms. Cooper was just a reason to rifle through his things. He'd been gone for almost two weeks, and in her mind there was something that would pin-point his whereabouts. His truck was like his home, and if there were signs of infidelity, it would surface beneath a rug, underneath a seat, along the door panels, tucked inside some secret compartment, or pocket. She preferred to snoop, rather than ask.

Roy strolled through the house, doing a bit of his own inquiring. He stuck his head inside the master bedroom. She didn't have much besides a bed, armoire, and a flat screen, but everything had a place. She preferred open and airy. A cluttered home equaled a cluttered life.

Her bathroom was squeaky clean. No traces of hair scattered along the tiled floors. No soiled pads or dirty clothes anywhere. He took a leak, flushed and washed his hands. Before leaving, he did the ring check. He pulled her shower curtain back, and noticed that her tub was spotless. No brown rings looping the ceramic tub, no pubic hairs, no soggy soap slipping from corners. He was impressed. Everything whistle clean. Everything except the toilet. The seat. It was up. Something he hadn't realized until after he pushed the chrome handle.

Twenty minutes later she came running through the door, kicking off her boots, tossing her sweater coat onto the sofa, and ran towards the kitchen sink to wash her hands.

"Guess who I bumped into while picking up these?" She tossed him the box of rubbers.

"Who?"

"Shauna."

"Really," he said dryly.

"Was she buying condoms too?"

"No, but she probably should have been considering she was holding a two-pack pregnancy test when my buggy bumped her booty by accident. You should have seen the look on her face."

"That's nice."

"What's wrong babe?"

He stared into her eyes. "Nothing, sit down while I make the plates."

"Oh no, allow me. You relax."

He grabbed her hands, firm grip. She looked at him. He forced a smile to his face. His energy, it was different. She looked around the kitchen, spotted the pack of incense.

"Let me take care of you for once."

"Let me burn an incense."

"Fuck them incense, just sit down," his voice boomed.

She placed a hand against her chest. "You're scaring me."

He pulled her into his chest. "I'm sorry, okay."

After dinner they headed straight to the bedroom to make passionate love. Roy's attentive hand, roamed her body in search of the truth. He'd be damn if let somebody step in on his good thing. *Fuck that!*

It was time to talk, a conversation well over due. His for sure thing wasn't feeling so for sure anymore. His sweet moment was turning bitter the more he thought about that toilet seat. He raised himself up on his elbow, looked down at her. She closed her eyes, drawing him close for a kiss. Their lips pressed together. He got back into position, looking down into her eyes, searching.

"You scare me."

She giggled. "Why?"

"I'm not the one to trust no female."

"You can trust me."

"Can I?"

"Have I given you any reason not to?"

He didn't answer.

"Look, I know you didn't intend for this to go far. I'm not exactly your type," she winced, regretting the way she said that.

"Hold on now, what you talking about."

Her voice cracked. "Come on Roy, I know you're doing your thing. I'm not stupid. You're in the streets for weeks at a time. Somebody holding you down when I'm not, so don't lie to me, okay."

He respected her wishes.

"Let's not spoil the evening. We haven't seen each other in a while now. Can I enjoy you?" she asked, trembling.

He held her.

The question of fidelity never came up, not that she was naive or desperate for a man. It just didn't. A stickler for protection, she strapped him up every single time. He liked that about her. Good, clean and wholesome ways said a lot about her character. However, exclusivity, never once mentioned.

"I found the toilet seat up."

He kept looking at her, waiting for her say something, anything. She pushed away, sat up on her own. The sharp breath she took scared him. *Naw, not my lovely, not my Queen.* His dark eyes now piercing her body. *Definitely not my wiz, my baby.* He kissed her breasts, her lips, her neck, and back to her lips.

"It happened once."

She heard a pop in his jaw. Clinching muscles made her draw back the sheets. She lowered her eyes in shame.

"When?"

"Last night."

He hopped out of bed. "Did you at least change the fucking sheets?"

"It didn't happen here."

"Where, in the kitchen, bathroom, where?" He demanded to know.

"His apartment, he brought me home, asked to use the bathroom."

He grabbed her arm, snatching her halfway off the mattress.

"Don't lie to me."

"I wouldn't lie, I promise. No one other than you has been in this bed."

He released her. His eyes, blazing with anger. "Why Sonny?"

She sunk her head into her hands. "Because… I was lonely, okay."

Her reasons were valid, justifiable. Roy's disappearing acts drove her into the arms of another man. That truth hurt him to the bone.

"While at the traffic light, on the way back home, when I parked in the driveway, I went through your things. Found something."

A shifty look passed over his face. He took his time cleaning out that truck. There was no way she could have found anything.

"Something like what?"

She shook her head. His sharp instinct told him it was something heavy, something that she couldn't just let go. There he was chewing her out about giving away his cookies when he'd been giving away her rod.

"What you find?" he asked again.

"New York hotel receipt."

He opened his mouth to explain, she cut him off.

"Roy, don't lie to me. If you have to lie… just don't say anything."

Damn, I should have brought my ass home days ago, he thought. And just like that, he let the toilet seat issue go. After settling back into their groove, Roy took care of his woman, loving her with no end, making her feel like the only one.

At that moment, she was.

CHAPTER 24

Sickness claimed her. That was her story and she was sticking to it.

Flu, migraine, stomach cramping, but this time it was her asthma. She was experiencing tightness in her chest. Her pump had two squirts left and she needed refilling. And on top of breathing difficulties, she was catching a head cold, or was it her allergies flaring up? By the time Sonny hung up with her boss, and settled back into position with Roy, the lie that slipped from her lips was a complete haze.

"You really should stop doing that."

"I'm tired of working there."

"Thought you loved it," he said, twirling her coiled hair between his fingers.

"You don't know the half."

"Tell me the half, or the whole, or whatever."

She giggled. "You don't want to hear about my day job, but you can tell me about yours."

Her request made him uncomfortable. "You've never been interested in what I did before."

"Like-wise," she said sarcastically.

"Does this mean were growing?" he asked.

"Does it?"

"Why you keep asking a question with a question. I hate that."

"Sorry."

"Don't apologize, just stop doing it."

"Thought you liked me this way," she said.

"What way?"

"Don't ask, don't tell policy," she said exasperated.

"Does that bother you?"

"A bit."

"You seemed okay with the Don't ask, don't tell policy."

Her head slightly rolled. "Guess I've changed."

"Guess we've both changed," he said a bit too loudly.

She jumped at the sudden hostility in his voice. The toilet seat issue was emotionally taxing. Mentally, he kept going back to that moment. Just hours ago when she'd dropped the *truth* bomb on him, his heart shifted. She avoided his eyes. Her lids closed, as if she were asleep.

"You okay?" she asked softy.

"Yes," he murmured.

"Don't lie."

He was hot-blooded, unstable, and ready to say something that would hurt her feelings. Her gut told her to tread lightly, perhaps examine her words prior to releasing them. She cleared her throat. "You know, everything happens for a reason."

He suddenly felt cold. "What's that supposed to mean?"

Her eyes rolled towards the ceiling and back. "Forget it."

"It's probably best that we do."

His silence left her lonely. She now knew what her mother felt for so many years. Her daddy went into his shell back in the eighties and never returned. Living under the same roof with someone didn't exactly mean you conversed. Her daddy went his way, and her mother did the same. Speaking first was a sign of weakness. A game her parents played without cease.

"Silence is deadly," she said.

He watched her from his peripheral.

"My parents were practically strangers because of it."

He said nothing.

She took in a sharp breath. "They never addressed their issues head on. Instead, they just stopped talking. As if silence would remedy whatever ailed their relationship. Guess that's why I'm a talker, yapper, blabber, jaw jibber, big mouth…" She watched him. "Ah, is that a smirk?"

He tightened his jaw. Reluctant to give in. *Just like her daddy.*

"Thought your childhood was a creative one, musical, artful?"

"It was quite colorful if I might say. My mother danced professionally. She landed a few Broadway shows in her day. When Broadway stopped calling, she taught the craft at a local college. When she got bored with that she opened a studio. It was small, smelled, and had stains in the hardwood, but my mother kept her vision goggles on. With a little elbow grease, time, and the help of a few good friends, the studio sparkled like new."

"Sound nice."

"Better than nice. The studio is known throughout the East coast. Debbie Allen once visited. Momma used to tell me how she met Ms. Allen during one of her runs on Broadway. Daddy said it was a lie, and you know us girls, we believe whatever Daddy says."

She looked at him, waited for him to jump in, participate in the conversation, but just like her daddy, he just listened. "So when Ms. Allen showed up with her entourage of long leg, flexible dancers, daddy became an instant groupie."

Roy chuckled. "Back in the day Debbie Allen was the shit," he added.

"Absolutely beautiful. Even today she's still a looker."

"True."

"Daddy was a saxophonist, and could handle a piano."

"Sexy instruments," he said with a smile in his voice.

"We had a piano at home, nothing fancy but Daddy kept it tuned. Music filled our walls. That was my parent's commonality. Momma danced, daddy played, that's how they made love. I guess you can say they did *it* their way."

"Nothing wrong with doing *it* your own way."

"True, but there was still that silence that kept her lonely, vacant, at times sad," she said with a slight whimper.

"You ever talk to her about it?"

"Once. It was right before I was to marry Erick." She stopped, looked at him. She never spoke about her ex. He was her past, made no sense in drudging up murky memories.

"And."

"Well, I was unsure, had doubts. Hell, I was looking for her to give me a reason not to. My mother could never say a bad thing about anyone."

"Sounds like someone I know."

She smiled bashfully. "We were at the table, sipping wine she brought back from Spain over three decades ago. She was saving it for a special occasion."

"Nice."

"I asked her why she sometimes looked lonely... she grabbed my hand, whispered words I'll never forget. She said, *baby never compromise yourself. When the world says you're not equipped, show them just how magnificent you really are.*"

"What did she mean by that?"

"There were several meanings, *I think*. That was Momma. She would drop a one liner and walk away from a topic."

"A person of very little words, but her presence is always felt. I think that describes me."

She cocked her neck. "You think?"

"I'll admit. I'm not big on repeating myself. I speak perfect English, my words come through clearly and I feel it's a waste of my time, energy, oxygen to say things a second time. Speaking twice on the same topic makes me violent."

"You one liner people expect folks to get it the first time. Momma was like that. Daddy made her that way. Since he never talked, and barely looked in her direction, she kept it short and sweet, but always impactful."

"That's deep."

"Her words stuck to the four corners of my mind for days leading up to my nuptials. She told me to never compromise myself. I think that's what daddy hated the most about her. She never compromised her gifts, her talents, her vibrancy. She rocked Broadway, traveled abroad, collected collectables, and filled the plastic pages of her album with photo's that reminded her of her youth, and Daddy, he envied her for it."

"No."

"Yes. He did. It took me awhile to really understand what she meant that day at the kitchen table. See, Daddy didn't make much money as a musician. He wasn't exactly the poor struggling artist, but he wasn't a big name that closed out symphony halls either."

"Wasn't he good?"

"Daddy was one of the best, but you get out this world what you put in."

"True dat."

"He paid bills, contributed like a man should, but Momma was the bread winner. When Daddy couldn't land a gig, my mother would pull a few strings; call in some favors for him. Odd jobs like painting, trash collecting, and warehouse work filled his time while in-between gigs."

"I bet he hated that."

"Despised it so much he left once, went to New Orleans for six months to earn some cash. Daddy had to show Momma that he could stand on his own two. When he came home from his *extended stay* they argued non-stop. Daddy wasn't a violent man, but he would throw things to vent his anger."

"At least he didn't hit her."

"I know, thank God for that. When Daddy came home, Momma had a friend. Mr. Ned. He was Cuban, a gorgeous specimen from the New England part of Connecticut. Mr. Ned had this exotic multilingual accent that inspired me to write my first ballot."

"Mom dukes replaced Pops after six months?"

"More like thirty one days. When Daddy didn't call, write, bring his musically *inclined-ass* home, she moved on."

"Sounds familiar," he said, now finding his thoughts hours in the past. The toilet seat issue rising from the dead. She snuggled up against him, broke down his wall of anger. "*Wait*, did your pops at least bring that bread home?"

"Some, not much... truthfully I don't believe he made the killing he'd hope for."

She looked at his ashy knees, grabbed the lotion. As she massaged cream into his skin she thought about that day her father returned home. He was casket sharp. New suit, crisp button down, and some black shiny boots with the metal plate across the toe. Her mother wasn't the least bit impressed with his "new" look.

"Daddy insisted that she stop seeing Mr. Ned, and she did. Things were okay for a little bit, they spoke a little, he played music, she danced, home felt like home again. Until one day the vacant lot next door to Momma's studio went up for sale. She'd been talking about expanding for years, growing the studio into a full fledge facility. She not only wanted to teach ballet, but she wanted to teach other forms of dance. Hip Hop, Tap, Jazz."

"What does your mother know about Hip-Hop?"

"At the time *nothing*, but some of her students expressed interest in it. Seventy percent of the girls truly loved ballet, the others were there because their mothers made them show up. Those girls, Momma took an interest too. She was their sounding board. She listened. So when the lot next door went up for sale, she grabbed it."

"A woman with an eye for opportunity. Love her already."

"Daddy hit the ceiling when she told him."

"I bet he did. She made a big move without consulting him. Even if she was the bread winner, you just don't buy into something without talking to the other, right?"

She shrugged. "Daddy never cared one way or the other. The fact that she was still growing, reaching new heights bothered him."

He opened his mouth to defend a man he never met, and up until that day never thought about meeting. That toilet seat had him feeling a certain way. He was off his square.

"What were you going to say?" she asked.

"Nothing. Thought I had to yarn," he lied.

"She enlarged her territory, equipped her establishment to welcome all forms of dance. There was even room left for a small private parking deck."

"Where'd your mother get that kind of bread from?"

She paused. His brow arched.

"Mr. Ned owned the lot. He was in real estate back then and he'd owned a few lots downtown. Before Daddy came home, I recall hearing Mr. Ned talking about demolition, developing, rehabbing buildings in the district where we lived. My mother never spoke on it, but I think he sold her the lot."

"Sold or gave? There's a difference."

She inhaled. "Either way, she got the deed to it. Don't know how she pulled it off."

"Pussy is a powerful tool."

"Please don't put that image in my head."

They both laughed.

"How are your parents now?"

Her voice became soft, almost childlike. "Daddy passed a few weeks after my wedding. Stroke."

"I'm sorry."

"Momma's accolades lined the wall of our living room. Trophies and metals dated back to when she was just two. She was accomplished. Daddy wasn't. This divided them. I believe that killed him."

Sadness covered her face. Her eyes watered as she looked across the room at her own accolades. She was accomplished just like her mother. Just like her daddy, Erick hated it. "My mother is still kicking. She's at the studio five days a week, dancing. For an old broad she's got killer legs."

He laughed. "I bet she does."

"When my daddy went home, it was rough but she kept her dazzle. She was determined to show the world she was still *equipped*. Mr. Ned proposed recently."

"Wow, your moms is getting re-married?"

"Yep, got a colossal diamond on her finger too. Mr. Ned rich as hell. Before 9/11 he sold most of his properties, preparing for his retirement."

"Lucky bastard pulled out just before the market crashed."

"Sure did. Now he owns a consulting firm. Works remote most of the time, other times he's managing the books at the studio. Mr. Ned insists that he and Momma vacation every three months. They slip away to some island every ninety days to refresh and recoup. They just returned from Bali," she said with glee.

"Your mother chose wisely the second time around."

"The old broad didn't do too bad the first time. Daddy was a good man, just lacked her ambition. They were unequally yoked. Two peas from different pods. Not cut from the same clothe."

His voice broke through her heavy thoughts. "Let's talk about your day job."

She drew a long breath.

"You don't have to. Just thought it would be a nice step in another direction." Roy winced. He felt silly. He felt like a punk. Just hours ago his wiz, his main chick, his baby just told him she let another dip into his honey walls. Now he was saying cornball shit like, *Just thought it would be a nice step in another direction.*

He gritted his teeth, tried to reclaim his masculinity but the moment was stolen with hot passionate kisses. He wanted to push her away but couldn't. His hand was on her back. Loving strokes made her purr.

"So you were saying?" he asked, trying hard to restrain himself.

"You know I don't like complaining, especially when I don't have a solution."

"Let's call it venting."

She cleared her throat. "My boss is such a prick. He's a dick head with a PHD." She took a deep breath, started to laugh. He joined her. "Damn, that felt good."

"Continue," he said.

"It's just hard working with a group of people who can't seem to leave their issues in the parking lot. Don't get me wrong, we all have bad days but these folks bring their drama to the work place every day. It's exhausting hearing about Bridget's baby daddy ducking child support, or Alison's son becoming a career criminal, or Monica's IBS, or..."

"IBS?"

"Irritable bowel syndrome."

He laughed. "Okay."

"Jade's confused. She's a lezzy one day, and the next day she's throwing herself at Harland."

"Who's Harland?"

"This very handsome older man who works in Billing. That child doesn't know whether she wants beef or fish. The girl is a hot mess. And I wish she would stop forcing me to eat those damn vegan snacks she brings in every other day. I mean damn how many times can I say no? And *Dr. Jesus, Gonzales, Morales* has his way with all the ladies," she said in her best *Chris Tucker* voice.

"All the ladies?"

"All except *muah*, and Sandra who's engaged to a very fine surgeon."

"This doctor is a player huh?"

"He's a cunt chaser."She covered her mouth. "Did I just say cunt?"

He nodded, suddenly turned on by her bad girl side. Sonny never cursed, never talked bad about people, and to see this side of her made him want to spread her legs and call her all sorts of dirty bitches while screwing her doggy style. He shook the urge.

"Yes, you said cunt. Continue."

She took a deep breath. "Okay, so he's screwing the new chick that works the front desk."

"How you know?"

"*Man* everybody know. He got them drawers her first week. I mean the chick didn't even get her first pay check before spreading eagle to Mr. Latin Lover."

"The Latin Lover must be a smooth talker."

"Yes, he's always talking that smooth Español, all up in my face. I told *Hector Javier Hernández, Santos, De La Cruz t*o keep out my way before I pinned a case against his sleazy ass."

"You threatened the man?"

She lifted her brow. "Human Resource is on the third floor. Anyway, the chick at the front desk was hired to make sure we had enough beds available, enter data, prepare discharge papers, *etc.* One day last week I needed some information on a new patient. The woman had a failing liver, and some other issues. Anyway, I buzzed the front desk but she never answered. I'm thinking the girl went to lunch or something. When I got up front this heffa was on a PC."

"What's a PC?"

"Personal call."

"Ooh, that's bad."

"Not only was she on a PC, but she was logged into that social network thingy everybody is crazy about."

"Did you rat her out?"

She gave him the sister girl neck roll. "I could have, but I didn't. Told that trick she better get her act together before she finds her ass at the unemployment office."

"And all this drama bothers you?"

"It's not just the drama, it's the energy required to sustain in this field. We're trained to remain empathetic, somewhat compassionate, but we are never to get too involved, *attached*. However, lately I find myself hugging patients, consoling family members, offering prayer to the afflicted."

"What's wrong with having a heart?"

"My job description doesn't exactly give me permission to offer physical affection. I go overboard."

"Nothing wrong with being a hands-on kind of person," he said.

"You don't understand."

"Make me understand."

"It's emotionally draining seeing people die of AIDS. My heart aches when I see our youth riddled with bullets. Last month, this one boy got shot in the face and..."

"The new 50 cent," he said jokingly.

She sucked her teeth.

"My bad, you were being serious."

"Very serious." She inhaled. "50 cent was one of the lucky ones. This young man was a vegetable. The machine kept him alive until the family decided to..." She shook her head. "Watching the patients suffer, witnessing the families go through it, hearing my colleagues discuss how terrible their lives are is slowly driving me a bit crazy. Lately, I'm questioning my path."

"Sounds like you want to try something new."

"It's not that I'm no longer passionate about being a Nurse. Maybe too passionate... too caring... I take my work *too* serious. Guess I should be more like my colleagues."

"Maybe you need to step away from it, take a break. Do something different. You can always go back to being a nurse."

"I've thought about it."

"Take some time off. Focus on writing some music."

She jumped out of bed. "Be right back."

He heard her tinkle, flush; wash her hands and before he could adjust his position she was back. She stood in the window, looking out onto the neighbor's yard. "Did I tell you the house next door sold?"

"No."

"Sure did. I met the new owner yesterday." She knocked her knuckle against the window, waved. Roy jumped out of bed to be nosy. "Is that her?" he asked.

"No, that's her realtor. The lady, who bought the house had to head back home, gather her things, handle her daughters transfer papers, and tie up loose ends."

"Damn you nosy," he chuckled.

"Look who's talking," she said, elbowing his side.

Roy couldn't help but stare. The woman had hard to ignore features. Ghostly like skin, dirty blond locks hung pass her shoulder blades with a crinkle at the tip. She was Albino to the bone. Tall, flat booty, and top heavy. He watched the realtor replace the *"For Sale"* sign with one that read, *"Private Residence"*.

He jumped back into bed. "Is your new neighbor nice?"

"She seems cool."

"Where she from?"

"She's a Jersey transplant, newlywed, has a daughter who's five. Just landed a job with the CDC here in Atlanta, and her husband is an out of work Business Analyst."

He smirked, shook his head.

"I'm pretty nosy aren't I?"

"Yep. Real nosy," he said, laughing.

"I need to lose weight." She waited for him to say something, but he didn't. Roy shook his head dismissively.

"What was that for?"

"You've got a serious complex about yourself."

"Oh please, I do not. I'm *very* confident."

"Some days you are Queen Sheba, walking and talking like nothing or nobody can faze you. On other days, the slightest glance will throw you into this big girl frenzy."

She covered her mouth. "Am I that bad?"

"Yes, and it drives me crazy."

That *truth* bomb was exploding between them once again.

"Some days I don't feel like Queen Sheba. Some days I feel like whale blubber," she said after a long moment.

"Baby, you're no whale," he said, and licked his lips.

"And if you are, whale sure does taste good. Give me some blubber any day."

She swiveled her hips, licked her finger tips, and made the cinch noise.

"That's more like it," he said, loving when she loved herself. She plopped back down onto the bed. "You feel better?" he asked.

"Yes, but tomorrow I'm still faced with the same issue."

"This is true."

"Maybe I should quit, pack up Ms. Cooper and head west, or maybe further south. Better yet, I should cash in my 401K, become a gypsy, see the world, and travel to another continent."

"Take me with you."

Her eyes lit up. She perched her back, crossed her thick leg over the other. Pudgy foot bounced. "Come here," she commanded. Just as their lips were to connect, Roy's cell vibrated.

"Thought I turned that off," he said, reaching for his phone.

Earlier, he'd made a trip to the bathroom to release his guts. Carrots did that to him. While he cleansed his colon, she snooped. His phone had zero numbers stored. There were no texts, no voice messages, no call history, no nothing to pin-point his whereabouts for the last two weeks. He was off the radar.

"What time you talking?" he asked the nuisance on the other end.

She got up, walked towards the window, looked out onto the street. She was mad, angry, annoyed with herself for not turning his phone off. *That's what you get for snooping.*

"Where the hell is Locust Grove?" he asked in a hush tone.

Locust Grove, what the hell is he worried about that hick ass part of town for?

He looked up at her, whispered into the receiver, "Now?"

The dip in Sonny's brows told Roy she wasn't about to let him go easy. He read her thoughts, felt her energy. When the phone call ended, she immediately began to babble.

"We should go to the movies. There's a ton of new stuff out. I hear Snow Mountain Park is nice this season. We should head over there and act our shoe size for a couple of hours."

"Sonny."

She snapped her fingers, squealed. "Better yet, my home girl Freda invited us to her annual Christmas party tonight. From what I hear she really does know how to throw one *helluvah* party. I heard last year she booked a local gospel group to sing *Joy to the World* outside her doorstep, like in the movies." She brimmed with excitement.

"Sonny, listen..."

"We don't have time to head to Lenox, but if we go to Stonecrest Mall I'm sure we can find something snazzy to piece together.

"Sonny, baby, you gotta listen to me..."

"I can't wait to show you off to all the girls. They'll be there with their washed up husbands and I'll have you on my arm. They will be so damn jealous of me." She snapped her fingers in a zigzag pattern. She covered her mouth shamefully. "Good Lord, I'm getting ahead of myself. What's gotten into me?"

Roy couldn't help but chuckle. Her new found blunt nature was gratifying. Deep down Sonny desired to be that mouthy bad bitch who said whatever was on her chest.

"*All black everything.* Shirt, tie, suit, hard bottom Stacy Adams would do you well. I'll hit up Ashley Stewarts for something festive. I've got a fifty dollar gift card from one of the ladies at the job. My secret Santa was this nice lady by the name of Geraldine. Lovely woman recently widowed. She had gastric bypass and looks stunning."

"Sonny, baby..."

She scurried off towards the kitchen to fix something to eat. Roy appeared minutes later, dressed in dark clothing. A knit trapper covered his head. He watched her from the archway as she whipped up his favorite cheese omelet. She refused to look at him. Pouty lips were seen from the side. He walked up behind her, cut the fire to the stove off. He reached for a plate. Egg omelet slid off the non-stick pan and into the dish effortlessly.

"I need to make this run."

She sat, looking down at his boots. They were laced and tied with precision. Flawless, without a scratch. His jeans cuffed a mere inch above the boot, showing off the tree symbol. "Don't go."

"I have to."

"You just got home."

"I know babe, but this is important. I'll be back," he said with certainty.

"When, next week sometime?" she asked dryly.

"Tonight."

"Whatever, Roy, just go."

He pulled a wad from his pocket, and handed it to her.

"Buy yourself a nice dress for the party. Get one of those sleek black numbers that shows off your jugs." He jiggled her coconuts. "Pick me up something too. You remember my shirt, slacks, and shoe measurements?"

She cuffed his nuts. He coughed, as he wasn't expecting her to do that. "Boy, I know every square inch of you."

"Good."

CHAPTER 25

T hey were way off the reserve someplace far.

Deep into the country backwoods, where no one could hear you scream, let alone stumble across your corpse. They remained low in the wilderness amongst the unknown, the hunted. Three hundred and sixty degrees of forest surrounded them. Weeds shoulder high, naked trees, and open skies. Miles away from civilization, inside a tilted one room shack.

Lou-Lou peered through a set of binoculars. They were high tech night visions. Military grade goggles used in combat. Ace occupied himself with a swig of whisky he'd found tucked away in the makeshift pantry. Expired cans of sardines, beans, chilly, stews, lined the weak ledges. He grabbed a rusty can from the shelf, and wiped away the remnants of time.

"It went bad June of 1999." Curiosity got the best of him. Aged foods told a story. "Tomato soup with a stamped date of..." he struggled to read the print. "I think it says 2002, could be 03'though."

Daddy long legs crept out from behind the can. Horrified, he dropped the stale soup, and began stomping the tired floors with the soul of his boots.

"*Shush.*"

"Sorry, fucking tarantula tried to attack me." He exaggerated.

A rash of itchiness crept across his body. "I hate spiders."

"Me too," she said, never breaking her eyes away from the goggles.

"My cousin Isis used to love watching that movie *Arachnophobia*."

"Don't mention that hellish movie."

He itched and scratched, and itched. "Need a bath."

She giggled. "That's what you get for touching stuff. You're supposed to be on stakeout."

Lou-Lou and Roy had managed to flawlessly take over the small shipment without casualties. Ace's only request was that Roy left the driver breathing. He knew the man's wife by first name. She was a sweet woman who baked him cookies once a month, usually on pay day.

"You look happy scrappy."

"I am," she said.

Lou-Lou smiled, one hand jammed inside her pants pocket, the other holding binoculars, looking on as Roy transacted the deal. But that was a cover, a facade she displayed in order to keep her true feelings in check. Back at Ace's apartment, things turned for the worse.

He did things to her she'd only seen in movies, but for the love of money, she was determined to hold her peace. She knew that night would be their last night together. She knew if she didn't get as far away from him as soon as possible, somebody was going to get hurt.

"Come here."

"Can't, gotta watch Roy's back."

That she did without blinking. She kept a close eye as Roy and the Aryan brother unloading the last of the guns into the stolen utility van. His peoples from Dade couldn't come up with the dough, so the crazy white boy closed the deal. *Unfortunately.*

"Come give me some of that ass."

"Just gave you some back at your apartment. *Don't you remember?*"

Of course he didn't. He'd had another spell. Ace slipped back into that dark place, transformed into some sadistic monster. His true cards were laid out, and there was no telling which suit he would follow next.

"That was a few hours ago. Need to be refreshed."

She gave him a curt shake of the noggin. *Not today, not tomorrow. Never again!*

"Now's not the time."

"Baby, relax. Roy can handle this guy."

"I don't trust that swastika wearing, skin head. Did you see how he looked at me?"

"You're beautiful. Ray Charles can see that."

He turned on the small outdated television. Local channels came in fuzzy.

"Your cousin got a problem with me."

Her eyes shifted towards him. "He's alright once you get to know him."

"I've been around long enough to know when somebody aint feeling me," he said with a slight chuckle.

"He's just not that into dudes, yah know."

"Seems like he's more into you," he said in an insinuating undertone.

A single brow rose, and froze. "What are you implying?"

"Ya'll real cousins or fake cousins?"

"Real, why?"

He shrugged. "You know how folks do, especially black folks. We call everybody our cousin. You got baby pictures with him?" he asked, rather harshly.

"Wow." She giggled, dismissing his last remark.

"I don't know much about you," he said.

Here we go. She thought, wanting him to shut his trap so that she could concentrate on her *play-play* cousin. They weren't blood related, but they were family. And she wasn't about to explain or attempt to validate their unusual connection.

"So ya'll grew up together?"

"Same tiny ass apartment in the projects," she lied. "Our grandmother took care of us."

"So his mother and your mother are sisters, making you two first cousins?"

"That's right."

"That's funny. You two look nothing alike," he said as if he knew she was yanking his chain.

"How'd you get access to a place like this?"

He rubbed his jaw, obviously deciding whether or not to push the issue of kinship or not. They were first cousins, but they looked nothing alike. He was in the mood to interrogate, get some clear answers. He looked at her, noticing her level of discomfort. Ace chose not to press the issue any further.

"The land spreads out over two hundred acres. It's been in the family close to a century."

"Damn, that long huh?"

"Big Bo, my grandfather used to bring his floozies up this way to cheat on Big Momma."

"Why you call him Big Bo, why not good old granddad?"

"My mother said he never adjusted to the idea of being a grandfather. See, my mother got knocked up in middle school. She was in the sixth grade, I think. Not uncommon back in the day, but it sure as hell wasn't permitted in their household. Big Bo was thirty-*ish*, a young man still sowing his oats. When he found out my mother was pregnant with me, he beat her until she lost conscious."

Lou-Lou broke away from Roy and the white supremacist for a second to look at Ace. "Sounds like a real son-of-a-bitch if you ask me."

"I didn't, but since you brought it up, the motherfucker was mean as a snake. He was a real monster off the whisky. Rumor has it Big Bo came home, not here, but the house in Atlanta where my sister Kema stays..."

Location, location, location.

"Wait, you guys inherited another house besides this one?"

"Sure did. My grandmother was the brain. She kept the land in the family, even when the greedy ass white folks came trying to steal it. She fought tooth and nail through the courts, and when the system failed her, she resorted to violence. Big Momma made sure the papers were straight on the land before she passed on."

"Interesting." She moved from the entrance, forgetting all about Roy.

"Big Bo came home drunk as a skunk, talking smack, having been caught cheating with some lady name Gladys. Big Momma said she left Big Bo at the table to argue with himself, and when she came back the next morning he was dead.

"How?"

"Big Momma said he choked off his own saliva, or something crazy like that. Folks in the family see it differently though. Word has it the potato salad killed him. See, after drinking like a fish all night down at the juke joint Big Bo usually came home expecting his supper. Big Momma had his plate waiting. Fried chicken and potato salad. Folks say she spiked the salad with rat poison."

Lou-Lou shook her head. "See, that's why I don't eat everybody potato salad."

"First she said he choked, then she said he had a seizure which explained the foam around his mouth, but no one really knows. Back in the day the coroner showed, bagged and toe tagged, asking very little questions, especially if you weren't the right skin complexion."

"Damn, Big Momma was nothing to play with."

"Who you telling. She used to whip my ass with an extension cord for getting out of line. Kema and I stayed with her every summer. Talk about miserable. The damn house lacked central air, was falling to pieces and Big Bo's spirit still looms the old place. My sister refuses to sell. I recommended demolition, rebuilding on the property but no. Lil' Sis wants to hold on to some spooky foundation, in hopes of keeping our grandparents memory alive."

He turned the knob on the tube, switched channels. *Good Times* came in a bit snowy. Florida Evans was scolding her son Michael for placing a photo of black Jesus next to the white one.

"I hate this show."

A look of shock spread across his face. "Okay, I'm revoking your black card. How can you possibly hate *Good Times*?"

"Because, they never make it out the projects," she said, turning the channel.

"Hey, turn it back."

"No."

"It's not like they didn't try."

She rolled her eyes. "Try meets a fail any day."

"Damn girl, why you gang-banging *Good Times*?"

"Remember that episode when Thelma married that football star? He'd just signed a contract to earn millions to play in the pros."

"Yes, one of my favorite episodes."

"*JJ* ruined that opportunity by tripping him, damaging his knee, causing him to lose his contract. Guess what happened next?"

Ace couldn't stop laughing.

"Thelma's new husband ended up moving in with them, in the projects. His ass started drinking, and that was all they wrote."

"Ah *C'mon*, what about *JJ*? He always had ideas, some lucrative ones too."

"Remember the episode where *JJ* discovered the voice on that young girl?"

"Yes, another favorite. That girl could really blow."

"*JJ* had done all the leg work to get the girl a gig at the show. He basically groomed her to sound a certain way, look a certain way, hell *he managed her*. As soon as the big executives caught wind of *JJ's* girl, they..."

"...stole her right underneath his nose." He finished her sentence, laughed.

She rolled her neck. "Oh baby, it was to his face."

"Okay, you're right."

"Remember the episode where..."

"Alright, I get your point."

Her goggles back eye length, focused on Roy. From what she could see, things were just about finalized. The white boy and Roy gave each other dap, than to her surprised they hugged. *Interesting!*

The **US ARMY** commercial came on. Large white letters on a military back drop appeared. ***JOIN US!*** His eye started to twitch, breathing accelerated. Ace jumped into a crouching tiger position, and beat against his chest like King-Kong.

"*Allahu Akbar.*"

"Whoa, you alright?" Lou-Lou asked, taking a few steps back.

Arabic words slipped from his tongue fluently. His arms spread apart, his head rolling counter clock, his eyes cold and dangerous.

"*Allahu Akbar- Allahu Akbar- Allahu Akbar*"

Ace was clicking, obviously experiencing a mental break-down of some sort. He grabbed his face, nails penetrating his skin. He kicked the television off the table.

"*Yo*, chill the fuck out before you blow this deal," she warned, looking back over her shoulder. The last thing they needed was for that Nazi head to feel threatened. So far, everything had gone according to plan.

"*Allahu Akbar- Allahu Akbar- Allahu Akbar*"

She twisted back to look at Ace, but saw nothing but heat pointed at her face.

"This here is designed to blow a motherfucker to pieces." His sinister laugh made her leak urine.

"Ace, baby it's me, Lou-Lou"

"Who the fuck is Ace?"

Running into the blackness, heat clogged his lungs. Dust from burning bodies burned his eyes. Bullets whizzed past his dome. He'd just broken out the cage. *POW* for far too long. Tortured by skin darker than his. Scared of shadows, mostly his own. The voices in his head made him do things. The voices made him lose sleep. The voices turned him into a vampire out for blood.

"Lower your weapon soldier," her voice, as demanding as it could be with an AR15 pointed at her head.

His eyes stretched further. Ace was in another place, another time, another realm of life altogether. And in order to stay alive she had to role play.

"Can't Sarg, we won't make it back alive if I do."

"We'll get back. We always do. Lower your weapon."

"Trust me Sarg, we busting out this cave tonight. Got that fucking Towel-Head in my scope."

Lou-Lou stood statue still. If only she could convince him to lower the tool, maybe she'll have a chance. *Maybe.* "*W*-wrong target," she screamed in hopes of getting Roy's attention.

He placed the tip of the barrel to her forehead. "Right target motherfucker."

She began to breathe last moments of desperation.

"I got that *S* on my chest Sarg, ain't afraid of these cowards."

"Big man, *chill, chill, chill...*" her voice lowered, just barely above a whisper. She didn't want him accidently discharging the tool. "You got my back right?" she asked.

"No question."

"Will you kill for me?"

"Kill all these sons-a-bitches. Blow their ass to pieces."

"Will you die for your country?"

"No doubt. These motherfucking Towel-Heads sacrifice their lives every day to prove a point. I'm willing to do the same. I'll die for the cause."

Dedication, loyalty, his finger still caressing the trigger. *Fuck me!*

"Sarg."

"Yes." her voice shrilled in fear.

"See them Rug-Riders?"

"Where?" she asked, trying to prolong her death. Every precious second counted.

Roy was still making a deal with the devil. *Shit!*

"Sarg, look closely at them Sand-Niggas, especially the one right there."

She looked into his dark evil eyes. Her fear mirrored back. *Towel-Heads, Rug-Riders, Sand-Niggas, Caves.* He had gone off the deep end for sure.

"I don't see any Rug-Riders. You better point em' out."

He yanked her arm, shoved her to the floor. Her head knocked against the old wood burning stove. Out like a light, but only for a few minutes. When she came to, Ace was hovered over her, taunting her with the rifle.

"I'm going to fuck you in the ass you Towel-Head bitch. Fucking Sand-Monkey. Camel-Riding-Whore."

"Soldier, she's not worth it," she struggled to say.

"When I'm done, you can have a piece too Sarg," he said, loosening his belt buckle.

She tried to stand.

"Stay down Rug-Rider. *Stay the fuck down.*"

"Okay, okay, just don't shoot me."

"Turn around, spread that pretty ass."

"Ace, please."

"Who the fuck is Ace?"

"Who are you, what's your name?" she screamed.

Hate tears spilled from his lids. Her question triggered something on the inside of his soul.

Who am I?

What's my name?

He was in a faraway place, doing what he was programmed to do. *Kill.*

Her question suffocated him, squeezed his lungs. Finally, he exhaled paranoia. He turned, started pacing, grabbing his head.

"I don't know. I don't know. I don't know."

She tried to stand.

He turned the burner back on her.

"Stay...the fuck... down."

She did as she was told.

He lifted the AR15 in the air, and shouted, *"Allahu Akbar- Allahu Akbar- Allahu Akbar"* One minute he was a US soldier fighting a war on terrorism, and the next minute he was the terrorist. Somewhere in the middle of both worlds, Ace was struggling to find his way back home.

CHAPTER 26

R oy's first thought was to shoot Ace dead.

Putting one in his head to silence his ranting was an easy solution. He would have laid him out cold and left him for raccoons and deer to feast upon, but knew they would never make it out the wilderness without him. Ace was their human map, their guide, and without him they'd never make it to the main road, which wasn't for miles.

They've traveled over rough rugged terrain, driven over some fragile overpass, passing over a creak of streaming water, rode several miles into deep forestry with dirt and rocky landscapes, and wild life on all four sides. Night had fallen and without Ace, Roy and Lou-Lou would be supper by morning.

Lou-Lou was in distress, balled into a fetal position, looking up into the barrel of death. Ace chanted and praised Allah every few seconds, thrusting his arms in the air and shouting *God is the greatest.*

Roy saw an opportunity to disarm Ace, so he moved in. His arms propelled beneath Ace's. His praise for Allah cut short as Roy's forceful hands pressed against the back of his neck. A *Full-Nelson* wrestling move had been administered properly, causing Ace to lose breath, slowly losing consciousness. After weakening Ace into submission, Roy released him seconds before he blacked out.

Thump.

Ace crashed to the floor, inhaling deeply. He coughed and hacked, struggling for air. Roy stood over his body, contemplating on which body part to attack next. With all his might Ace held up a single finger, declaring his surrender. He coughed, hacked, head pressed against the floor for support.

After a few seconds his breathing became more regular, normal. The crucifix move applied by Roy had Ace partially dazed. He couldn't recall why he'd been subdued. He couldn't recollect sounds, feelings, movements. It was like being asleep with both eyes opened. He couldn't explain why Roy choked him out, but he knew it had to be for a good reason.

He gazed at Lou-Lou as she advanced cautiously in his direction. She was crying hard. *What have I done?* He didn't know, couldn't remember, and had no clue. The evils within controlled all things.

She lifted the big tool, pointed it at his head. Knowing if she discharged his noggin would explode into a million watermelon pieces. He stared at death. The vicious look in her eyes clearly described her rage. She wanted to destroy him, but Roy firmly demanded she be cool. They needed him.

"We got a problem?"

Every head in the room jerked towards the door. Scalped bald, white skin, thin lips, pencil nose, racial tats branded his cause. The blue eye demon that stood in the passage way represented *White Power*.

"We good," Roy said calmly.

Skin head stepped one foot into the shack, stood poised. He eyed Ace, who was sprawled out against the floor. "What's up with your boy?" Lou-Lou's jaw tightened at the way the word *boy* slipped from his lips.

"I said we good." Roy's voice was too relaxed to question.

Blue eyes shifted towards Lou-Lou and back towards Ace. He ran his tongue across his teeth, squinted. "Good. Let's get the hell out of here."

Ace rode shotgun as he guided them back the way they came. Lou-Lou sat in the backseat with the burner pressed against the rear of his head. White power trailed them to the main road. He cruised generously behind, high beaming them the entire way.

"He's a smug superior bastard," Lou-Lou said angrily.

Roy said nothing. Instead he kept his eyes on the dirt path ahead. White or black, money was money. There wasn't a *Code of Ethics* handbook he was obligated to follow. He looked over at Ace, who looked a few cans short of a six pack. He knew by first glance that the guy wasn't all there. He tried telling Lou-Lou that Ace's elevator stopped at the third floor. But you can't tell a black woman shit. Roy had no earthly idea what transpired between Lou-Lou and Ace back at the cabin, and he wasn't about to ask for the 411 now.

Strange noises emitted from beyond. The wilderness was hungry. All doors were locked, all windows rolled up with a slight crack for ventilation.

"Me and my sister Kema got lost in these very woods."

The truck stopped. High beams flickered from behind signaling them to move. Roy clinched the steering wheel. His eyes shifted towards the rear-view mirror. He watched her for a long moment. She barely moved a muscle. The cat was out the bag and Roy was vexed.

Claw like noises against the passenger's side door made Roy eased out of position. They continued down the narrow rocky road. Tree branches slapped against the truck, lashing its twigs in anger. High beams lit their path.

"My grandmother had taken us to the cabin for the weekend one summer. We spotted a fawn, and tried chasing it. Somehow I lost track, ended up way off the reserve by that old creek," he pointed up ahead.

"I was scared but I had to be strong for Kema. She looked up to me. So, we decided to try catching fish until I came up with a plan."

"Shut the fuck up," Lou-Lou demanded.

So he did. Silenced by her obvious dislike for the story, Ace only spoke to give directions. There was a dip in the terrain. More water, a stream cascading over rocks slipped alongside them. The colossal moon beamed brightly above. Lou-Lou nudged the back of Ace's head with the pistol.

"I don't remember this," she said. Her stomach was churning with anxiety.

"Me either," Roy added, peering through the windows. "I think we're lost."

"We're good. Just stay the course," Ace said confidently.

So they did. They had to.

"Your sister name is Kema?" Roy quizzed.

"Yeah. She's all the family I have. She takes care of me and my moms. I caught a bullet in the noggin overseas and…"

"Didn't I tell you to shut the fuck up?" she cut him off.

Roy glared at Lou-Lou. She sucked her teeth, refusing to feel guilty for not revealing that small little detail. A girl was entitled to keep some things to herself, right?

"You caught one to the head?" Roy continued with genuine curiosity.

Ace hesitated before speaking. Roy was obviously in control, but Lou-Lou didn't seem to fold under his authority. There was an apparent power struggle between the two.

"Still got the slug in my head to prove it," Ace said, flinched. He braced himself for whatever Lou-Lou had in store, but the blow never came.

"Damn, that's crazy," Roy said, truly intrigued.

"No, this motherfucker is the one that's crazy," Lou-Lou spat.

Roy growled, "*Yo*- on the real, calm that shit down."

She calmed down but kept the burner steady. Roy didn't know Ace like she did. Any sound, thump, or vibration might set that whack job off.

"If you know what I know, you'll keep small talk to a minimum. Never know what might set him off," Lou-Lou said, keeping her voice leveled, which took great effort. Roy wasn't all there either. The last thing she needed was for him to start tripping. She blew out a sigh, and hoped for the best.

"She's right," Ace confessed, "I'm crazy. Haven't been taking my med's lately. I hear voices. These voices tell me to do bad things. Terrible things like harm, rape, kill. Dr. Scallion diagnosed me with *Paranoid Schizophrenia*, and *Bi-polar*, along with that I suffer from *Post Traumatic Stress* disorder. I'm sick." He shook his head. Lou-Lou lost her aim. The handle came down, landed against his shoulder. Ace released a wail.

"Don't move," she yelled.

Roy's face grimaced. She sucked her teeth, rolled her neck justifiably. Roy didn't know the half. She'd been forced upon, offered up as sacrificial tokens to Ace *Hades*, and damn near sucked the tip of his AR15. *So you can kiss my black ass!*

Paved road up ahead signaled they were easing back into civilization. Wild life seemed further out of reach as the sound of a neighboring highway jilted their senses. There were less trees and more sky. Things were looking familiar. Roy lowered his window, extended his arm upward, willing his Nazi friend the right-of-way. Flickering lights indicated the deal was sealed. The utility van whizzed pass them, and disappeared.

Roy parked several yards away from the freeway. The ditch on his left seemed like a perfect location to start a family plot.

"Get out."

Ace blinked nervously but obeyed Roy's command. Roy wasn't much bigger then he, but the burner in his hand gave him the advantage. Ace surveyed his final resting place for a second. A cluster of rocks would have to serve as his tomb.

"Hurry your ass up." Lou-Lou barked.

Hard dirt balanced his steps around the nose of the vehicle. Lou-Lou was on his heels, burner stuck in his spine like acupuncture. Tortured by a sudden case of acid reflex, he stopped, held his chest. Slow burn attacked his esophagus. Or was it a heart attack? Death snatched most of his relatives that way. The old ticker usually gave up on his kinfolks as they neared the big *five-o*. He and his sister Kema had made a pact to surpass those stats, and live. But now there he was, a young man about to take his dirt nap. *Not here. Not like this. Not without a fight.*

Wobbly legs gave way. He collapsed beneath the headlight. Slow burn intensified. Chest tightened, pressure caused him to suck back air. Ace gripped the metal grill guard, held on to it for his life. He held on as if his boat had just capsized in the middle of the Atlantic and all he had was an oar to keep him afloat. He held on as if he were hanging from metal beams eighty-eight floors high when the first plane struck the south tower. He closed his eyes shut, imagined himself dangling midair, looking for his rescue team in the thick of smoke. *Help!*

Lou-Lou stood frozen, not wanting to create any more foot prints. Just in case this area became an official crime scene. She wanted to leave the least amount of evidence as possible. Roy lifted his pistol, aimed it.

"Get up."

Ace held onto the grill, pleading for his life. He wanted them to give him a pass, overlook his malice actions. He had a disability, a real handicap. He'd served his goddamn country, shouldn't he be pardoned? Wasn't his life worthy of a second chance? Where's the goddamn president when you need him?

Roy moved in, grabbed Ace by the collar. He lost his grip against the metal. His body scrapped the ground, finger nails filed down to a bloody numb as he dug into the earth's crust for support.

Roy released his collar, drew back his foot and sledge hammered his face with the sole of his boot. Ace's pain echoed, followed by whimpering and tears. Lou-Lou eased closer to examine the bloody mask. Roy did some damage for sure.

"Make him take his clothes off."

Roy gave Lou-Lou a puzzled look. "What the hell for?"

"Just cause."

Lou-Lou wanted to toy with their victim, and she probably had good reason to do so. Roy on the other hand hated to prolong the inevitable. Sonny expected him home in a few. Shit needed to end, *now*.

"You heard the lady. Remove your clothes."

Ace disrobed down to his briefs and socks, begging for more time. To live, breathe, get right with God.

"Socks and drawers too," she commanded.

Shit was going too far. Roy turned his back as Lou-Lou had it her way. He inhaled the dampness around him. If he never saw another tree for as long as he lived he wouldn't be mad.

"She's so extra," he said.

Roy was simple. Pull the trigger and get ghost. He didn't have time for playing games. This wasn't the damn movies. Roy glanced back, saw Ace standing stark naked, pleading for his life. Sickened by the display, he shouted, "Hurry up!" He popped his head into the back seat, stared at his small fortune. Since Ace was as good as dead, a third of the profit now would be divvied down the middle. That made him smile.

"Can't take it with you Ace," he said with not even an ounce of remorse. He had to take a leak, been holding his fluids since they left the cabin. He surveyed the area, found a spot by a big tree.

Noises from beyond caused Lou-Lou to jerk her aim away. And in that split second Ace gripped her neck, lifted her off the ground, both feet dangling in the air. She let out a shrill scream.

"*Roy.*"

The first crack of the bullet was aimed for Roy's head but derailed when Lou-Lou gouged Ace's eye socket. He tossed her into the ditch. Roy took cover behind the tree. Precise shots chewed through bark. *Sharp shooter.* Roy slithered on his belly into the wilderness, seeking refugee. Ace let off shot after shot.

Click

Click

Click

Chamber empty.

The night went silent. Everything stopped moving. Even the wilderness obeyed the code of stillness. And then the wind whistled a sweet tune of death.

Roy groaned, rolling onto his side. He went for his tool, let off several intended shots. He hoped to God Lou-Lou had enough sense to stay low. He bit down on his bottom lip, felt his lower leg. It burned. *I'm hit.*

Roy pressed his hand against the wound. Blood oozed. He sat up in a midway crunch, teetered back and forth, inhaling, exhaling pain. The smell of iron in the blood attracted wolves. He struggled to stand, but flattened when he heard movement.

CHAPTER 27

B ury me upside down so the world can kiss my ass Bitch was what the keychain read. She couldn't help but laugh out loud. It defined her to the letter. *I'm in touch with my inner Bitch. It's Miss Bitch to you. I'm the Bitch my mother always wanted to be. Cold hearted Bitch. Queen Bitch. Hot Bitch. Sexy Bitch. Drink Up Bitches. Head Bitch in Charge. 100% genuine Bitch. Shut up or get Bitch slapped. Bee-yotche, Pleazzzeee.* The last keychain that dangled didn't belong in her Bitch collection. *I do what the voices tell me.* Her fingers gripped those words, laughter muted. She took in air.

"I hate this one."

She hated it because it was her brother's truth. The voices in his head ruled him, propelled him into everyday life like a puppet. Controlled by the whispers, the mental chatter governed his on-n-off switch.

"Ah, the infamous Bitch arsenal of keychains. What's cooking good looking?"

Kema twisted back, and smiled at seventy years of class, charm, charisma. A lady's magnet, a power held humbly in the crook of his smile. From what she's heard, Mr. Peterson was gifted.

She jiggled her keys, "My kryptonite to keep the scrubs away."

"Well, that ought to work," he chuckled.

"So Ace got him a new lady friend I see."

"*Ugh*, don't even mention it," Kema said, with a grimace.

"She seems pretty nice, and might I add she sure was a looker."

"You mean hooker?"

He laughed. "I think Ace may have hit the jackpot this go around."

"No one will ever be good enough for Ace."

She quickly assessed the items in Mr. Peterson's plastic bag. Wine, french bread, cheese and fruit.

"Someone has a date?"

He winked. "I aim to please."

Bet you do.

She watched Mr. Peterson retreat inside his apartment. Lou-Lou buried her smile the best she could. The old man was fine as aged wine, and if he hadn't been a close friend of Ace's, she may have allowed him to offer her a history lesson.

Kema refocused, located the spare key Ace had given to her months ago. She intruded on his privacy often, especially when she had a hunch he'd missed his medication. Ace started having his spells again. The voices inside his head were causing him to act irrationally.

He made her promise to use the key *only* if she felt that he was in danger of hurting himself or someone else. Kema being the hard head she was used the key whenever she pleased. If he caught her snooping, she would look him square in the eye, tears and all, claiming how she felt in her spirit something was wrong.

That day, that feeling settled on her like God himself tapped her on the shoulder, and whispered her brother's name. While visiting her mother, his face kept flashing before her. Although they weren't twins, and had more than a decade of time between them, they mirrored each other's feelings. Positive, negative, in-different emotions amplified between two siblings as if they shared the same womb at the *same time*. Kema could feel the danger surrounding him. Something was definitely wrong.

Index finger ran across a piece of furniture. "Clean-Freak."

The wall-unit was spotless, dust free. The Army taught him how to be tidy, uncluttered, and meticulous about the space in which he rested his head. She glanced up at her senior photo and almost gagged. She was a pimpled faced train wreck her last year of high school.

She eyed the eccentric art that decorated the wall. Her favorite piece, a mirror made of wire and glass. She winked at herself, loving the skin she was in. "Baby piss, who would have thought?"

She smiled at a photo taken of them both at *Tybee Island*. Sand between their toes, hot sun beaming on their head, phenomenal water view slowly brought her dear brother back to reality.

"Bro, you needed that trip. *We* needed that trip," she whispered.

The Department of Veterans Affairs offered free counseling, but their efforts seem to cause more harm than good. It was vital they sought treatment away from Base in order for Ace to begin his long journey of healing. These sorts of treatments of course didn't fall within the guidelines of his health coverage, so once again Kema stuck her hand way down deep into the pit of her empty purse, and magically produced funds to help cure her brother's trauma.

Over a dozen recommendations led her to a pricy Institution in Savanna. A safe, nurturing environment was essential. They specialized in *Bi-Polar, Depression, Schizophrenia* and other behavioral disorders. She assured Ace that his stay would be more like a retreat than hospitalization. This fully accredited, serene facility gave hope to the hopeless, and helped to piece together the broken.

After three months of therapy, Ace was worse off than when he went in. The medication they administered could knock a whale on its ass. Seeing her brother immobile, silent, eyes practically dead made her rethink her decision to have him admitted there in the first place.

That hot June morning she'd driven from Atlanta to Savanna with her ink pen ready to sign his release. She spotted Dr. Scallion trotting from room to room, visually examining the residents from a small port in the steel door. He jotted down reminders on his trusty pad, and nodded his big bobble head.

"Dr. Scallion." She called out. "May I have a word with you?"

Dr. Scallion looked up from his specs, smiled.

"Good Morning Ms...?"

"Kema... Just Kema."

They shook firmly. "Alright, just Kema. What can I do for you on this glorious morning?"

"Well..."

"You know God is good?"

"Yes Dr. All the time, but we need to speak about…"

"Yesterday's service was a God send. I tell you the Holy Spirit was jumping all over that congregation. The Lord…"

It was the same old conversation every time she stopped to speak with him. He always had a word from God. Kema felt his reference to God and the bible was unprofessional, especially within their setting. As far as she was concerned the facility wasn't a bible based facility. Its mission statement said nothing about God, or the heavens, or prophesying to members of the family each and every time they came for a visit. She had nothing against praising the lord, but Dr. Scallion was overkill.

"Look, don't mean to be disrespectful, but I'm here to sign my brother out."

"Is that so?"

"Yes. And I would like to handle this business as quickly as possible."

"Is there something wrong? Why the sudden dismissal?"

"God said this isn't the right fit for him. So, if you don't mind."

Her reference to God made him nod his big bobble head in acceptance. They proceeded to walk down the narrow corridor. The main office was just a few steps ahead. Dr. Scallion stopped, looked at her with concerned eyes.

"Do keep in mind your brother is a very sick man. He needs around the clock care, evaluations, counseling."

"I'm well aware of this."

"Post Traumatic Stress Disorder is just the tip of the iceberg. We've recently diagnosed him with Paranoid Schizophrenia, and Bi Polar Disorder." He could tell that this news bothered her.

"You weren't made aware of this?"

"No."

"My assistant placed several calls to you."

She cursed herself. The *burnout* phone she had turned off weeks ago. She had a new number and failed to provide the center with an update.

"My fault Dr. Scallion, I've had a recent number change and…" immediately she quit rambling. There was no excuse for her behavior.

"So you do understand how important it is for him to continue treatment at our facility?"

She gave the doctor a sideward's glance. *Tell me anything in order to keep me paying. Paranoid Schizophrenia my ass. He's just fucked up from the war. That's all!*

"My decision to remove him is final."

"There's nothing I can do to change your mind?"

"No sir."

"If you don't mind me asking, where will you take him next?"

"Tybee Island," she said with glee.

A cynical laugh escaped him. "The Beach?"

Kema gave the Dr. a scornful look. *Bobble Head* needed the shit smacked out of him but she chose to remain civilized. The last thing she needed was for Dr. Death to stick her with a hypothermic needle, fading her thoughts with tranquilizers. He looked like the type to lock you up with the crazies just for being disrespectful. She saw what happened to Leonardo DiCaprio in *Shutter Island*.

She layered her lips with Vaseline, manufactured a smile.

"Dr. Scallion, I appreciate all that you've done for my brother during his short stay. Your staff has been nothing but good to him, but I know what he needs. The sandy beach will do him some justice."

He opened his mouth to speak, she interrupted.

"Sand and sun hasn't touched my brothers toes in God knows how long."

"You can't erase his memories."

"Yes, I know, but what's wrong with creating new ones?"

"Paranoid Schizophrenia and Post Traumatic Stress Disorder is a dangerous combination." Dr. Scallion leaned in close. His eyes leveled hers. "He comes and goes, in and out, fading into the darkness, back and forth between the present and the past. He's a soldier one minute, the next minute he's a suicide bomber ready to give his life for Allah. He's high risk."

Oh my God. Lay it on thick why don't you. She kept her smirk buried beneath her tight lips. *Keep it real. You want him as a case study.* Dr. Scallion wanted to toy, examine, and poke at the three marbles Ace had left. She knew the deal.

"I'm pressed for time. Can we handle the paper work soon?"

"Consider a one day pass."

"No thanks."

He nodded his bulldozer head. "Right this way."

They took a few steps forward, stopped at Ace's door. They looked in; saw him staring at the concrete wall. No blinking, no movement, stiff as a board. Dr. Scallion gripped her firmly at the elbow. His freaky eyes, bushy brows and enormous head made her extremely uncomfortable.

"A little sand and sun has never hurt anyone. However, if for some reason *your kind of therapy* proves to worsen his condition, promise me you'll bring him back."

"Yes, of course."

Kema shoved the thought of Dr. Death aside and headed towards the kitchen. She opened the fridge. A bottle of red wine, three tall neck Coronas and a bunch of five hour energy shots lined the door. She shoved aside the gallon of 2% milk, jar of jalapenos, squirt bottled mayo-ketchup-mustard, and grabbed a plastic container. She pulled a fork from the drawer and dug into the wedding cake.

"Ace said this cake was good, but *damn*." She smacked her lips.

Three bites made the cake disappear. She swallowed milk straight from the container, belched. Still hungry, she grabbed a loaf of potato bread from the top of the fridge.

"Fuck."

Half the loaf slipped from the plastic, landing on the floor. She shook each slice, kissed it to God, placed it back into the bag, and twisted the tie. No longer hungry she headed out the kitchen, but halted her stride. A stack of mail, mostly bills was wedged between a metal napkin holder. A letter from the Savanna Institution sat on top, unopened. She tore into the thick envelope, and read. They wanted to evaluate, assess, and pump more downer drugs into her brothers system. He was a peculiar observation, guinea pig; a subject worth mentioning in Dr. Scallion's next published Psychotherapy *Best-seller*.

"Not on my dime."

She rummaged through a drawer, located a lighter, burned the tip of the letter and dropped its ashes into the sink. An envelope marked *One Hour Photo* graced her finger tips.

"Look at this fat fuck Vick."

She couldn't help but laugh. She skimmed through the wedding photos, stopping at one in particular. It was a photo of Ace and the new bride. His hand at the small of her waist was without a shadow of a doubt inappropriate. There were two glasses inside the sink, one with a shade of bronze on the rim. She replaced the photos, and headed towards the rear of the apartment.

Kema opened the bedroom door and was greeted with an awful odor.

"What died?"

The room was immaculate. The bedding had not a single wrinkle, yet the joint stunk. She figured he'd had some funky chick in his bed who didn't know the meaning of soap and water. She hit the switch on the wall. The lights and ceiling fan came on at the same time.

As the funk circulated, her eyes glanced towards the dresser. She jumped at the old spooky sculpture Ace made while over in some third world country. Somehow he'd managed to smuggle the wooden piece back into the states. It stood four inches tall, two inches wide, camel hair glued at the throne, dried sheep's skin wrapped the body. Three black candles circled the ugly figurine. A bowl of water, rock, and wood peace pipe lined the back, near the attached mirror.

When she asked him about the significance of the sculpture his eyes grew to the size of dinner plates. He yelled something in Arabic, and then told her to never touch his *Hades* which from a biblical stand point meant *grave, hell.*

"Nut job."

Ace's mental equilibrium was off the scale at times. His logic of life surrounded his *Hades*, his *grave*, his *hell.* She felt helpless, alone, and afraid for her brother. With the stress of her mother's illness, and now Ace's mental sickness, Kema turned to the one person she could trust. Chief Edward Burnett wasn't just Ace's old college crony, he was family. She confided in Chief about Ace's new found reality *(Paranoid Schizophrenia and Post Traumatic Stress Disorder)*, but to her amazement he begged her to keep quiet. *Give him time,* he said. According to Chief, many soldiers came back a little messed up. Most, if not all had witnessed the unimaginable, done the unforgivable, and couldn't forget, couldn't stop feeling, hearing, dreaming.

According to Chief, Ace wasn't that bad off. He'd seen worse, and to disclose Dr. Scallion's tentative findings would ruin her brother's squeaky record. *He'll be labeled as a loon, Kema.* So, she kept quiet under the conditions that her brother's combats days were over. Chief pulled some strings, called in a few favors and helped Ace land a communications position. His job on base as a dispatcher kept him tied to a desk, in constant communication with *real* people.

"Ace, you are one sick puppy," she muttered.

Kema recalled the first call she received about her brother's psychosis behavior. Hanna was his girlfriend at the time. She was a cute red head lieutenant he'd fallen madly in love with during his short stay in Budapest. Hanna was from Tennessee with a thick country-fried accent that drove Kema batty.

"Calm down, speak slowly."

"Ace done did it again."

"Did what?"

"Wet my goddamn bed."

"Huh?"

"He sprayed my damn bed again."

"*Ah,* Hanna I don't need to know that my brother is giving you golden showers. Better yet, keep your freaky business with Ace to yourself."

"Sweetie, you're not hearing me. You better come get him before I have his ass committed."

"Why, for what?"

"This is his third time, I can't take this... he's crazy."

"His third time, what the hell are you talking about?"

"It started with the dreams. He would wake up in a pool of sweat, breathing hard, eyes stretched across the room, like he was possessed."

"What kind of dreams?"

"Reoccurring ones. The same dream haunts him over and over again. Sort of like that witch dream. You ever had that feeling a witch was riding your back and you couldn't move, get up, or scream for help?"

"It happened once. When I was a kid."

"He goes days without sleep. He's afraid of the dark. Afraid to close his eyes and be in blackness. He's terrified that he might not wake back up. My light bill is sky high."

Hanna paused. "Then there's moments he prefers darkness. The night soothes him. He forbids me to turn a light on. I make my way in the dark. I can't live like this. He's paranoid all the time. Everyone is out to hurt him. Your brother needs professional help."

"Is this a joke?"

"No joke Kimma. No fucking Joke."

"It's *Kema* and where is he?"

"He's rambling through the kitchen drawers looking for his keys." Hanna called his name. "He wet my damn mattress. The first time he blamed it on the alcohol. He said he was so wasted that he couldn't move. The next time the witch was riding his back. This time I found him sleep walking, speaking Arabic, spraying my bed, my furniture, throwing jabs, fighting the air."

"Talking Arabic... Sleep walking... Pissing on furniture... Fighting the air. What the fuck Hanna. Did you give him something?"

Kema's accusatory tone made Hanna suck back air. "Me?"

"*Yeah you bitch*, what the fuck did you slip my brother?"

"I don't believe this."

"You white bitches like that acid. You drugged him?"

"I would never. How dare you..."

Kema heard Hanna scream, then her voice silenced. She heard Ace speaking in a language she'd never heard before. Maybe it was the Arabic tongue Hanna just warned her about, either way she had no idea what he was saying. Suddenly his voice became low, menacing. Hanna sobbed hysterically as he spoke death to her.

Kema's cell broke into her grim thoughts. She shook away Chief, Hanna and Ace, looked at her phone. It was an **1877**- toll free number flashing on her screen.

"Take me off your list okay." A chipper voice came through offering her a new package on her mobile phone plan. "I don't want a damn upgrade; I've got three thousand minutes, unlimited mobile to mobile, free internet, so stop bugging me."

Click.

The *Hades* was giving her the creeps so she decided to head back into the living room. She stopped at the oversized dresser on the way out. Sheets of paper stuck out the top drawer. She opened the drawer slowly, careful not to disturb the *Hades*, or shift the candles, or interfere with whatever séance he'd preformed last.

She grabbed a small laminated map, and paper, and just as she was about to close the drawer, she noticed her brother's cell phone buried beneath socks. It blinked, indicating he'd had a missed call. She shoved the phone into her pocket, even more convinced that something was wrong. "He never leaves home without his phone."

Once inside the living room she laid the documents out against the coffee table. A small map of South Georgia, papers detailing a truck route, and receipts from The Home Depot sat before her. She looked at the map pensively, having seen it before. It took her just a few minutes to realize it was a map of her grandparents land out in Locust Grove. The old document had yellow highlighter circling a prime location. She examined each receipt. Shovels, gloves, rope, hourly rental for a forklift.

"Okay, what the hell are you up to?"

Her fingers traced each page, not exactly sure what she was looking at. That wrenching feeling at the pit of her stomach was back. Her cell phone, once again interrupted her thoughts. It was a blocked call. She started not to answer. She figured it was another telemarketer trying to up-sale her on her mobile services, perhaps it was someone trying to convince her to apply for a home loan, or it could have been some organization looking for another donation. Then she thought about Roy. Kema called him back to back, leaving several messages until his box no longer accepted her whiny voice.

"This is Ms. Chambers calling from Spalding Regional. You were listed under ICE."

"*ICE*... what's that? Who is this?"

"*I.C.E... In case of emergency*. You were listed as point of contact on a medical ID bracelet belonging to Aaaameeria.... Amirea...hum I think it's...."

As the woman on the phone struggled to pronounce her brother's name her eyes filled with water. Ace wore his medical bracelet at all times, even slept in it.

"...forgive me dear, but we have a Mr. Anderson here. He was involved in a shooting."

Her heart stopped.

"What's your relation?"

She became lightheaded. She felt herself slipping. Knees collapsed. She fell to the floor, facing East. Bent over, forehead pressed against the carpet. She prayed.

"Ma'am, what's your relation to the victim?"

Victim.

She blinked once, and a flood of tears made way.

She swallowed hard. "Is he..."

"As of now he's in critical condition. May I have your relation please?"

"Sister."

***

"Ma'am yah can't park here." The flashlight cop stated strongly as he wiped powdered donuts from his lips.

Kema continued through the sliding glass doors, up towards the information desk. A line of folks stood before her. The wounded and sick filled the waiting area. Stretchers and wheel chairs lined the main corridor. *Ace, hold on...I'm coming.* With no time to spare, she bypassed the long line and headed straight for the elevator doors. Face wet, heart thumping, nerves rattled down to the core. *As of now he's in critical condition.* She recalled the severity of the nurse's voice. The extremity of the word *critical* alone meant danger.

"Ma'am, move yah vehicle or I'll be forced to have yah towed."

She snapped her neck in the guard's direction. Eyes blood shot red, swollen at the rim. "Tow my car and I'll kick your ass old man."

"*No Parking Zone.* Can't yah read the cotton picking signs?"

She swung her large designer bag, using it as a weapon. The guard backed away, grabbing the can of pepper spray from his waist. He held steady, waiting for her to make another move. She thought of accepting the challenged but remembered why she was there in the first place. Ace had been shot and was listed in critical condition. That reality scared her.

Go Kema. You don't have time. Go.

"My car better be there when I get back or else," she warned the old man who tugged at his trousers, exposing the bulge in his pants.

"Or else what?"

She mashed for the elevator several times. Foot tapping against the floor, migraine throbbing her temples. She stared at her own reflection in the shiny doors, realizing how swollen her eyes were. Nostrils clogged with worry. Mouth agape so that she could breathe. *Maybe I should take the stairs.*

Over her shoulder stood the old man calling in something over his walkie-talkie. She twisted her spine, and glared. "Look soggy nuts, don't fuck with my car."

The old man shifted his dentures in his mouth, completely stunned at her blatant disrespect. He shook his decrepit finger in her direction. "I know yah."

"You don't know me so back off grandpa."

"You that gal who lifted my wallet. Me and my buddy Harold were having lunch in Atlanta the other day."

Oh Shit!

A shifty look passed over her face. She leaned in, pushed for the elevator again.

"You stole my goddamn wallet *you… you crook*!"

Heads turned in their direction.

"Hey Phil, everything okay?" another flashlight cop half the man's age hollered a few feet away. With backup in route, Kema whipped her head in all directions in search of the nearest staircase.

"This… this…this gal here took my wallet."

The elevator finally arrived, and was thankfully empty. She hopped on, pressed for the fifth floor and headed straight to the Intensive Care Unit. Kema lifted her legs high, and ran as fast as she could down the corridor. The length of the hall seemed like forever with no end. By the time she reached the room she noticed nothing but chaos. Doctors and nurses traveled frantically in zigzag patterns performing life saving techniques. She pushed through the door.

"Ace!" she screamed.

"Keep her back," someone yelled.

Kema fought through medical officials, struggling to reach his bedside. White coats tried to subdue her but the love for her brother overpowered their attempts. By the time she touched the hem of his garment it was too late.

Too late to say goodbye.

Too late to say I love you.

Too late to place a hand against his chest and feel life beat, *one last time.*

***

Through slit eyes everything was one big blur. The sound of friction rubbing, the smell of lavender, movements of someone meandered their way about the small room. Kema lifted her lids a bit more, noticed a full figure in pink scrubs, big puff hair, holding a clipboard and pen.

"Hello," the nurse spoke in an angelic tone.

Kema groaned, tried to sit up but failed in her attempt. Her head was spinning at the speed of light and any sudden movements would surely throw off her balance.

"What happened?" she whispered.

A gentle hand planted against her cheek. "You fainted. Don't you remember?"

Ace. She closed her eyes tightly, gripping the metal rail. Agonizing tears slipped from her lids, spilling along the sides of her face. Tormented with the truth, plagued with sudden grief made her lean over the side and vomit. One good hurl left her empty. She wiped her mouth with her sleeve and cried.

Realities of Ace being hooked up to that morphine drip crept back in. Bright red string of light blaring from the cardiac machine as he flatlined made the air back up in her lungs.

"I'm sorry, but he didn't pull through."

Kema's scream was agonizing and heartfelt. The nurse rubbed her back in circular motions as Kema gagged and coughed. Ace was dead. Her brother was dead. Her best friend was dead. *Who would want Ace dead* was the million dollar question? Ace was a lame. He worked a desk job, and stayed to himself.

The full figured nurse side-stepped the vomit, and scampered across the room to grab bottled water, and a box of Kleenex.

"Thanks."

"Welcome."

Kema pulled a single sheet, blew her runny nose. She pulled another sheet, dapped her eyes but the tears kept coming. "This is unbelievable."

"It always is."

Kema looked up at the woman who'd smelled of lavender body spray, and whose demeanor was all so soothing, yet commanding.

"Was he your husband?"

Kema sniffled. "Brother. Only one."

"I'm sorry."

Kema grabbed her throbbing forehead, squeezing tension away from her mind. It was all too surreal. The only person in the world that kept her grounded was gone.

"God will bring you through."

She gave the nurse a wayward glance and shrugged pathetically. Her faith in the big man had diminished down to a single pulp. Her blood boiled in her veins as she felt her adrenalin pumping. *I need to find out who did this.* She sat up, planted both feet firmly against the floor. The smell of vomit beneath her heels heightened the disinfectant, and beef burrito she'd eaten just hours ago.

"Maybe you should rest," the nurse suggested.

"I'll sleep when I'm dead. Right now I need answers."

Kema whipped her head in all directions, eyes bulging, mouth agape. "My bag. Where's my bag?"

"Check the closet."

Suddenly equipped with enough energy to run a marathon, she sprang to her feet. A sigh of relief escaped her. Her contents within remained untouched.

"By the way, I'm Nurse Sonny."

"I'm Kema."

The lady with the big puff hair looked over her shoulder nervously, then back. Kema could tell she wanted to say something.

"This ain't none of my business, but I thought you should know Detectives were here asking questions."

"What kind of questions?"

"They suspect your brother to have been involved in some robbery," Nurse Sonny whispered.

"Robbery?"

"*Shush.* That's the word."

"They got the wrong guy. My brother was many things, but a thief wasn't one of them," Kema protested. She took a seat in the big leather chair, placing her throbbing head into the palm of her hands.

Nurse Sonny looked over her shoulder a second time, closing the curtain shut. "I can lose my job for administering this, but here." Kema grabbed the two pain pills and swallowed dry. "Your brother was shot six times in the chest. He was found..."

The sound of walkie-talkies brought their conversation to a screeching halt. Nurse Sonny quickly busied herself with the fallen bodily fluids left at the bedside. Kema stood, tossed her purse over her shoulder, and straightened her clothes. Voices squawked over high frequency waves. Fuzzy static stood still outside the curtain, then turned down low. Two plain clothes officers popped their heads in, intruding on Kema's hour of grief.

"May we enter?" Tall, lean, big feet, big hands, low afro faded at the neck spoke up first.

Kema inhaled the stench in the room. "I was just leaving."

"I'm Detective Marshall, and this is Detective Olive. We would like to have a word with you?"

Detective Olive was black as tar, a wide receiver for the Falcons. She was a real beast. Kema glanced down at the pebble on her finger and couldn't believe somebody actually wifed the creature.

"Okay. Let's talk," Kema managed to say as she watched both detectives get comfortable. Detective Marshall positioned his leanness against a wall, with both legs and arms crossed. Detective Olive grabbed a chair, and straddled it. She wet the tip of her pen, and scribbled something against her pad.

Nurse Sonny slipped off soiled gloves, dumping them into the receptacle, and was heading out the door when Kema called her name.

"Yes."

Kema leaned in, gave the woman that smelled of lavender a massive hug. Human affection was something she needed, even if it had to come from a perfect stranger. Everyone needed love. For a second, the nurse hesitated on returning the embrace. Kema could tell that she was trying desperately not to get too involved.

Screw it! Nurse Sonny wrapped her big arms around Kema and held onto her as she sobbed hard into her shoulder.

"Thank you," Kema whispered.

"God is in control."

Kema sniffed back a nostril full of mucus, swallowed. Nurse Sonny cringed. Mucus was meant to come out, not be sucked back in, and swallowed, only to rise again. *Yuck!* Kema stepped away, wiped her wet face with the back of her sleeve. She watched Nurse Sonny disappear, leaving her alone with Detective Marshall and Detective Olive who were patiently waiting.

"Your name?"

Kema looked at both detectives, confused.

"Simple question," Detective Olive said peering up at Kema.

"Kema. That's spelled *K.e.m.a.*"

"Last name?"

"Look. Do you have any leads on who killed my brother?" Kema asked, feeling her skin bubble. She had done so much, and there was no telling what they actually knew about her. Detectives did detective stuff like researched next of kin, pulled records, files, studied the history of those closest prior to examination. They looked for motives, an alibi, and witnesses to paint a picture. She knew the drill and there was no way in hell she was about to slip up and say some bull that would have them looking at her sideways.

"Ma'am this is protocol."

"Well, excuse me Detective Olive if I don't seem enthused to follow protocol. My brother lost his life tonight. I'm in no mood..." she inhaled, trying desperately to stop the tears from rolling. "Unless you got some information to share with me, there's nothing to talk about."

Detective Marshall bounced off the wall, shuffled his way across the room with purpose. "That relentless trigger finger is still out there," he said pointing towards the window. "A trucker found your brother on the side of the road, naked."

That information took her breath away. Deeply disturbed by the details, she took a seat. Kema hadn't been briefed on the specifics leading up to Ace's discovery. All she knew is he'd been shot, in the chest, and was now pronounced dead. And there was that bit of information Nurse Sonny spoke of. *Robbery!*

"Naked, as in no clothes?" Kema asked, massaging her temples.

"Not a stitch, except for his medical bracelet," Detective Olive chimed in, scribbling notes against her pad.

"Detective Olive is following protocol, just asking a few preliminary questions to piece together what actually happened. So please, give us your time and attention."

"But I don't know anything."

"Let us be the judge of that."

CHAPTER 28

Military issued gats stolen. Ace called in sick from his dispatch job, but subsequently ends up naked, riddled with bullets on the side of the expressway, and *dead*. They had nothing but an assumption, a theory at best. As Detective Marshall and Detective Olive kept Kema cornered with questions, Military police seized the moment to search Ace's apartment. They would find nothing for Kema possessed the documents which linked Ace to the heist.

He-Man bitch, Olive kept a skeptical eye planted on Kema's purse. She referenced how nice the bag was, how expensive it looked, how it looked roomy enough to hide things. Kema had what they needed and for some reason, Detective Olive sensed that. What she possessed on the inside of her bag would connect the dots; bring their case to a close in less than 48hours.

As Detectives realized they were getting nowhere with Kema, they left, leaving her each with a contact card. She promised to telephone in the event she remembered some crucial detail that would help them do their job effectively.

Outside the hospital Kema decided to take a tote of some earth to relax her nerves. She unzipped her bag, looked in, knocked evidence around, and finally located the pack of smoke. Inside were five nicotine sticks, the other white boys were laced with that *Kush*.

"Damn, where is my lighter?"

She searched her bag, but came up empty. She stuck the tightly rolled *J* at the corner of her mouth, slipped her purse over her shoulder, and patted her pants pockets. Her face lit up when she felt her flame. She also felt her brother's phone.

"I almost forgot I had this."

She lit her desire, took a few totes, and started doing a bit of her own investigation. It took her a few seconds to crack the security code. It was her birthday, the month and the year. Tears welled up.

"So damn predicable."

She immediately hit the menu button, accessing the phonebook option. There were a total of four numbers stored, one being hers. The others belonged to Chief Edward Burnett, Mr. Peterson, and finally the last was locked in under initials *LD*.

"So damn secretive."

The phone buzzed in her hand. Up popped a reminder for Ace to take his meds. Her fingers turned ice cold. She began to tremble. Dismissing the reminder, she continued to source for information. Her fingers navigated towards the missed-call log. There she noticed the last missed call came in from *LD*. The call log indicated Ace called *LD* back two seconds later. Their talk-time was exactly three minutes and twenty-two seconds long. Kema dialed the mysterious *LD*.

"No answer. Generic voicemail." She dialed it again, but got the same results.

Ace wasn't crook material. In fact he'd never stolen anything in his life. He was one of the good ones, which was why his death came as a shock. The details surrounding his murder were so mind boggling.

Six to the chest.

She pulled strongly at her joint. Background noise faded and all she heard was her heart, thumping wildly. Pounding beats inside her chest, eyes focused on the pavement. She blinked once and they fell. She swallowed, made herself breathe.

Robbery.

Shredded in anger, feelings of betrayal, overthrown in traumatic revelation had Kema struggling to keep her balance. Her topsy turvy stance required a bench. She took a seat. Body postured slouched in defeat. She clinched her fist.

Military issued gats.

Her leg bounced. Agonizing truths rushed through her like a tidal wave. She stood, began to pace. Onlookers watched as she walked back and forth from the main entrance to the corner, ranting on and on about killing the responsible. Pain slipped from her lids, and froze in their tracks. The chill outside did that.

Naked.

A berserk rage gripped her, took her on a roller coaster ride of homicidal thinking. She had thoughts of the responsible dying a long, painful death. A bullet to the head was too quick, too easy, too much like doing them a favor. She wanted the responsible to feel it, simmer in pain, and beg for their life to end.

Ouch.

The *J* singed her finger tips; bringing her back from that dark evil place in her mind. She spat onto the concrete, shook her head. The muscles below her right eye began to spasm. Uncontrollable twitching caused her to close her eyes tightly, and breathe.

Calm down.

She jammed her frigid hands into her coat pocket and stared off into the wooded area adjacent the hospital. Pain blanketed her; anger wrapped its hateful hands around her heart and squeezed love out.

Don't stress.

The muscles beneath her left eye caught up with the right eye. Both sides now contracting, pulsating, throbbing. Fresh tears presented, making new tracks against her skin. She stood breathless and motionless for a while, thinking of her brother. Seeing him lying there with umpteen tubes running in and out of his fragile body made her sick.

Focus.

Finally, the twitching ceased. She parted her lids slowly, looked around, and checked her surroundings. Just then, she noticed her Lexus being hauled by the nose. Her baby was hitched and was off to see the wizard. Soggy nuts stood at the corner smiling and waving.

"Gotta read the signs," the old man yelled across the courtyard.

Kema charged in his direction full speed ahead. Both fists were balled tightly. Anger wrapped her face like a raged mummy. She stopped just inches away from the old man and jabbed her pistol arched finger into his birdcage chest.

"Old man I'll put you in a fucking bag."

He huffed. "Oh yeah. Do it."

Noticing the security cameras in the sky, she backed away, growled. The gat wasn't too far, tucked neatly at the bottom of her purse lie the old man's death. "How the fuck am I supposed to get home?" The old man slapped his knee several times, and galloped. "Gal, yah figure it out."

She cocked her arm back, and was about to knock his old ass into the middle of next year when she noticed a black Crown Victoria approaching at a snail's pace. Tailing the Vic was a black Grand Marquis. Both indestructible vehicles painted in heavy tints, factory wheels clean as a whistle. The window to the Crown Vic fell. Behind the wheel was Detective Marshall. He pointed and winked.

They were watching.

"Kema is everything okay?"

Kema twisted in her stance to see Nurse Sonny gliding gracefully towards her. Fleece sweater and pink earmuffs made her prettier then she already was. There was something about her that Kema couldn't quite put her finger on.

"No. Everything is not okay. My damn car just got towed," Kema said hoarsely.

"Poor thing. If you want, I can give you a lift. I'm parked on the lower deck."

Kema turned her anger towards the old man. "Where the hell did they take my car?"

He shrugged. "Don't know. Guess yah best be making some calls, *ah.*"

"Now Mr. Carlson, be nice," Sonny said in Kema's defense.

"But Ms. Sonny she's evil. Best not let her in your vehicle." He leaned in, cupped his hand around her ear. "She's got the sticky fingers. The gal will take lent from yah pocket."

"Oh Mr. Carlson. This is no laughing matter. She just lost a love one." Sonny sighed.

"No joke Ms. Sonny. The gal is a clepto. She stole my..."

Kema swung her purse. "Who picked up my Lexus?"

The old man whistled a tune, galloped.

"Oh Mr. Carlson please tell her?"

He looked at Nurse Sonny with compassionate eyes, stubborn shoulders fell slump. "Well, alright." They watched the rigid man pull a business card from an old faded leather wallet. The one Kema lifted was much nicer, newer. It had a metal clasp which held everything in place. The one he had now was torn down the center. A couple of threads connected the two halves. He held the card loosely between his finger tips.

"Oops." He dropped the card, rubbed his chin dramatically.

"Gotta bad back darling."

Kema mean mugged, now itching to pull her burner from her purse. She settled down, took control of her rage. Besides, unleashing her fiery on the old man would truly be un-fair, but he could get it, all of it.

"You son-of-a-bitch." She knelt down to retrieve the flimsy stock, but it was swept away by a strong wind. Mr. Carlson fell out laughing as he watched Kema chase down the runaway card. Nurse Sonny held her head in embarrassment.

As Kema waited curbside for her ride to the pound, she decided to extend a call to Roy. He was the only person she could trust, and the only person she knew who would help her devise a blueprint for retaliation. With each ring her hands shook, her tears rolled. Disappointed to hear that his voicemail was *still* filled to capacity.

She dug into her purse, searched for her smoke. Two puffs in, she noticed a tiny red bug whirling around the corner at an alarming speed. The Mini Cooper blew pass the yellow pedestrian-crossing sign and stopped at the corner. The door flew open. Kema looked in. *You have got to be kidding me.*

"Ms. Cooper has a strict No-Smoking policy."

Kema took one last drag, flung the butt into the drain and hopped in. She cracked the window, releasing the over bearing stench of nicotine from her clothes.

"Nurse Sonny, I really appreciate this."

"I'm off duty. Call me Sonny. Where we headed?"

"Ellenwood. Head back north on 75, merge onto 675, get off at exit 5, make a right, then another right at the BP station, location approximately a quarter of a mile from there."

Sonny hadn't realized the trip would require trudging two major highways. She had plans with Roy. She tapped her fingers against the steering wheel, thinking of a short cut. There had to be some back road that could link them to another back road, and perhaps cut their trip down the middle. Mr. Carlson was one spiteful old man. There were several wrecker services in the area, but he'd gone out his way to call the one located the farthest. She made a mental note to speak with him about that.

"I understand if it's out the way."

"No, that's not it." Sonny fished out her cell, made a call. "Hey baby, it's me. I'm running behind schedule. Call me when you get this." Sonny dropped her phone back into her purse.

"Had to leave my man a message. We've got plans tonight," said Sonny, regretting the fact that she'd answered her bosses call. Shortly after Roy left on his top secret mission she hustled towards the shower, got dress, and was two steps away from the door when the phone rang. She doubled back, answered. Her boss practically begged her to come in. *Just for a few hours to help fill in, please.*

"Are you okay?"

Sonny nodded, smiled. "Yes, of course. I was just thinking of... never mind."

"Don't worry; I've got you on the gas."

"Alright bet, but only the good stuff for Ms. Cooper. Can't afford to put that cheap mess in, make her hips knock the wrong way."

Kema couldn't help but giggle.

"Was that a smile?" Sonny teased.

Kema buried her grin, slipped her seat belt on and they took off. The casket on wheels cut through traffic with swiftness. Kema suddenly felt claustrophobic in the tight space. She lowered her window, taking in more fresh air.

"I apologize for Mr. Carlson. He's a bit over the top."

"A bit?"

"Well, let's just say he's been securing grounds at the hospital for over two decades. He's pretty much seen it all."

"Seems to me he's taking his job a bit too serious," Kema said, wiping back her tears.

"Oh honey don't cry. If I were you, I would report his behind to Human Resource. Write a letter, document exactly what happened. I'll even step in as a witness. Mr. Carlson was out of line this time."

"My tears don't belong to Mr. Carlson. Just don't know how to break the news to my mother that her only son has gone home before her."

"Oh."

They drove down Hwy 75 in silence. Traffic was starting to thicken, and those eighteen wheelers were making it difficult for Sonny to maneuver. Kema took in the scene as she rode shotgun. Half the people operating vehicles were either on cell phones, texting, eating, shaving, reading, singing, dancing, looking for CD's in the back seat, and applying make-up.

Sonny's phone buzzed, and just like the hundreds of other distracted motorist on the road, she answered. "Hi baby, you got my message?" Sonny's grin seemed to fade slowly as she listened. Something was wrong, real wrong. Her hand shook like a leaf, her mouth agape, speechless. "Where are you, are you okay?" Sonny sucked back air, gasped. "Oh no."

Ms. Cooper swerved, crossing lanes, and refocused onto the tarmac. Sonny clenched the wheel, holding her breath, nodding her head as she gave all of her attention to the caller. Every fiber in her being was sucked in, retained by the voice on the other end.

"Oh God, Oh God, Oh God," Sonny sniveled. Her foot made of led. "I'll be there as soon as I can. Just elevate the leg. Keep it wrapped until I get there."

Sonny dropped the cell in her lap, both hands clinched the wheel. Her eyes were now glossy and looking to release a stream of worry. Sonny leaned across Kema, opened the glove compartment, and grabbed a soft pack of Kleenex. She dabbed her eyes.

"Is everything okay?" Kema asked with genuine concern.

"My man...he was..." Sonny shook her head, applied more pressure to the pedal and sped up behind a two-toned Malibu. She honked the horn, zipping around the junker, only to be stuck behind an RV carrying a load of wrinkled white people singing *Kumbaya*.

"My man needs me."

They hit a pothole and the contents within spewed out the glove compartment. Kema noticed one item in particular that looked familiar. She grabbed it, felt it, and examined it.

"My man bought me that. Isn't it beautiful?"

Kema held the unique watch up, inspecting its validity. It was official. No knock off. She glanced at Sonny who was wiping back obvious tears.

"I have a watch just like this. Can't seem to remember where I left the damn thing."

Sonny held out her hand to retrieve what belonged to her.

"Pretty isn't it?"

"Pretty expensive. Your man must love you cause this watch ran me close to ten stacks."

Sonny took in a chest full of air, sniveled. "Yeah, Roy and I have something special."

Did she just say Roy?

Kema saw red. Her neck twisted slowly towards Sonny, teeth clinched, demonic horns protruded from her head. Although challenged with keeping her hands steady, she demanded herself to relax, chill. *Patience*, she knew it well. She knew the dangers of speaking too quickly on impulse.

"So, your man Roy, is he hurt or something?"

Sonny waived her hand. "It's nothing major."

Kema's eyes landed on the watch. It wrapped Sonny's arm perfectly. She inhaled, blew out slowly. "Why all the tears?"

"I'm just a big O cry baby that's all."

Kema sized up Sonny for the first time, laughed. *We can't possibly be talking about the same Roy.*

"What's funny?" Sonny asked.

"Oh, nothing, just laughing to keep myself from crying."

Kema tried best not to seem intrusive, but she had questions, straight forward, inappropriate questions. She fumbled with her phone for a second. Her heart started racing. Could it be possible that she was his *wifey*, his *Wiz*, his *Queen*, his *number one*?

Roy was certainly an *ass* man but she couldn't picture him being into a chick with that much future behind her. Her body measurements weren't exactly breathtaking. He was no chubby chaser. Maybe she spoke of a different Roy. Her thoughts ran like brush fire through *LA*. She felt incinerated with envy.

"Music?" Sonny asked, already mashing buttons and skimming through stored CDs in the changer.

"Sure."

Jill Scott's voice streamed in like a ray of light. Kema watched Sonny's head knock, body rock all while zipping in and out of cars.

"You like Jill?"

"*Loooovvve Jill*. She relaxes my nerves. My man Roy got us tickets to her show at the Fox last week."

Kema made a face. *Last week... he was with me last week. All last week and the week before that*, is what she wanted to say but didn't. "Did you two enjoy the concert?"

"Roy and I had a ball. Jill did the damn thing. Afterwards we stayed to get a picture with her. She was so cool. *I love, love, love* me some Jill."

Relief covered Kema like a security blanket. They obviously had two different Roy's. She reclined her seat and enjoyed Jill for the rest of the ride.

CHAPTER 29

"Am I back? Didn't know I was gone," Bradley said arrogantly, lounging in a chair, one leg crossed over the other. He poured himself another drink. Not a nip, but from a gallon of booze he'd purchased from the bar and subsequently had billed to the room.

"*Johnny baby*, listen to me, you can't miss this party. Everyone will be there. Janet from Aspens, the Takumi brothers from Japan, Mary Murdock from Denver, Double Chin Charlie from Wichita, Lester Patel from Tulsa, Sterling Malone from Palm Beach, Joey and the family."

He lifted the knife, sliced into his tender steak, dapped a bit of sauce at the tip, opened wide and chewed. "*Ah, C'mon for Christ Sake, Joey and the family are harmless.*"

Offending one of the wealthiest men in Atlanta would serve to be social suicide. He laughed silently as his affiliate griped about their last gathering.

Vegas, the *Venetian* hotel was the perfect set-up for a night of million dollar gaming. Johnny had Joey and his brother Antonio in the hole an easy *mill* apiece. Johnny was happily satisfied with his earnings and was looking to cash out. Joey and Antonio didn't take kindly to Johnny walking away without an opportunity for redemption. Rumor had it Joey and Antonio extorted Johnny for double the amount, sending him back to Atlanta with a gimp leg.

"*Johnny baby*, security is air tight. Plus, bring your own guy."

Everyone knew Joey and Antonio's reputation. They were Bronx style bullies. Their bloodline was full of crazy Italians, but money was money. Bradley needed Johnny's deep pockets on deck.

"Awesome. I'll have my guy contact your guy with the details later tonight. *Chow!*"

Bradley had no guy. He was a one man show, looking to score big. With Lou-Lou's financial backing, and his billion dollar plan, he'd be back on top in no time.

He sliced into his meat, popped a corner of cow into his mouth. *Delicious!*

He took another sip, "Fuck Betty Ford. I'm getting wasted."

Bradley finished his meal, refreshed his drink, stuck his cell into his pocket, and staggered towards the bed. Thoughts of slapping his father with a wad of cash made him chuckle.

"I'll show you, you fuck-face."

"Who are you talking to?"

Bradley jumped up, spilling his drink along the sides. His back, vertical and rigid. His eyes, colossal and glazed.

"*Shit*, I didn't hear you come in."

Lou-Lou placed the bag, which looked as if it weighed a ton, onto the floor. She quickly chained the entrance, breathing rather quickly. Both palms pressed against the door. She leaned in, and peeked through the peep hole.

"What's in the bag?" he asked, eyeing the oversized black duffle.

"*Shush.*"

"Who's out there?"

"*Shush.*"

As she backed away slowly he noticed she was covered in dirt, mud and blood. Dry twigs and crumbled leaves scattered about her long hair. Her jeans were torn at the knees, both scraped and bloodied.

"What hole did you climb out of? What the hell happened to you?"

She turned, looked at him for the first time. There was a nasty bruise above her top lip. A lump the size of a silver dollar dressed her forehead. Evil eyes stared at him, gave him goose bumps. Bradley stuck out his chest, *big man style.* "Who did this to you?"

"*Shut the fuck up,*" she said through clinched teeth.

His puffed up chest deflated. She turned on her heels, headed towards the window, pulled the thick drapes closed. She ran back towards the door, both palms pressed against the frame, peering out into the hallway.

Lou-Lou had been on pins since she received a call from Ace's cell phone. Two calls, back to back made her beyond skittish, downright paranoid. She couldn't blink without seeing his face. Her ears rang with *Allahu Akbar* causing her to call for *Jesus*.

But that motherfucker dead. I pumped his ass full of led, she thought.

"I made sure of it," she whispered.

"You made sure of what?"

She shot him a look that told him to *fall back*.

They heard heavy footsteps in the hall.

The sound stopped just outside their door.

A shadow loomed their quarters.

"Someone followed you?"

"Will you shut the fuck up," she said acidly through a set of tight lips.

She moved across the room, unzipped the black duffle and brandished the biggest gun he'd ever seen. Heat pointed straight for the door. Everything became still, *silent*.

He looked into her vicious eyes, knowing well that she wouldn't hesitate to empty the damn thing if she needed to. He sucked back the last of his drink, blew out fear.

His cell chimed.

Her face twisted.

He ran to silence the ringtone.

There was a knock. Not just any knock, but a hard bang. Was Ace still breathing? Was it the police? Had Kema received word, and deployed her troops into combat? Bradley pulled a cigarette from the pack, stuck it in his mouth. His hands shook like a leaf as he lit the stick. He pulled strongly at his only source of oxygen. He savored the flavor of the Marlboro as if it would be his last.

Determined knuckles knocked again. Bradley inched towards the door.

She turned the tool on him. "Stay back."

"But it could be the bottle I ordered from downstairs."

"*Fucking Alchi.* I said stay back."

He backed away, pulling strongly at his smoke.

She stood, aimed, ready to let them *thangz* go, but the shadow that loomed their quarters inched in the opposite direction. Footsteps echoed away from the door. The *ping* from the elevator meant nothing. It was merely a distraction. She knew better. She side stepped, still aiming at the door. A long slithering pulsating vein ran diagonally across her forehead.

"Pack your shit."

Bradley outted his smoke, dropped the bud to the carpet and moved quickly, stuffing clothes and shoes, and whatever he could get his hands on.

***

They headed north. Up 400 towards Alpharetta, where they'd checked into some off brand hotel. It was cute, inconspicuous, a real posh type place you took your special creep too. Bradley chose the spot, which made Lou-Lou's antennas shoot straight up. He handled check-in. She wasn't exactly in her most appropriate state to do so. During the ride, she'd managed to cover her busted knees with those noisy nylon jogging pants which made a *swish* with each step she took. Shiny gold LV logo covered her baseball cap and printed her scarf, and dark square shaped frames covered her eyes. Her coat zipped up high, concealing her bruised neck. Ace's prints embedded her skin. *Evidence.*

Her quick wardrobe fix managed to conceal her filth, but she couldn't hide her pain. She'd taken a blow to the knee. Hard rock, the size of a mini boulder shifted, torn, rattled a few things.

He slipped her the plastic keycard. "Room 502. I'll be up in a sec."

She gripped his elbow, removed her shades. He winced at the bruise.

"Where you going?"

She had to keep him in eyesight distance. Couldn't risk having Bradley snatched up. She still needed him. Big money was still in the works. Her financial freedom was at stake. She needed him glued to the hip for the next twenty four.

"Relax. I'll be up in fifteen minutes. If I'm not back, call the National Guards."

His joke didn't sit well. In fact, it made her stomach churn in all sorts of ways, made her bust a sweat, made her think of Ace. Poor Ace felt her vengeance. But he was still alive, breathing, or was he? *Damn!* She let them *thangz* go, at point blank range. Slug after slug, until there was no life left, at least she thought. Her eyes went cold, all color lost from her face.

"You don't look well," he said, pulling her close.

"I don't feel well," she felt the need to throw up.

Bradley looked around, saw people watching them. He nudged her gently in the directions she should go. "Room 502. Go now, you're scaring the white people."

"Fuck these people," she snapped.

He covered his brow with his hand. A group of rambunctious teens flooded the lobby. If they didn't know any better they would have thought J. Crew and Nautica were holding casting calls in the hotel. Striped polo tops, light weight sweater draped the shoulders, sleeves tied at the center of the heart. Starched khaki pants for the fellahs, high waist pleated skirts for the ladies. Crisp and pristine blonde hair, blue eyes, stick thin figures were everywhere.

"It's the Ken and Barbie invasion." Her joke went unheard. Bradley was in Becky heaven, and from the looks of his darting eyes she could tell he was assessing the options. A manufactured smile crept up against her lips, she held her rage.

"Room 502 babe," Bradley said as a reminder, just in case she didn't hear him the first two times. She was cramping his style.

She decided to let him play. Besides he was broke as a joke, and wouldn't get far. A few steps towards the elevators she halted. *Wait, Room 502. Fifth floor. That won't work. We need street level access, just in case we have to evacuate suddenly. Need a room with a window that opens, preferably a patio door that slides. A quick get away!*

"What's the problem now?" he asked, interrupting her master mind for escape.

"Get a ground floor room. One with a patio door."

"Fifth floor offers the best views. You'll love it."

"You know from experience?"

"No, I've heard. A buddy of mine said..." he stammered himself mute. *Busted!*

She zeroed her evil eye in on him. But before she could act a fool he got the hell on and obeyed. As Bradley made the necessary changes with guest services Lou-Lou placed a call to Roy.

"I didn't think you would answer," she said in relief. Hearing his voice meant he was still alive. Hearing him breathe meant she wasn't in this by her lonesome.

"You good?" Roy asked in a husky voice.

"Can't shake this feeling."

He groaned. "What feeling?"

"Like I'm being watched. Had to book up and change hotels"

"Got that same feeling," Roy admitted.

"You sound like you in pain."

"Nothing a player can't handle," Roy said, then chuckled. "You sure you didn't clip me on accident?" he asked, this time seriously speaking.

"Promise it wasn't me. That fool..."

"Not over the horn," he warned.

"I fucked up," she admitted.

"This is true," he layered her guilt, and then grew silent. A second later she heard him groan in pain.

"That white boy got shit under control?" Roy asked.

She twisted back, looked at Bradley as he flirted with the blond from guest services. *Damn, all you had to do was switch the room number.* She hissed.

"He says it's a go, but I'll double check the specifics, make sure everything is everything."

"Do that."

"You heard from Kema?" Lou-Lou asked in her panic voice.

"We spoke."

"And?"

"Somebody bodied her brother."

She started to breathe again. Ace was dead, and dead men told no tells, but there was that call that came in.

"Got a call from his phone. I'm spooked."

"Don't worry about that. Kema wants to meet up, discuss some big money moves."

Lou-Lou touched her lip, flinched. "You trust that?"

"Verdict still out, but she seems sincere. In the mean while, stay low. Kema's goons got night vision. They'll sniff you out, cancel your contract."

"Roger that." she ended the call, still feeling enormously paranoid.

Bradley returned with their new room key. First floor, garden view, walk-out balcony, straight shot to the parking lot if need be. She placed the plastic card inside her purse, zipped it.

"I'll meet you in the room in ten," said Bradley.

"No, we stay together."

"Will you relax already? Go to the room. I'll be there in a sec."

"Just tell me where you're going, so I won't worry."

He released a long exaggerated breath. Her sudden clinginess wasn't cute nor was it sexy. "Gift shop," he grumbled.

Twenty minutes later, Bradley returned. He found her pacing, still dressed in those noisy *swish* pants. Her cap found a spot on the floor, right next to her coat, sunglasses and duffle bag. Dried blood packed at the top of her lip. Hair in complete and utter disarray. Eyes bulging from there to Timbuktu made Bradley even more curious to know why they had fled their previous hotel. Why was she covered in twigs, dirt, and blood?

"You said ten minutes," she snapped.

"My bad. Ran into an old friend downstairs."

She eyed him suspiciously. "What old friend?"

"More like an ex-fling. Val from Marietta." He waved his hand, turning a shade red.

"She was married, *is* married. Saw her and the hubby down by the elevators. Got to chatting. They've parted from the kids for the night." He laughed. "That was always their issue. Life revolved around their kids, and old buddy boy worked himself like a slave, and there was never *ever* any time for... well you know."

She wondered if he and this Val chick frequented this hotel. Did they have a special room? Perhaps room *502* was a favorite? Depending on the ambiance of the hotel, and assuming he'd gotten lucky, Bradley would almost always request the same room on each visit. *Repeat offender.*

Bradley dug into his bag of tricks, *literally*. She'd watched him scamper off, holding one of those eco-friendly, reusable totes they sold just about everywhere these days. She pulled back the drapes just enough to see into the garden. She gripped the handle, slid the patio door open. Year round foliage, evergreen shrubs added necessary privacy. Low dim from the moon cascaded above, lighting a fleeing path.

"Come inside."

"Let me sit here a little longer. Need to think."

"Not an option my dear."

***

A million stilled, frothy bubbles filled the Jacuzzi tub. Scented votives, bath beads, massage oil, deck of cards, a bottle of strawberry champagne, chocolates, and a loofah that cost twenty three bucks, were laid out for her pleasure.

"I kind of went gift shop crazy."

"I see."

She unzipped her sweater, exposing a murder scene. As she peeled the bloodied clothes from her body, stripping away soiled garments, Bradley scooped every stitch into the tote bag without question. He decided not to press her for details, but instead introduce her to a world of relaxation.

She moaned as he scrubbed her back, penetrating natural oils into her skin.

"This feels so good," she said, eyes closed, trying hard to enjoy the moment, but flashes of the nights events invaded her thoughts.

As he buffed her skin, and stirred her circulation, he spoke softly into her ear. His voice, so damn relaxed, hypnotic, mesmerizing as he dropped words on her she'd never heard before.

"What language is that?"

"French."

"I didn't know you spoke French."

"I'm far from fluent, but can read a menu, hail a taxi, and order me a drink." He smiled.

"Interesting."

"You can trust me," he whispered.

No I can't. I trust only me.

His breath against her lobe made her wonder, say *what if*. She hated that *what if* shit, hated wondering *what if* she'd handled things differently. *What if* she'd been a bit more tolerant, offered some guidance, perhaps applied the *softer* approach. Maybe, just maybe his million dollar plan would have surfaced then, instead of after the fact.

"You like that?"

She looked into his eyes, loving the twinkle they possessed. She had a soft spot for the jittery white boy with a periodic coke habit, who loved sipping that Crown.

"I scanned the box; saw they had pay-per-view channels. We can rent us an XXX show, or watch regular tube for the cost of this God forsaken room. Or..."

He ran the loofah across her chest, unclogging pores, releasing toxins, and exfoliating unwanted dead skin cells.

"... I say forget the tube, and rediscover *us*."

She shoved the loofah away, and stood. He was on standby with a warm towel. After pat drying her body, he lifted her cradle style, and carried her towards the king size bed. He laid her upon a ruffled spread, spreading her legs, dripping macadamia nut oil onto her dampness.

"*Boy*, you better quit."

"*Girl*, you better relax."

She laughed. So did he.

"Champagne?"

"No doubt."

The cork eased out, followed by a small pop. He tilted the flute, filled it midway.

"Thank you."

"Don't mention it."

She waited for him to pour his drink, before lifting her glass.

"Here's to a shit load of money," she said.

"Cheers."

They clanked flutes, sipped. She rolled over, made room for him. Bradley hopped into the sack. He'd already removed his garments. Briefs covered his ass like second skin.

"What's up with the punk panties?"

"The what?"

"The tighty whiteys are cutting off your nut circulation."

"You got jokes?"

"Briefs are so gay. You need boxers homey."

"Hey, there's nothing wrong with holding my nuts in place. A little support ain't never hurt nobody."

"Those bad boys are supposed to hang, not be restricted with elastic."

"Says who?"

"The brothers."

"Who's brothers?"

She giggled. "In junior high, The Patel's used to get beat up for wearing punk panties."

"The Patel's?"

"The Indian boys," she said, sipped.

"Wow, that's so racist."

"The Indian kids would attempt to slip into their gym shorts quickly without being spotted by the brothers. If spotted they got beat up."

"That's insane."

"Where I come from, that's a violation. You might as well stick a sign on your back that reads *homo*."

He grabbed her left boob. "There's nothing wrong with having an underwear preference. You prefer bikini cuts and thongs over hipsters and boy-shorts. Some woman like underwire and some don't. You prefer no bra at all."

"Got that right. These suckers cost me a fortune. I meant cost *you* a fortune."

He adjusted the pillows behind his back, sipped.

"You scared me back there."

Weariness overcame her. She didn't want to talk about it, didn't want to think about it. However, she knew he wouldn't let up. Her empty hand clinched into a fist. Her eyes closed just the same.

"There's another side you don't know," she said in a child like whisper.

"Do tell."

She drained her glass, held it out for a hit. He poured midway, pulled the bottle back, and watched the bubbles burst and settle.

"Can't. The less you know the better."

"How can I protect you if I don't know whom or what to protect you from?"

"I don't need your protection. But if anyone asks, I was with you all day today."

"Oh so I'm only good as your alibi?"

"Don't take it that way."

A sudden thud, followed by an earsplitting scream made them both jump. He grabbed her arm, halted her movement.

"Relax."

Her eyes beamed across the room. The tool lay across the dresser, safety off. She denied his request, bounced off the mattress, headed towards the door, burner in hand.

"It's probably that group of college students we saw in the lobby. Chill."

Her tune suddenly changed. She was up on her toes, pacing again. *Relax. Chill.* Two luxuries she couldn't indulge in until the time was right. And now wasn't the time.

"In the mean while, stay low. Kema's goons got night vision. They'll sniff you out, kill you." Roy's voice rang in her head like a bull horn.

"You made those calls?" she asked.

"I did."

"How many on board?"

"Babe, listen..."

"Answer," she snapped.

"Six confirmed, four tentative, and two unanswered."

"That's not good. We need at least ten on deck to make this happen."

"Don't worry. Got it covered."

She eyeballed him. "You secure the spot?"

"I'm scheduled to meet Rose for coffee in the morning. She's invited me to her estate to go over evacuation plans, rules, regs, legal mumbo-jumbo, the norm. My organizer, Kate will be on site setting up tables, stocking bar, food, even got two massageologist on deck to relax these sons-a-bitches."

"Scratch that. It's overboard."

"Trust me babe. When I start raping these rich fucks for all their worth their going to need a back rub."

"Just do it."

"Okay, you're the boss."

The noise receded down the hall. College students disrupted the quaintness of the hotel and Lou-Lou insisted that Bradley report the interference.

"Babe, they're just kids," he said passively.

"Well those *kids* are interfering with my peace. You call them or I'm walking down the hall and fucking them white bitches up."

"You wouldn't."

"Try me."

He laughed.

She grabbed a pair of crumbled jeans from her bag.

"*For Pete's Sake...Wait*, okay, I'll call. Man you're uptight."

"Whatever, just call."

Bradley requested that hotel management handled the situation. His voiced laced with authority. His demands, met. Riffraff, muted. *White power!* Their atmosphere, silent and peaceful, for well over an hour until the shrill from her cell caused the muscles in her neck to stiffen. She flung both legs out of bed, stood erect. Someone was using a dead man's phone.

CHAPTER 30

The phone rang three times, and then stopped.

Jazzman ignored the pest that tried cock blocking her well anticipated affair with *Mark Wahlberg*. As a young girl she'd long to have him in her clutch and finally her wishes were coming true. In the early 90's his Calvin Klein ads showcased much more than her naïve mind could absorb. Having him there, lying next to her with his tight physique made her think back to the day she first saw his massive billboard in New York's Time Square. Her mouth fell open as she trotted through loads of tourists, while being yanked along by her aunty to keep up.

"You look even better in person," she said, flicking her tongue at his lips.

Marky Mark taught her how to tongue kiss. Her lips pressed against her wall, flicking her tongue at his gorgeous lips, dampening her *New Kids on the Block* poster board made her strawberry shortcake undies moist many nights.

"You're so sexy," she told him delving her eager tongue into his slightly parted mouth. She had a thing for the thuggish white boy with killer abs. With him finally in reach there was no way in hell she was letting him go.

She spotted him in the hotel, at the piano bar, looking devilishly handsome. Their eyes locked from across the room. *He,* being the gentleman that he is offered to refill her glass. *She,* being the boss that she is declined. Mark was big time Hollywood, so it was nothing for a woman to fall at his command. She offered to pay his tab, and then extended an invite for cocktails in her suite. He wanted her just as much as she wanted him, their mutual needs on the verge of being satisfied.

The phone rang three more times, and then stopped.

Mark savored her, feasting relentlessly without coming up for air. She was on the cusp of having the biggest one yet. Only in her dreams did she receive that much pleasure. Only in her dreams could she have Mark *"killer abs"* Wahlberg, aka Marky Mark in such a way. Her legs locked around his neck and just when she was about to explode...

The phone ranged.

Ugh. "This better be important," Jazzman barked into the receiver.

"I've been trying to get you on the cell."

Jazzman sat up quickly, lifting the flap to her eye covers, and checked her cell phone.

It was dead. *Shit.*

"Lou-Lou, how the hell did you get this number?"

"Your baby daddy gave it to me."

Jazzman sucked her teeth. "Snitch."

"Don't be mad at him. I practically begged for the number, and when that didn't work I threatened to blackmail."

"Blackmail?"

"Never mind that. Shit is official. It's going down tonight. Are you in?"

Jazzman wiped the drool from the corner of her mouth and rubbed the crust from her eyes. "What's going down?"

"Time is money, so don't play dumb. You either in or you're out."

Jazzman yanked the cover back angrily, slipped her size seven's into a pair of plush complementary house shoes, and made her way towards the commode. The wall length mirror made her halt her stride. That pudge in her belly was getting a bit out of hand.

"You and Roy need to chill. Besides, I've already accepted the job."

"Fuck that job. We need you."

"What you mean fuck this job?"

"You and I both know it's a six week pilot. At best you'll squeeze out three months before they eliminate your position, than back down to unemployment you go."

"That was rude."

"Don't mean to rain on your parade, but it's time to face the facts Sunshine. Job security doesn't exist. It's about taking matters into your own hands. Besides, you have too much of an entrepreneurial spirit to be taking orders. You're a Boss Bitch. Start acting like it."

That made Jazzman smile. "You sound real desperate."

"I am."

"Where is Roy?"

"We're still in the ATL. Waiting on you."

Jazzman rolled her neck. "Why are you still there?"

"Nothing's coming in or out of LaGuardia, JFK, and you can forget about re-routing to Newark. The whole East coast is crippled by the blizzard," Lou-Lou said, sounding like her battery was on full charge.

"Are you serious?" Jazzman grabbed her laptop off the nightstand which was already on. Music from her playlist had led her into dreaming erotic dreams with imaginary men. Her fingers moved quickly across the keypad, accessing NewYorkOne.com.

Mayor, *Michael Bloomberg* was holding a live press conference. It appeared that the city was smacked with a whopping twenty inches of snow, and with the recent layoffs it seemed as though the Department of Sanitation was ill equipped to handle the job.

"Damn, I better call Jacob. Didn't call and say goodnight last night."

"He's eating Mickey Mouse pancakes with his daddy."

Lines from her satin cap penetrated her forehead. She loosened, rubbed, squinted. The bottle of wine she killed last night made her slip into a comatose sleep. Orientation had gone smoothly as expected, but then she spoke to Rick, and all hell broke loose. They argued mostly about Tony. As much as Rick claimed to support her decision, he obviously felt threatened. Who wouldn't?

"Did you fuck him yet?"

"What do you mean yet?"

Their call disconnected. Not because she hung up, but because her battery died. She had all intention on recharging it, and calling home to check on her son, but the bottle of Chardonnay she'd ordered from downstairs arrived.

"Schools closed?" Jazzman asked.

"*Everything* is closed. That's why you need to get on the two o'clock flight into Atlanta. Ticket already paid. Just get there two hours before hand."

Jazzman placed her cell on the charger, tried to turn it on but the thing was as dead as a door knob.

"But you said everything is canceled."

"Everything North, the dirty is still wide open. For now."

"You sound strange this morning."

"Feeling strange. Tell you all about it when you get here."

"I've got a little time to talk. Tell me now." Jazzman insisted.

"No, I'll see you when you touch down. Be on the lookout for that Similac coup."

"The who?"

Click

***

Delayed. Canceled. On Time.

Styrofoam cup, plastic cap, piping hot Columbian roast filled the center. Jazzman hustled through the crowd of angry travelers. With thousands of flights canceled due to the storm, the scene before her was looking like the Superdome after Katrina. Those who were lucky secured proper seating, others camped out on floors and small compartmentalize areas near the check-in booth.

Katrina caused the largest displacement of people in American history, and the East Coast blizzard had been officially ranked the most ferocious since 2006. Jazzman wanted to be home with her son, but the reality was she wouldn't be able to leave Houston for seventy two hours. So, Atlanta made sense.

A mob of people complained about one thing or another. Everyone had an issue.

"But I'll miss my damn connection."

"What's going to happen to my luggage?"

110

"This is madness. It's not even snowing in Florida. Why the hell is my flight delayed?"

"My mother is diabetic. She needs her Insulin."

"Seventy two hours! I need to be in Brooklyn tonight...Hotel, do I look like I can afford a damn hotel room? I spent my last on this flight. I'm out of dough, my baby is hungry, he got a shitty diaper on and I can't afford to buy none. So somebody better open this fucking gate because I can't be here for no damn seventy two hours."

That particular complaint tugged at Jazzman's heart string. She knew all too well what it felt like not being able to provide the essentials like diapers, wipes, sometimes food. She identified with the young girl whose pants were far too tight, and whose weave was far too long to be believable.

Something told her to stop, make an about face, and head back. Tears streamed down the girl's brown face as she held her stinky baby in her lap. Her arms wrapped him like a receiving blanket. The stench was evident, and the fact that no one offered to help the girl and her baby was terrible. Jazzman slipped through the cracks, trying best to avoid touching anyone.

"Excuse me."

Wild hair, red rimmed eyes, narrow face looked up, sniffled. The two year old she bounced on her knee felt a sense of comfort with a pile of poop on his booty.

"What you want?"

Jazzman was taken back by her hostile tone. She worked around the girl's aggression, smiled. "I overheard you talking and I wanted to help."

The girl stood, baby on her narrow hip as it poked out to the left. She smiled big showing off her bottom row of crowded teeth.

"Here's a hundred... no better yet, here's two hundred dollars. Get your baby a pack of wipes, diapers and some food. Can't help you with a room, but this should hold you over for awhile."

The girl leaned in, hugged Jazzman.

"Ma'am for-real, you just don't know how much I appreciate this."

Feeling awkward, Jazzman stepped away from the unexpected embrace, and patted the stinky kid on the head. Realizing her purse was opened she got paranoid, checked her things.

The girl did say she was from Brooklyn, or was traveling to Brooklyn, or needed to be in Brooklyn... can't fuck with them Brooklyn chicks.

Satisfied that all her belongings were in place she smiled one last time at the girl and her son, grabbed the handle to her suitcase and began a brisk walk. As she approached her terminal she noticed two men arguing over an electrical outlet.

"How dare you touch my plug?"

"There's other people who need to juice up there devices. Your laptop has been charging for the last hour."

"That's right. I need to juice up my cell, and this lady here needs to juice her IPOD, and this gal over here needs to plug up her laptop... and you sir, you've been hogging the outlet. Give somebody else a chance."

Their loud voices escalated to pushing and shoving.

Jazzman lifted her luggage and broke out into a light jog. When she reached her terminal, passengers were boarding. Thankfully her flight to Atlanta was still on schedule.

CHAPTER 31

Hartsfield Jackson International Airport was full of the same faces, same attitudes, same issues plagued travelers who so desperately needed to go North. She stepped out the terminal, onto the curb and looked towards the dark clouds that hovered above. Just then a slight drizzle fell. She stepped back beneath the covered port and waited. Five minutes passed before a shiny baby blue Bentley came inching over speed bumps.

"Similac coup, *I like.*"

Jazzman slipped her luggage into the trunk, walking slowly back towards the passenger seat, admiring the vessel before her. Leather Interior. Wood Grain Dash. *Damn this ride is sweet!*

"You doing big things I see."

"Get in."

Jazzman caressing the leather, checking out the gidgets and gadgets, played with the visor. She checked her make-up, scanned her tongue across her teeth.

"I did a good deed today."

Lou-Lou hit the blinker. Her brows dipped inward, her grip on the steering wheel unflinching.

"Gave money to a young girl stranded in Houston. I feel good about it."

They eased behind the shuttle bus bound for the College Park, Marriott. Jazzman glanced over at her friend for the first time, and jumped.

Suddenly alarmed, she asked, "Lou, what the hell happened to your face?"

"Shit. Everything," she blurted.

"Talk to me."

Lou-Lou pulled heat from beneath the seat, sat it in her lap. Bad nerves made her left leg shake. Every car that passed had her on pins. Every horn blown made her cringe. Every watchful eye made her mind scramble in fear. She felt Kema near. Felt her lethal energy right around the corner, sucking her peace through a straw.

"That's for *show* or do you plan to use it?"

"Have you ever known me to hesitate?"

Jazzman released air. "Guess not."

"I think we fucked up," Lou-Lou said in a tone that made Jazzman nervous.

"We who?"

"Me and Roy... last night went all wrong... we had to..."

Lou-Lou's eyes shifted up. She pointed at the blue button.

Jazzman placed her hand over her brow, sunk down into the bucket seats.

"I should have kept my ass in Houston."

They drove in silence.

The smell of desperation made Jazzman claustrophobic. She glanced over at Lou

Lou every few seconds to find her mumbling words. She'd asked her to pull over at the nearest gas station three times, but for some reason Lou-Lou acted as if she was suddenly hearing impaired.

"You hungry?"

Lou-Lou side glanced. "No."

"Well, I'm starved. Let's grab a bite."

"We don't have time."

"We have time. I'm hungry. You wouldn't deprive your best-bud of a meal now would yah?" Jazzman said, trying best to make light of the situation.

Lou-Lou made the *Tsk* sound. "So we best-buds now?"

"Look, I'm hungry. Now unless you want me to get medieval on your ass you best be finding me a damn restaurant. No fast food stops, but a *sit down-may I take your order-check please-* damn restaurant."

Lou-Lou growled. "You always hungry."

"I'm a stress eater."

"It's showing in your hips."

"*Ooh*, so we fighting below the belt?"

"*Fuck it.* One quick bite and then back to business."

Jazzman leaned over, pinched her cheeks.

***

They sat across from one another in an upscale Buckhead Japanese restaurant. Red wood paneling, heavy textured walls, water sculptures, and sliding rice-paper doors provided a relaxed atmosphere. Their private dining room was the perfect setting for confessionals.

"I'm so hungry."

"You always hungry."

"Shut up Lou."

Mixed vegetables, shrimp, steak and chicken sizzled against the Hibachi grill. Jazzman applauded as the sliced onion volcano erupted. Fire shot up, then subsided into a fizzled steam.

Jazzman sipped Miso soup, while Lou-Lou kept her eyes glued at the sliding rice doors. Their waiter walked in and out, checking their comfort levels. The chef juggled knives, oils, and food, providing the ultimate culinary experience. When the show was over, Jazzman lifted her fork and dug in. She made a face of pleasure.

"Damn this is good."

Paranoia overshadowed Lou-Lou's hunger. Her eyes glued to the rice-paper partition. Her purse in her lap, heat just a snap away. Noise from patrons applauding the onion volcano presentation made Lou-Lou whip her neck in all directions.

"*Whiplash,*" Jazzman said jokingly, sipping Sake from a tiny cup made from bamboo.

Lou-Lou stared at her with intense eyes. "Don't take what I'm about to say lightly."

Jazzman braced herself, "Okay, what?"

"We hit a small shipment of AR15's last night. Things were running smoothly until Ace started spazzing."

"Stop. I don't wanna know."

Lou-Lou's index finger touched the center of her forehead.

"He pointed the tip of the barrel right there."

Jazzman gasped. "I don't wanna know."

Lou-Lou looked up; made sure their waiter wasn't in ear shot distant. She decided to back up her story, rewind, and tell Jazzman everything. She felt the need to confess the whole story, just in case something happened to her or Roy.

***

After mulling over Vegas style party plans with Bradley, Lou-Lou received a call from Ace. It sounded as if he'd been hitting the bottle. At first she wasn't much interested in anything he had to say. Bradley's conversation included a return on her investment, so naturally gravitating towards him was a smart move. It wasn't until Ace mentioned the shipment that she felt a bang in her spirit.

"You got the route?

"Ran a copy before I left the office," his voice slurred.

"Tonight's the night."

She pounced to her feet, adjusted the volume on the small radio which sat on the end table, right next to the Bible she'd taken out the drawer. "Why tonight?" she asked.

"Because tonight is a perfect night. I need to see you first." She smiled, and twisted back to look at Bradley.

"I can work that out, but first let me call my cousin, make sure he's got a buyer."

She hung up with Ace and quickly dialed Roy's number.

"It's gotta go down tonight," she said as soon as she heard Roy's deep whispery voice. Lou-Lou noticed Bradley staring at her. He had a gift for reading lips so she took her conversation with Roy into the bathroom.

"What time you talking?" Roy asked.

"Two hours tops. Locust Grove," she said, feeling charged up.

After hanging up with Roy, she dialed Ace back. He answered on the first ring.

"Hi beautiful."

"I'll be there soon."

"Good. Hurry up, I need to see you."

He wanted to taste her kitty before business. She had no problem with filling his needs before the heist. It was her pleasure to pleasure him. Money did that to her. It made her senses vulnerable to the touch. He could have his happy ending, just as long as she had hers. Money talked, and Ace was speaking her language.

When she arrived at Ace apartment he had the music bumping, drinks flowing, a celebration was in full swing. She stepped in, looked around for the remote.

"Don't turn it down baby. I want my neighbors to know my name."

"Funny, but we need to get serious."

"Don't be such a Debbie Downer."

"Whatever. Where's the route?"

He stared happily at her.

She blushed. "What?"

"Would it be too soon to say…"

A faint like cry echoed from the bedroom, interrupting their moment.

"What was that?" she asked, looking over his shoulder.

"What was what?"

"That sound?"

He broke into a light jog towards the bedroom and quickly returned. He handed over the schedule. She scanned, nodded, and said, "What are you holding?"

He slapped the old tattered paper against his hand. "The map."

"Silly I can see it's a map, but of what?"

He cocked his head, eyed her with suspicion. "Can I trust you?"

"What kind of question is that?"

He rubbed a nervous hand over his head. "I need to know that I can trust you."

"Yes, you can trust me." She returned the scrutiny. "Can I trust you?"

"I've been on the up and up with you from the beginning."

She dialed back her anxiety, adjusting her tone of voice. Ace was a sick puppy, and she didn't want to set off any alarms within his mixed head. He slapped the map against his open hand a second time. If only she could read his thoughts. She was losing him. That distant look in his eye, shutting her out of his world. *No, come back into the light.*

"Ace."

"Huh."

"What's up with the map?"

He opened the map against his chest, pointed. "This is the drop location. We transact here."

"Brilliant."

Her sensitive lobes picked up whimpering sounds. "You hear that?"

"What?"

"Sounds like a baby crying."

He laughed. "Rented a small fork lift to transfer the heat out the rig, got some rope, and other material to make sure the plan runs smoothly. You got the van?"

"Got that all covered."

"Did your cousin inform the buyer that it's going down tonight?"

She gave him a sound yes.

"Maybe you should call him, double check."

"No need. My cousin is a man of his word."

Ace came at her strong, hands rubbing her breasts, hips, thighs. Now that she had the play book she couldn't refuse his loving. He wanted to do it in the bedroom; she wanted to handle business on the living room sofa. It made no sense in prolonging their ecstasy. After some pushback she decided to oblige.

He pulled her into his world. Darkness surrounded them with the exception of a few flickering candles. The alter like set up made her tense. Fire, water, rock, hideous doll strategically aligned against the dresser. She ran her hands along the wall, trying to locate the switch.

"I need light."

"Relax."

"You're scaring me."

He gave her a sharp look. The flames from the candles mirrored in his eyes. He yanked her close, attempted to kiss her lips. She squirmed in discomfort. A boyish smile found its way to his face.

"Let me have you."

She kicked herself for not paying attention to the floor plan. She needed to navigate herself towards a switch, a lamp, some sort of artificial lighting. Sweat burst from his pores, trickled down the sides of his face. His eyes, olive shaped. She wondered if he was on something other than liquor.

"Can I have you like this?"

She could smell his desperation for her. "Ace, I prefer to see what I'm dealing with."

He sulked, and then shot her a twisted smile. "Don't spoil the fucking mood okay."

She slid off her jeans. He took off the rest. She rode him with her eyes shut until her released a wicked shrill.

***

"Okay, my heart just skipped," Jazzman said holding all ten fingers against her chest, interrupting Lou-Lou's story. The details were far too much.

"This shit will haunt my dreams, Lou."

The waitress returned with more Sake. This time Lou-Lou poured herself some to ease her trembling limbs. Instead of the traditional sip from the tiny bamboo cup, she poured a huge measure into her glass and tossed it back like a pro. Her face tightened, and then loosened.

"Please don't tell me this dude is practicing magic."

Her eyes now fixated on her untouched plate. Lou-Lou told Jazzman about Ace's multiple disorders. Jazzman sat in disbelief. She drew breath as she listened to her friend describe the sacrificial ritual performed against her will.

"He laid me on my back, cuffed me to the bed, dripped cat's blood on me."

"Cat's blood?" Jazzman asked as if she hadn't heard her clearly the first time.

"Black cat. He gutted it right there in front of me with four inches of stainless steel. I just knew I was next."

The waitress returned but Jazzman halted her movements with a stern hand. Sensing the tension in the room, the small framed woman bowed and disappeared.

"He laid the cat across my belly and started chanting. I didn't fight him. I just laid there and let him..." she stopped talking, knowing Jazzman needed time to absorb the madness.

Lou-Lou scratched her head. "I need weed."

"Focus. How did you get loose?"

"My phone buzzed against the window ledge and Ace was back just like that," she snapped her finger.

Jazzman mocked the gesture. "What do you mean just like that?"

"He has this thing with bells, whistles, buzzing, clapping. Some noises trigger him, sets him off, and then brings him back. It's crazy."

"No, he's crazy. He's a fucking psychopath."

"No kidding."

***

That buzz came in just in the nick of time. Ace snapped back into the "now". Seeing her chance for survival, she started kicking and screaming. Dead vermon slithered from her belly, onto the mattress. Remnants of the bloody massacre saturating beneath her. He looked down at her, at his shaky hands that held four inches of steel, wondering how he got there. His distant looked frightened her to the bone.

"What happened?"

"Unlock the cuffs."

"Oh God, What I do?"

"Nothing baby, just unlock the cuffs," she said real sugary.

He scrounged for the key. Pillows shredded, feathers descended into the foul air. The scent of death permeated throughout. He rummaged through is jeans, found the shiny *get out of jail* free card. He held it, hesitation plagued his next move.

"Ace, unlock me."

"I *be* bugging sometimes and I don't know what I may do next."

"Unlock me Ace."

"Didn't take my pill in a couple of days, been feeling better, normal since you've been in my life."

"Take the cuffs off and we can talk, okay."

"Oh man, look at all that blood. Did I hurt you baby?" He began an intense body search.

"Ace, stop fucking around and unlock me."

"Will you ever forgive me?"

"Already forgotten, now unlock the damn cuffs."

With an uneasy feeling in her belly, Lou-Lou still went along with the plan. Money was still money. And as long as a quarter of a million had her name on it, she would turn the other cheek to Ace's sacrificial antics.

***

"He bludgeoned a black cat, and dripped its blood onto your skin. He smeared the word *Hades* against your damn skin idiot. Why the hell would you move forward with the plan?"

"Quarter of a *mill* not a good enough reason?" she said light heartedly.

Jazzman's face viciously twisted. "Is that all you're worth?"

"Don't judge me for wanting more," Lou-Lou protested.

Jazzman dug into her purse, pulled a compact mirror out, checked her teeth.

"You're a hypocrite," Lou-Lou spat.

"Excuse me?"

Lou-Lou stood. Jazzman grabbed her arm, forced her to sit.

"Lou, I'm sorry. Okay."

Who was she to judge? Who was she to throw stones when she's compromised herself on so many different levels for Tony? Lou-Lou wanted to lash out, tell Jazzman a thing or two, but she didn't have the energy. She had bigger issues on the table.

"The payoff was too big to walk away from. Roy was already involved. He had a buyer. Who in their right mind walks away from that kind of bread over a small mishap?"

"No explanation needed. I assume all went well with the buyer."

"Smooth as butter. Roy came through as always."

Jazzman braced herself for the next bit of information to leave her lips.

"So, I've got my eyes on Roy, and Ace and I are having small talk. Nothing serious. Didn't even bring up the cat situation for it was water under the bridge. He had a sip of some crap he found at the cabin, which I thought was a bad idea from the getty-up. When that Army commercial came on, he lost it."

She shielded her eyes with a shaky hand. Jazzman pulled up the chair beside her friend. "He started chanted, talking to me like I was some damn terrorist, pointing the barrel at my head. My life flashed before me." Lou-Lou sniffled, wiped away her water works with a napkin.

"Roy showed up, saved my life. While Ace was in his right frame of mind we bounced, got the fuck out those woods."

"Where's Roy?"

Her swollen eyes shifted towards Jazzman.

"Roy went to take a leak. I got distracted. Ace overpowered me, took my gun, and threw me in a ditch. This nigga Ace running around naked and shooting at Roy... the clip goes empty...and...and..."

Jazzman's breathing backed up into her lungs. "...And what dammit?"

Lou-Lou poured more Sake, guzzled. "He caught one in the leg. Flesh wound."

Jazzman let out a sigh, mostly relief. She couldn't lose him twice. "So he's alive?"

"Roy got nine lives or something," Lou-Lou said, still in disbelief herself.

"What happened next?"

***

Stuck in a pit, surrounded by dirt, rock, and snakes caused her survival instincts to kick in. Lou-Lou was a big city girl, a true New Yorker. She made it out the concrete jungle, and by all means she would make it out the backwoods of Georgia *alive*.

"Come on. You can do this," she murmured, channeling her pain into strength, endurance. *Think positive thoughts.*

While Ace's eager trigger finger unloaded in Roy's direction, she'd discovered a way up and out the ditch. Down on her knee's she moved towards a narrow opening which connected to an icy ravine. Running waters caused her to slip on a boulder, adding more traumas to her already bruised body. *You can do this, Lou. Don't give up.*

She forged on, climbing up a steep mound, landing alongside the interstate. Eighteen-wheeler blew pass, and it was at that moment she stared freedom in the face. Now faced with a decision to flag down a ride, head back into Atlanta, and lay low until the coast was clear. But something told her Roy was still breathing. Her instincts told her he was alive. *You can't leave him.*

Wet, cold, bruised. She knelt down, retrieved her .22 which was latched at her ankle. She headed back up the twisted trail to save her fallen comrade, but didn't have to go far for she noticed Ace running straight for her. She could almost smell his insanity as he neared. Ace was gone, some place dark and evil. His eyes said so.

She lifted her heat, aimed.

His naked body paused, shivered, laughed.

He pounded his chest like a gorilla, daring her to finish what she started.

The way he came into this world was exactly the way he was about to leave.

CHAPTER 32

Kema watched *One-Time* circle the block before she parked. Morrow was a fairly decent city, and wasn't known to house the riff-raff, which was why she was surprised to see the law. *Three cars deep.*

A large U-Haul was parked in the driveway with the hatch opened. *He didn't mention anything about moving,* she thought as she neared the truck. She stopped at the rear, look in at all the boxes piled high to the left. To the right there was a plasma television sandwiched between a dingy futon cushion, pissy twin size mattress, and torn box spring. Headboard and footboards were covered in cartoon stickers, flimsy dresser, mismatch end tables, four plastic patio chairs, foldaway card table, and an old rusted barreled bar-b-que smoker crammed the space.

Her cousin approached, two black Hefty bags slung over each shoulder. He tossed the bags in, and was just about to close the hatch when his girl, Fantasia came running out. *"Mike-Mike don't forget the toaster oven."*

Mike-Mike's unattractive face turned angry. *"Just leave it. It's broke."*

Fantasia slouched, pouted and waved. "Hey girl."

Kema forced a smile to her face. "Hey Fantasia, you guys are moving?"

"Me and my landlord had it out. Decided to cut my losses and just move before she starts complaining to a judge. Got my first certified letter the other day, and you better believe there's more to come."

"How are you holding up these days?" Kema quickly wished she hadn't asked.

Fantasia shook her head, broke down and started to cry.

Mike-Mike lifted his sagging jeans, and thug limped his way back towards the porch. He held Fantasia, kissing her tears as they fell. Kema couldn't stand to look in Fantasia's direction of fear she might see her guilt. See the truth. She took a seat on the bumper of the U-haul, gripped her head.

Because of her, Fantasia's *only* brother was in a body bag. And now because of some twisted rule designed by the man up top, her *only* brother had received the same fate. She looked towards the sky and wondered if this was God's punishment. Her cousin laid a firm hand on her shoulder. She refused to look at him. He would know. They all would know.

"You crying?"

"I didn't mean to upset her," she stood, wiped her fallen tears.

"Police have any leads on who canceled Flap?" she asked, sniffling.

"Homicide Detectives just left before you pulled up. They don't have shit. Everybody in that house got aired out. No witnesses," he said angrily.

The best witness is a dead witness.

She broke. Right there in the driveway, she fell into his arms and broke into a sobbing cry. Knees buckled, face buried into this armpits, dreading having to deliver the bad news. "Somebody bodied Ace."

He gripped her shoulders, shook her. "What you say?"

"Ace is dead." Her voice crackled.

He released her, rubbed the top of his head, and looked towards the clouds.

"Not my cuzzo."

Kema didn't believe Mike-Mike's slumped face could twist any further than it already was, but surprisingly it did. His nostrils flared as she told him all that she knew. And what she knew was nothing. Just like Flap, they had no witnesses.

"Detectives said Ace was supposedly involved in some robbery and ..."

"Robbery? Ace? No, they seriously mistaken."

"Military burners. A shipment came up missing, poof, disappeared. They have good reason to believe he orchestrated the hit."

"*No*, they seriously mistaken."

"Six to the chest. He was left on the side of the road naked. Trucker found him, got him to the ER. When I got there, it was too late."

As Mike-Mike struggled to process his thoughts, Roy crossed her mind. She'd left him three urgent messages and he had yet to return her call. His sudden strange behavior wasn't sitting well. She'd been driving all morning trying to locate him, speak with him, but he was nowhere to be found.

"He always calls back."

"Who?"

"Nothing, just thinking out loud."

She gave him a moment to deal with his pain. He looked as she did hours ago when she first swallowed the news. Ace and Mike-Mike were damn near inseparable as kids. They spent every summer joined at the hip, doing what mischievous boys do. He eyed her for a second, and was about to say something but heard the screen door open and slam shut. He looked over his shoulder; saw Fantasia struggling with the last few bags of clothes.

"Leave it there. I'll get it," he barked.

They watched Fantasia return inside the house, brokenhearted.

"Don't yell at her. She's going through a lot."

His jaw squared. She backed off, decided to stay in her lane when it came to him and his woman. Mike-Mike had his situation in check.

The wind kicked up, tossing her curly-frie weave in the air.

"Military officials and detectives practically set up shop in Ace apartment. They won't let me in, and ain't shit coming out."

"Bet their going through his things with a fine tooth comb."

"And you know this," she looked towards her ride. Thankfully it was untouched and unharmed by the ruthless tower from the pound. Her purse sat in the front seat. It possessed all they needed to know.

Map, receipts, schedules, motive, intent to steal and resale, all rubber banned together.

The screen door opened and slammed shut, breaking her thoughts. Out walked Fantasia's youngest. Snot nose, nappy head brown boy yelled, *"Daddy, momma needs your help."*

Mike-Mike winced. "Tell her I'll be there in a minute." He kept his voice leveled when he spoke to the child. Yelling publically was a sign of abuse, and Fantasia already had an open DFACS case pending. Her oldest was a habitual high school ditcher. One more unexcused absence from school and Fantasia was facing ten days in the county.

"Handle your family matters. I'll be in touch."

"Wait, where you going?"

"Need to get up with this dude I know. From there, ain't no telling." Kema pulled a key from her back pocket, placed it inside Mike-Mike's hand. "This is a spare to Ace's Tahoe. It's parked at his apartment complex. I need for you to have one of your boys pick it up."

"Why can't you?"

"Detectives know me. They cornered me at the hospital, asking questions."

"What kind of questions?"

She became irritated. "Questions about Ace, his friends, his work, his day to day life. Anyways can't show my face there anymore." She thought about Detective Marshall, and Detective Olive. *They were watching.*

"Keep the truck for me until I figure out what to do with it."

"Consider it done."

CHAPTER 33

Roy shoved the urinal pan away, and stood on his own two.

"I'm not crippled," he snapped.

"I wasn't implying that you were." Sonny said, but just decided to shut up before she made matters worse. Rambling wouldn't do either of them any good.

Stalk naked and wounded, he stood at an inflicted angle. He was suffering but tried his best to mask the pain. He took one step forward, and shrilled out loud. She gripped her ears, wanting desperately to help him maneuver. He took another step and felt a burn like no other. The eight hundred milligram ibuprofen barely knocked off the edge.

Sonny gripped Roy's arm for support. "Let me help you."

He shook her away. "I got this."

"You've lost a lot of blood. You're weak. Let me help."

"I said I've got this."

Roy took a clean shot to the thigh. His entrance and exit wound stitched and bandaged with gauze. Inside the bathroom, Sonny watched from afar as Roy leaned his body in at an angle, both arms planted firmly against the wall for support. His organ filled with urine, guided itself, as he whizzed all over the toilet seat and floor. He normally had that technique in the bag, but today was different.

"Fuck."

"Baby, it's okay."

She looped her head underneath his armpit, held unto his waist. The distance from the bathroom back to the bed seemed miles apart. She laid him down, pulled the white sheet up to his chin. He was weak, vulnerable, and susceptible to attack. Roy hated feeling inadequate to defend himself, to defend her. If ambushed he could do nothing but accept his fate.

He thrust his arm back, slipped his hand between two pillows, felt the steel. *Aint shit wrong with my trigger finger.* His mind told him to get up, *man up*. His body told him to lay it down, *relax*. His heart sat at the edge of the bed with a Bible, reading verse after verse.

"You got something stronger?"

She broke away from the "word" and scurried towards the bathroom, opened the medicine cabinet, shoved a few prescription bottles around and grabbed one. When she returned she found Roy gripping his burner. Heat pointed directly at her. She dropped the pills.

"Jesus." She picked the bottle up, ran towards his side.

"Take half of this. You should feel nothing in about ten-twenty minutes tops."

He popped the half a pill in his mouth, swallowed dry.

"What is this?"

She placed a straw in his mouth. Orange fluid filled his lungs.

"It's Vicodin."

Night turned to morning. Roy's eyes parted to sunlight streaming in from the partially opened drapes. Blinded by the rays, he closed his eyes tightly, popping them back open. His vision adjusted. He turned his head slightly to the right and noticed food.

Sliced grapefruit, scrambled eggs and smoked linked sausages was placed neatly on one of those foldaway stands. Sonny was an infomercial junkie and saw two being advertised for the price of one. Across the room, the other foldaway sat an abstract piece of art. Hot oil balanced delicately at the throne of two outstretched hands. Tiny tea-light candle flickered at its core. Single flame emanated *Ylang-Ylang* throughout.

"Sonny."

Roy grabbed the link sausages, popped them both into his mouth, chewed. They were ice cold. He rocked twice against the edge of the mattress, stood. No pain, just slight discomfort. He extended his leg to and fro several times, working his muscle. He popped his neck, shoulders, back, feeling ninety percent back to normal.

"Sonny."

He slowly limped his way across the room, stopped at the steam, inhaled. *Ylang-Ylang* was said to be an aphrodisiac. A calming, soothing essential oil used to reduce insomnia, depression and lessened the angered. Sonny left the thing burning, probably on purpose. He couldn't blame her. He left in haste, on some top secret mission, only to return with a bullet wound.

"Sonny."

He looked down, noticed his gauze was saturated. He kept it moving.

"Yo' Sonny."

Each step reminded him of his Wild-Wild West encounter with Ace, and how wrong things could have ended up. Ace emptied the chamber in his direction and all he had was a flesh wound. He was lucky, or even blessed. Either way he was alive.

"Yo' Sonny."

He needed his thick and sexy nurse to bandage him up like before, make him like new again. Roy limped his way towards the front of the house, pushed the bathroom door in. *Empty.* Toilet seat, *down*, urine mopped up, everything smelling of zest. He headed for the kitchen, it too was empty. He doubled back, headed towards the rear of the house where there were two spare bedrooms. One she used for guests, which she rarely had. The other she used as her "Think Tank", her music room. Sonny retreated there only when feeling creative.

He pushed the door open, and found Sonny slumped over the electrical keyboard snoring. Next to her, an empty bottle of white wine and half eaten turkey sub. She was dressed in a leopard nighty, with red criss-cross spaghetti straps.

"Sonny," he whispered.

The acoustic speakers hummed a smooth, sexy, but sad melodic tune. Shredded musical notes scattered the floor. Amps, plugs, switches, cables and wires were connected by way of confusion. He scanned the room, noticed her daddy's old saxophone was out its protective case. From what he gathered she hadn't touched the thing in years. He opened the drapes to let some light in.

He heard her moan, then her sweet sounding voice, "Baby, is that you?"

"It's me," Roy leaned over, kissed her forehead.

She struggled to lift her head. "You hurting?"

"No, but I can tell you are."

"My head is pounding. Did I drink the whole bottle?"

"Unless you had company, it looks that way."

She straitened her spine, held her head high despite her throbbing temples. She was a lady first. "Did you get the breakfast I made."

"I did. Thanks.

"Good."

He turned the sound up, smile. "This you?"

"Your pain inspired me to create this piece. You like it?"

"I love it. Sounds bitter sweet."

She closed her eyes, popped her fingers, grooved to the music.

"Guess I should get shot more often, huh?"

Her eyes popped opened. She didn't laugh, nor smile. "Not funny."

"Okay, you're right. My bad."

A sudden rush of energy made her spring up from the chair. Her face was twisted, her lips tight. He knew that he was in for it, so he took a seat.

"Tell me what happened," she demanded.

"I told you, got hit with a stray."

"That's a lie and you know it. Roy, tell me what the hell happened."

"Look, don't trouble yourself with the specifics." He grabbed her hand, pulled her near. He rounded her hips, butt, and breasts with a set of eager hands.

"No, stop. You need to be honest with me. Tell me the fucking truth."

Shocked at her tone, he released her. She backed away, started pacing.

"This is the second time you've showed up at my house bleeding. First you were stabbed in a so-called bar scuffle, this time you're claiming you were struck with a stray."

"What you want me to say?"

"I need to know if being with you is jeopardizing my wellbeing."

Valid question caused his heart to sink. She had every right to feel unsafe, endangered, threatened. He toted a burner everywhere he went, even kept his heat locked and loaded at his bedside. He was ruthless, but careful. He knew better than to shit where he rested, and by all means he would protect her, even if it meant giving up his own life.

"Roy." She knelt before him, looking up into his eyes. "I love you, but I need to know if one day I may come home and find you bleeding from a place that I can't fix. I need to know if being with you mean's I need to watch my own ass. I'm scared."

He stood.

So did she.

"Don't be scared. I got you."

His response wasn't good enough so she proceeded to leave. He grabbed her wrist, spun her around into his chest. He grabbed her face, kissed her hard. The passion between them was real.

"I promise to always keep you safe."

Emotions and adrenaline running on high made them both hot. He snatched her leopard nighty over her head, pushed her up against the wall. Her thick leg hooked around his waist. He scooped in, penetrating her with every inch of himself. She screamed in pure numbing ecstasy with every push.

"That's my spot."

His tongue grazed her lips. "I know."

Wounded leg stopped nothing, but instead made him work harder to pleasure his Queen.

"Oh...oh...Roy. We need protection."

"This mine?"

"But..."

He stopped pumping, applied the brakes to their love making. *But*, wasn't exactly the response he expected to hear. He grabbed her face tightly, and looked into her eyes. His hard tool pulsated, made her twitch uncontrollably. Her body shook like a heroin addict needing a fix.

"No, don't stop," she begged.

"This mine?"

"*Yessssssss,* fuck me!" she screamed.

He sucked her bottom lip hard, and pumped her fast. Just the way she liked it.

"Have my baby."

"*Oh God, Roy....*"

"Marry me."

"Don't tease me."

"Marry me... have my babies..."

A resonated strength allowed him to lift her up, lock both legs around his back. She grabbed his face, kissed him harder than before. He rammed the last few inches of his thickness deep inside her. Her hips quivered and lurched against him, whimpering joyously at each thrust.

"I want you... need you... to be... my wife... have my babies..."

"*Yesssss.*"

"You sure?"

"*Yesssss.*"

"You love me?"

"*Yesssss.*"

He pressed his mouth against hers, feeling the warmth from her breasts touch his heart. He kissed fresh tears as they sprang forth and slid down her pretty face.

"Happy tears?"

"*Yesssss.*"

Her thighs trembled, middle twitched and tightened around his still erection. She nibbled his lope, whispered, "Let's make babies." He slowed his pace, caught up to the tune that dripped from the speakers. *Smooth*, *sexy*, *sad* melodic music forced him to take his time, restrain himself from exploding.

The moment had to be perfect.

He wanted her to remember.

CHAPTER 34

"Since when do you read *Business Week*?" Tony asked biting the tip of a greasy, piping hot, New York style slice. Bubbling cheese barely subsided.

Wayne winked. "Maintaining my image."

Tony laughed. "The rats you attract don't give a damn about you being business savvy."

"They're not all rats. I pull some classy ladies from time to time," Wayne defended.

"The caliber of woman you attract swallow DNA. They give themselves freely without expectation." Tony took another bite, but the heat was more than his mouth could handle. After a few huffs and puffs, he chewed, swallowed.

"Daddy, what's DNA?"

Tony glanced down at his son Jacob, patted his head. "Eat your pizza son."

"But it's hot. Can I have chicken fingers instead?"

"No fingers. Blow it."

Jacob made a face, pushing the bubbling slice away.

"What's wrong with fucking a chick with no expectations?" Wayne asked.

Tony shot Wayne a look, while rubbing Jacobs head. His son stared down at his cubically sliced pizza, frowning.

"I keep forgetting shorty sitting right there. He mad quiet, nothing like his daddy."

"You alright son?"

"I want chicken fingers."

Wayne stopped a waitress on the go. "Get the little dude some chicken fingers."

"With honey mustard, please," Jacob chimed.

"Yeah, with honey mustard," Wayne confirmed.

Two men and a boy watched booty bounce towards the kitchen to place the order.

Wayne took a good look at Jacob, and laughed. "*Yo* he looks just like your ugly ass."

"Mista I'm not ugly. My mommy says I'm handsome," Jacob defended himself.

Tony chuckled. "He's joking, son."

"What's wrong with *banging* a fine lady with no expectations? Wayne revised his question the best he knew how. Talking G-rated didn't come naturally. His kids, all three of them witnessed his unedited self. A vagina was a pussy. A penis was a dick. People didn't make love, they fucked. A Caucasian was a cracker, sometimes referenced as The Devil, a Hispanic a Taco, and a Black a nigga.

"That's cool while in your twenties, even somewhat acceptable while in your thirties, but your knocking on forty playboy."

Wayne swatted Tony with the magazine. "Thirty-five my man, and I'm still a young cat."

"Stop lying. Thirty eight, and yes your still young, but old enough to know better."

Wayne shifted in his seat. "What should I know guru?"

"Man, the chicks you mess with think a stimulus package is a sack of smoke. It's supposed to stimulate the mind. How is Biz Weekly going to help you in that situation?"

Wayne laughed so hard he accidently passed gas.

"*C'mon*, damn," Tony waved his hand beneath his nose.

"My bad man."

Jacob giggled. Tony fanned his pizza, dabbing paper napkins to soak up the grease from his artery clogging slice.

"I don't know how you eat that crap," Wayne said.

"Love this pizza."

Wayne grabbed his chest theatrically. "That's a heart attack waiting to happen."

Tony took another bite, chewed with pleasure. "Why you got it on the menu?"

"It sells. People love it," Wayne said nonchalantly.

"I personally wouldn't eat that mess. Honestly, I wouldn't eat half the crap I sell on this menu. Knowing what I know now, I would have stopped eating this shit years ago."

"I've been gone for a nickel straight, dreaming of this pizza. So, if you don't mind."

Wayne shrugged. "Your heart. Not mine." He straightened the magazine, scanned the page, stopped at the small business column. "How to navigate small businesses through economic turbulence."

"Stop fronting," Tony teased.

"Your BM still bugging over that dude?" Wayne asked, now talking in code.

BM equated to *Baby Momma,* and yes Jazzman had nutted up all of a sudden. She was throwing the cooch one moment, and taking it back all in the same breath.

"It is what it is," was all Tony could muster.

"I bet she flipped when you came home this morning."

Tony sat back, thought about changing the subject, bypassing the question all together. The Rick and Jazzman situation was becoming more than he could stand. In fact, it had him ready to take it to Rick's doorstep, tell him to back the fuck up off his woman. Thoughts of him sitting next to her on an airplane, elbow to elbow, sipping coffee and chewing complimentary peanuts was enough to drive any love sick man crazy.

Tony looked up from his clinched fist, stared at the space between Wayne's beady eyes. He gave a synthetic laugh, said "We had words. I checked her good."

"I bet, especially after Ms. Champagne took care of you."

Tony smirked, bit into his slice.

Wayne leaned in for the low down. "Details my nigga."

"C'mon, don't act like you ain't never sampled the product you pushing."

Wayne sat back, real dapper like, dusted his shoulders. *Enough said.*

They both cringed when two ladies dressed in blue hospital scrubs cruised through the door. Matching plastic crocks slid against the floors, transporting possible hospital bacteria into the restaurant.

"Wearing hospital uniforms publically should be against the law," Tony said suddenly getting a case of the hebejebes.

"I agree, especially when they dragging their diseased covered asses up in my restaurant. The emergency room is filthy. *Staph infections, Swine-Flu,*" Wayne spat. He stood.

"Where you going?" Tony asked.

"To kindly ask them to take their stomachs elsewhere."

"You can't do that, can you?"

"I reserve the right to be selective. They look unsanitary."

Wayne looked on as the two ladies took a seat at the bar. Neither went to wash their hands. As he approached the ladies from behind, a disgruntled voice grabbed Wayne's attention. Oiled stained overalls and beat-up work boots slammed his fist against the bar, causing Wayne to redirect his path.

"Big man what seems to be the problem?" Wayne asked.

"Me said no damn mayo. *No mayo.* Me can't eat this." Glass dish slid across the bar, tipped off the edge, and shattered. "Me done wit dis blood clot service."

Wayne looked down at the broken glass. The pastrami and cheese sandwich was layered in thick mayo. The wicked part of him wanted to shove the misappropriated meal down his throat, make him eat it, make him choke off it. If, and only if the city wasn't already looking to shut him down, he would have definitely opened up a can of *whoop-Ass.*

Wayne snatched the broom angrily. "You're welcomed to leave big man."

"Me no pay."

Wayne kept his cool, swallowed his rage. *I need to beef up security for the lunch hour*, he thought sizing up the disgruntle man. The dread was a big dude. He looked as if he lifted car engines, and lumber for a living. Wayne on the other hand wasn't the one for scrapping. His trigger finger was his mediator. His options to effectively pump led into the dread had become more enticing, but came with a price. With enough drama looming his establishment, he shook the thought.

The dread tipped the glass of beer, guzzled the last of the suds. Large belched escaped his belly. Empty glass slammed against the bar. Wayne peeked over his shoulder, saw Tony approaching slowly. The dread stood, cocked his head. Dookie locks hung heavily down his back.

"Wha mafucker...Wha yah feel'n?"

Wayne's fingers gripped the broom stick. "Big man, *chill*...It's on me."

"Yah blood clod boy wanna a piece of me ah?"

Tony slowed his roll, stood next to Wayne, hand behind his back.

"Big man, I said we cool. Just leave before things turn ugly," Wayne said as a final warning. There was so much disrespect he would be able to consume in one day. Tony's intense green eyes made the dread fall back a step.

"Me no come back *Earrr*."

"Fine by me."

Wayne watched the dissatisfied customer grab his tool belt, and head towards the exit.

"Damn, all that over a sandwich?" Tony brought both hands to the forefront.

Wayne laughed. "A bottle of ketchup, really?"

"Don't sleep on the Heinz. Where you think I got this mark from?" Tony pointed towards the gash above his eye. "One night after a party at club *Amazura*, me and this breezy headed to the *USA Diner*, off Merrick."

"Yeah, son, I know the place. Kinda hood, but it's the only spot open and the food is actually pretty good."

"Yeah well you know me; I planned on feeding this chick, than taking her to the telly off the Grand central."

Wayne smiled. "Kew Motor?"

"And you know it."

"My nigga."

"Man, guess who the fuck walks up in the joint, neck rolling, finger pointing, talking shit?"

"Your baby moms?"

"Exactly."

Wayne laughed so hard he passed gas again.

"Son, you need to chill with that."

"My bad, the wife got me eating cabbage at the crib. Go ahead, tell me what happened."

Tony pointed towards his brow a second time. "This is what happened. She cracked me over the head with the ketchup bottle. Saw stars for a second, then heard the chick I was with screaming and crying for me to help her."

"Did you?"

"Is you crazy?"

Wayne's eyes shifted towards the floor. Broken glass, globs of mayo slithered from the now soggy hero. He snatched a stack of paper towels and proceeded to gather the mess. He drew his hand back quickly, hissing through his teeth. *"Fuck."* Blood seeped from his thump.

"That's a nasty one," Tony said.

Wayne hissed again, sucking gently at this throbbing finger.

"Here's for the pizzas, and chicken fingers."

"Don't worry about it."

"Cool. Jacob let's go."

Jacob skipped towards his father but froze when he noticed an angry black woman storm in. Rage filled eyes, heaving chest, baseball bat in hand, vicious Rottweiler on leash. Jacob jumped into his daddy's arms.

"No dogs allowed," Wayne shouted.

Cujo barked three times. Wayne lifted the broom, ready to defend himself. Its master yanked its chain. Barking ceased.

"I'm looking for the owner."

Wayne wiped the sweat from his brow. Blood from his injured thumb smeared his face. "Who's looking for the owner?"

"Me, I'm looking for the goddamn owner. Are you him?"

"That depends. Who the hell are you?"

"His worst fucking nightmare."

The woman slammed the bat against the bar. A few patrons dropped their forks and flew towards the exit. Others sat back and watched the drama unfold. That was the hood for you. When a fight broke out, folks took a front row seat. Tony himself was glued to the action. He stood near the twenty-five cent gumball machine, with Jacob's legs wrapped tightly at his waist.

"*Whoa* lady, what's your damn problem?"

"Are you the owner, cause if you ain't this problem don't concern you."

Wayne backed away slowly; broom still in defending position, sweat pouring from the top of his head, finger dripping blood. Cujo stared at Wayne like he was supper. The woman holding the untamed beast looked to be in constant struggle. She held on as best as she could. Wayne parted his mouth to speak, but then silenced when he saw Raven burst through the door in tears.

"*No... it's not his fault Momma.*"

The crazed woman pointed the bat at Wayne. "Is this the man who got you pregnant?"

Wayne stood speechless. Murmurs erupted. Raven shifted from one leg to the next. "*Momma please... you're embarrassing me.*"

"Is this the motherfucker who knocked you up?"

"Look ma'am, I'm not sure what your daughter has told you but, you must have me mistaken with somebody else."

"*Wayne, how could you?*" Raven bellowed in tears. She folded her arms tightly across her chest and stomped like a five year old. She was immature, irresponsible, which was one of the reasons he fired her in the first place.

Two weeks ago, just hours after doing her young ass, near the jarred pickles, in the back office, he noticed Raven acting suspicious. She asked inappropriate questions, questions pertaining to money. Restaurant funds. The next night, right before closing, Wayne spots two unsavory looking characters parked outside the restaurant, scoping his movements. Raven swore up and down she didn't know them, but Wayne knew better. His sixth sense told him to fire her ass, and beef up security.

"You said you loved me." Raven cried a river.

The deranged woman swung the bat at Wayne, knocking his elbow. Pained surged up his arm, down his back, weakening his knees.

"You crazy bitch."

"My daughter is sixteen, you piece of shit."

Murderous Mommy slammed the bat against the bar, toppling drinks and a bowl of salted peanuts. Cujo chomped at the air, waiting to sink his teeth into Wayne's dark meat. With a hard swallow, Wayne moved behind the bar, reached for his Eagle, and gripped it.

Safety Off.

"Did you know that she was a minor when you stuck your uncircumcised dick inside her?"

Wayne looked at Raven in bewilderment. He wondered if Murderous Mommy had his exact measurements as well. Raven's eyes hit the floor, and stayed there.

"You better answer me or I'm letting this bitch go."

When Raven walked into his restaurant over a year ago looking for a job, she assured him that she was nineteen. She was legal to have his uncircumcised dick in every crevice, crack, and hole on her body. She had the ID to prove it.

"Wayne, I'm pregnant. I wanted to tell you... that night we did it... in your office... but then you, you fired me. I tried calling you, but you never called back."

"This is bullshit," he said seething.

"It ain't no game. I missed my bloody-show. Momma took me to Rite Aid, got one of them sticks to pee on." She smiled at him.

"We pregnant."

Murmurs erupted. Ro-*Neeka*, his new short order cook that replaced Raven stood in the frame of the kitchen door, shaking her head, chomping down on a freshly made pastrami and cheese sandwich lathered in mayo. Wayne gave Ro-*Neeka* a stern glare, and she quickly returned to her post.

"Ma'am, I can *A-assure* you; this has to be some kind of *M-mistake.*" His voice elevated several octaves. His pitchy, choppy range started a chorus of snickers. Raven stood twisting in her stance, fumbling with her knee length pleated dress. She looked younger and more innocent by the minute.

The Raven he knew came to work in a baby-tee, plunging neckline and jeans so tight it required paint remover to get them off. The Raven he knew popped bubble gum, switched her ass and always had something snappy to say. The girl standing in front of him that day played the victim role to the *T*. She deserved an Oscar. Hands down the girl deserved a damn Oscar.

Wayne looked at Jacob's innocent face, at Tony, at his workers, customers, Ro-*Neeka* whose head found its way back out the swinging door, at Raven, at her mother, at Cujo. He thought about his wife, his kids, his reputation.

"I don't believe this," he said nervously.

"Are you saying my daughter is a liar?"

"I'm saying I'm a married man."

"You weren't talking that married stuff when you asked me to go down on you. Remember, every night after closing, in your office?"

"You fucked my child in your office?"

Wayne held his burner tightly.

"She wasn't worthy of a room? You had to fuck my child in your greasy ass office?" Cujo barked. The leash loosened. She held the tail end of the strap.

Wayne's arm rose midway. "Lady, I *swear* to God... *if...* if you let that *Bitch* go I'm blasting."

"But Wayne what am I supposed to do?" Raven whined.

"Yeah, what is she supposed to do, Wayne?" Murderous Mommy reiterated.

"This is crazy. I never laid a finger on that girl. She's a liar."

Raven's eyes turned cold. She cocked her hip to the left, and planted both hands at her waist. Sassy Momma was back!

"Motherfucker you know what time it is. You gave me your dick. You said it was mine. You said that you would leave her. You promised."

"*Raven*... the language."

"Excuse me Momma, but he making me mad as hell."

"I'm calling the police," he warned.

"*Call em'... Call em' and tell em'* you had sex with a minor, and got me pregnant. Go ahead, make my day Wayne," Raven said, challenging him.

He looked mortified. "What?"

"Yeah, that's right nigga, *rape.*"

Raven stomped her way towards the counter, picked up a knife, sliced a hunk of chocolate cake from the swiveled dish. She ate a moist slice from the palm of her hand.

"This fucking restaurant will be mine."

CHAPTER 35

A sudden down pour had the interstate jacked up. Cars sat bumper to bumper, burning fuel. Wayne's loaner car was shiny on the outside, but was a true guzzler. With just a quarter of a tank, and five exits to go, Tony prayed the wreck would be cleared soon.

He turned back, saw his son slumped over, out like a light. All the commotion at Wayne's restaurant was enough to make anyone tired. His friend couldn't help himself. He had an appetite for the young tenders. He preferred to fish from a pool of juveniles instead of wheeling in a mature catch.

Murderous Mommy smashed up the bar, Raven shouted threats, Cujo was ordered to *sick-em*, and all hell broke loose. Tony held his son and hauled ass out the restaurant. Sticking around to see how Wayne's story ended was not in his best interest.

The temperature outside had fallen below freezing. He could see traces of his breath in the air. Kicking up the heat wasn't an option. He depended on that quarter of a tank to get them home. There was no telling how much longer they'll have to sit idle.

"Damn traffic."

The front and rear windows became foggy. Visibility poor, just like the road conditions, just like the weather, just like his attitude at the moment. He yanked off his hat, leaned over the steering wheel, and wiped a circle larger enough to see from all angles. He leaned over the passenger's seat, wiped and did the same for his left side. He heard sirens. Tony glanced out the side mirror, noticed the flashing lights from the paramedics bus riding the shoulder. Black Nissan zipped out of traffic, rode the bus coattail.

"Fuck it, I'm riding too."

Tony dipped out behind the Nissan and followed the leader. The emergency bus was doing an easy forty, the Nissan had to be doing thirty five, and Tony fell a few notches behind, giving himself enough room to stop in the case of any sudden changes in the road.

A half a mile into his pursuit he realized he was breaking the law. The imprint from the metal bracelets left a permanent trace against his wrist. The clanking sound of the lock that hinged him for many years resounded in his head. Metal doors, iron bars, restraints, the guard's boots dragging against the cold floors in the wee hours, peering into his cell with flashlights.

"When you know better, you do better."

He eased back into population. The Nissan kept it pushing, blowing past the rest of the sitting ducks. *Fuck!* He turned the heat on full blast for a couple of minutes, just to defrost his buns and defog the windows.

"Can't violate my terms. Stay low my nigga, stay low."

"Daddy, who are you talking to?"

Tony turned, saw Jacob rubbing his eyes and yarning.

"Talking to God."

"Mommy says God will always answer our prayers. We just have to believe."

"That's right son. Go back to sleep. We'll be home soon."

"Daddy, it's cold."

Tony unzipped his bubble coat, peeled it from his body, and handed it to Jacob. The coat covered his small frame from head to toe. He turned back to face the road, realizing there'd been some movement. As he proceeded to close the gap, an eager SAAB tried to penetrate the space. He honked the horn, but the vehicle continued to roll in his direction.

The lady behind the wheel carried four kids. All were screaming at the top of their lungs. The half crazed woman held the steering wheel with one hand, using the other to whack her children with a long plastic device.

"Are you crazy?" He leaned on the horn. When that didn't get her attention, he rolled down the window, shouted, "Pay attention to the fucking road."

She popped him the finger, swerving the nose of her vehicle into the back door. The impact caused Jacob to scream.

"Crazy bitch!"

The window to the SAAB came down. Frightened screams cut through the icy air. The woman fired racial insults, throwing her middle finger in his direction. Her apparent road rage had him at a loss for words. The SAAB straitened its wheel, and then came rearing its ugly head again. On impulse Tony reached for the opened drink that rested in the holder, tossing it into the window. *Tahitian Treat* splashed the driver in the face. *Bull's-eye.* He whipped the car onto the shoulder, and rode out before the angry driver could clear fruit punch from her eyes and copy down the license plate.

Tony called Jazzman immediately when he got home. An impulse decision he wished he could rethink, re-do, take back.

"You sure my son is okay?" Her voice quivered.

"He's fine."

"Where is he?"

"In the bathroom doing number two."

He could hear her breathing deeply. "Oh my God, I can't believe you got into an accident."

"That crazy lady hit me on purpose."

"Why the hell would someone hit you on purpose?"

"You didn't see the look in her eyes. That lady was crazy. Her kids were crazy too. She was whooping them with a stick... driving with one hand... beating their ass... I mean fucking them up... she must have gotten pissed when I blew the horn... the lady just rammed into me. I took off, didn't stop until I made it home." He left out the part about the drink tossing, and had already schooled Jacob on the same omission.

"You left the scene of an accident?!" Jazzman shouted into the receiver.

"What was I supposed to do?"

"Wait for the police, fool."

"*Shit*, fuck that. I got the hell on."

"Where's the car?"

"Garage."

"Just stay off the road okay."

"Don't worry; we're staying in for the rest of the evening."

"Make sure he's in bed at a reasonable hour. He's got school in the morning."

"I know this already," he said frustrated.

"Look, don't get no damn attitude with me," she snarled.

"*Yo*, for-real watch who the fuck you talking to."

"What?"

"Watch your fucking tone. I'm tired of you talking crazy."

"Fuck you Tony."

She ended their call abruptly.

He wanted to call back, stir up a fight but he had other pressing matters to deal with. "I'm a grown ass man," he mumbled. After placing the phone back onto the cradle, he went to check on Jacob. He knocked his knuckles against the bathroom door.

"You aight in there?"

"My tummy hurts."

"Told you not to eat those Fingers," Tony said.

"It hurt bad."

"You want me to come in?"

"No. I want Mommy."

"You want some tea?"

"No, I want Mommy."

Jacob started to sniffle. The boy wanted his mother. She was the only person on earth who could make it all better. Seconds later he heard the toilet flush.

"Wash your hands." The sink came on, and then turned off in zero point two seconds flat. "Scrub them with soap," Tony ordered from the other side of the door knowing a drop barely reached his palm.

Before long Jacob was back to his old self. He giggled, rolled, and bounce along with *Phineas* and *Ferb*. Seeing that his son was occupied, he headed out to the garage. He rubbed his chin, folded his arms, and kicked the tire. The massive dent in the fender made the car look ugly. He had to fix it, make it like new again, but he had no dough. He called Wayne to spill the news but got his voicemail. He figured his boy had enough worries dealing with his pregnant-teenage-mistress, so he refrained from leaving a message.

He circled the car, thinking of a way to come up with some cash. He stopped at the trunk. That Key of coke made the wheels in his head spin. "Walk the straight and narrow."

He shook the thought and continued to pace. The wall behind him held a custom cabinetry organizer. Overhead storage held boxes. One had his name on it. He reached for it, and placed it on the floor. Layers of masking tape had been sliced through with a straight razor of some sort. Since the box was already open, and it had his name on it, it wouldn't technically be snooping *right?*

The first thing he came across was the brown leather photo album. He couldn't help but laugh at his attire. Fashion trends had surely changed in the last five years. Everywhere he turned he saw skinny pants, and tight shirts with mo-hawks. He flipped through the pages and smiled at a picture of Jazzman. She sported a cap with the Lakers stamped across the front. Back in the day she loved LA because of Kobe, and then she became a Denver Nugget nut-holder. Carmelo Anthony was her baby daddy, and Jazzman would fight La-La Vazquez head-up for him. Since Melo's recent trade to the Knicks, Jazzman was repping her hometown to the fullest, *again.*

"LA...Denver...New York...*Traitor.*"

He continued to search through the box. There were a few jail house letters from him during his first year and some old clothes, but nothing of value. He placed the box back exactly the way he found it. He looked at the Mercedes, got mad all over again. Since there was absolutely nothing he could do about it now, he headed back inside where it was warm.

Jacob littered the floor with crayons, coloring books, and scotch tape.

"Are you hungry?" Tony asked.

"Not really."

"What are you doing?"

"Making Mommy a picture." Jacob looked up at his daddy.

"Do you know how to use a scanner?"

"A what?"

"A scanner?"

"No."

"How about a fax machine?"

He laughed. "Why?"

"Because, when I'm done with my picture I want to send it to Mommy."

"Huh, how about I take a picture and text it to her?"

Jacob got excited. He hadn't thought about that option.

"Okay."

He rubbed the top of the child's head and bolted up the steps. He stopped at the landing, stared at her door. It was closed. He neared it. Jiggled the knob. It was locked.

"Jacob," he called from the top of the steps.

"Yes."

"Time for your bath."

"But Daddy I haven't finished my picture."

"You can finish later."

"But Daddy..." Tiny feet trotted up the steps. When Jacob made it to the top he noticed his daddy facing the closed door. He tugged at his daddy's sleeve. "But's it's not even eight yet."

"Close enough. Go run your water."

A moment passed and neither budged.

"She put a new lock on it."

He looked down at Jacob. "When?"

Jacob shrugged his little shoulders.

"Do you know where she keeps the key?" He felt bad for asking, but kids knew more than adults thought they knew. Jacob was an observer, just like his mother.

Jacob shrugged again. "Don't know daddy. You want me to call and ask?"

"*NO.*" he said a bit too loudly. "I mean no son. That's okay." He patted his head, and then gave him a gentle shove towards the bathroom.

Sweet dreams captured Jacob moments after he finished his Picasso. As promised, Tony snapped a picture of his artwork, loaded and sent it via text to Jazzman. He scooped his son from the floor and brought him to his resting place. Covers pulled up to his neck, night light on, door cracked just enough to let the *Boogie Man* come and go.

Tony skated back down the steps, and was greeted with crayons, paper, glue, glitter, tape, toys and other crap Jacob had manage to pull out. He scooped everything into one bin, closing the plastic top, snapping the sides. Tony had the rest of the night to himself. He grabbed his cell phone. There was a missed call from Champagne. He licked his lips, smiled. There were two missed calls from Wayne, and one *Unknown*. Champagne took precedence over Wayne.

"You're so lucky it's a blizzard outside," she said.

"Why is that?"

"Because I would be at your doorstep naked, ready to give you all of this."

"All of it?"

"Yep, all of it."

He closed his eyes, gripped the phone, pulled in his bottom lip. With Jazzman out of town, and Jacob asleep, her timing would have been perfect.

"Don't play with me."

"Who's playing?"

"I'll jack a plow truck and shovel my way to you."

She giggled. "Now that would be some romantic stuff."

"Would you ride shotgun?"

"No doubt. Proudly."

"You mad cool Champagne."

"You aint too bad yourself, Tony."

"The other night, you did some shit to me that I can't forget."

"I told you my GPA was on point."

A beep interrupted his fantasy of Champagne's bodacious measurements. She placed him on hold, and came back two seconds later.

"Trigger, can I call you back?"

The way she said his street name made his toes curl. "*Ooh*, say my name again."

She giggled, made a slurp noise. *"Trigger."*

After hanging up with Champagne, Tony released the knot from his pants and fantasized. Relief landed on Jazzman's cashmere throw. More than satisfied with his happy ending, his eyes closed and he drifted off.

CHAPTER 36

J acob's tiny outstretched hands, and crusty smile was something he'd become accustomed to seeing. Having access to his son, twenty four seven was a blessing, a dream come true. He considered himself privileged and was determined to maintain his current situation for as long as possible.

Jazzman hadn't called to wish Jacob sweet dreams, which was strange. When Tony called her, the call went straight to voicemail. Things between them were worsening, and all he wanted was for them to be a family, *again*.

"No school, son."

Jacob bounced up and down on his bed, did a flip, landed on his hiny, and bounced back onto his feet. Charged on pure adrenalin, he ran towards the window, yanked back the drapes and waved his arms from side to side. *"Snow... oh yeah, huh-huh... no school."*

Jacob cart wheeled and back flipped his tiny frame onto the bed and proceeded to bounce again.

"Calm down before you break the bed."

"Can I go outside and play?"

"Not yet. Later."

"Can I watch cartoons?"

Tony rubbed his chin, prolonged his answer. "First brush your teeth and wash your face. You looking and smelling like a grown man these days."

Jacob didn't quite get the joke but he laughed anyways.

Downstairs Jacob copped a squat on the floor, surrounding himself with toys and his favorite *Pillow Pet*. Tony on the other hand utilized that time to seek some employment. With the city shut down, and everything at a standstill due to the blizzard, he knew the timing couldn't have been more perfect. *I need a job and fast.* The spare computer was powered on, in his lap for the first time since he'd been home. For the life of him he couldn't remember how to access the internet.

"Jacob."

"Yes daddy."

"How do you get to the internet again?"

"Find the big *E*, daddy."

The big E, the big... He fished the desktop for the big E, but there were so many Icons that he found himself breaking into a sweat. He felt a headache coming on. *Where the hell is the big E?*

"*Oh.* The big Eeeee.... *Dah...*Found it. Thanks."

Jacob giggled. His daddy was so funny.

His crash course on the *world-wide-web* was coming back. Jazzman showed him a few tricks which stuck, but lots of what she did teach him went out the window the moment she said it. He Googled: *Warehouse Jobs*. A list of Day Labor Staffing agencies popped up. He began applying for positions. Some he qualified for, others he didn't, but he wasn't about to disqualify himself.

"Have you ever been convicted of a felony?"

"What daddy?"

Tony looked up from the screen. "Nothing, son... just talking to my-self."

"Oh. Mommy said there's nothing wrong with talking to yourself. It's when you answer yourself back that you should get help."

Tony couldn't help but laugh. "That's true son."

He clicked *no* to the felony question, and proceeded to the next. "College. Some College. High school. GED?" He chose GED, and in the comment field listed some random online school he'd claimed to currently been enrolled into. While watching Maury he'd noticed over a dozen commercials advertising online education. It was the way of the world.

When Tony reached the work experience sector of the application, he didn't panic. Jazzman managed to doctor up a resume displaying his work experience dating back ten years. On paper, he was solid.

Salary expectations, "I need like a hunnit stacks a year," he snickered.

Full time. Part time. Weekends. "Anytime."

What position? "Shit. Whatever you got open."

When can you start? "Yesterday."

He'd managed to apply for over a dozen positions online, but was suddenly tired of looking at the screen. He shut down just like Jazzman had showed him, the proper way.

"Mommy didn't answer her phone," Jacob said in a whiny voice.

That bitch didn't answer last night either, he thought to himself. By this time Jazzman should have been made aware of the weather conditions. According to the news, all flight were canceled.

"Did you call the cell or her room?"

"Both." His brown face looked sad.

"I miss Mommy. When is she coming home?"

Tony glanced up at the clock. It was *9am* on the nose. Houston was an hour behind.

"She's probably asleep."

Jacob pouted, "I want Mommy."

Me too. Tony let out a sigh. "How about we make some Mickey Mouse pancakes?"

Jacobs's eyes lit up like a Christmas tree. *"Oh yeah, huh-huh, oh yeah, huh-huh."*

Tony and Jacob two stepped it towards the kitchen to make breakfast. Jacob was quite pleased with his daddy's skills. Mickey's ears were perfectly round, his face too. Sliced banana framed the eyes. A strip of turkey bacon formed a smile. Sticky hot maple syrup smeared their lips.

"Daddy, you make the best Mickey pancakes. Better than Mommy."

"And you know this man," Tony said in his best *Chris Tucker* voice.

"Just don't tell her that."

"Why?"

"You never tell a woman she's lacking in the kitchen."

"Why?"

"Because it's not polite, and she might not ever cook for you again."

"But if it's nasty shouldn't I say so. Mommy said to always tell the truth. She said the truth will set us free."

Tony held back his laughter. *What the hell is she teaching my son?* "Listen carefully son. Women are fragile."

"My mommy strong," Jacob defended.

"Yes. She is. But, she's still delicate, fragile, like a flower and needs to be told she's pretty, and smells good, and all sorts of nice things at least twice a day."

Jacob held up two fingers. "Twice."

"When you get older and find a girlfriend..." Tony stopped his lecture, looked at his son. "Do you have a girlfriend?"

Jacob blushed. He struggled with how to answer. "No, but there's this pretty girl in my class that always sharpens my pencil."

Tony threw his head back. "Whoa, what you mean she sharpens your pencil?"

"You know, she puts my pencil inside the sharpener everyday to make sure my point is pointy. She only does it for me."

Tony wiped his forehead, laughed. "What was I saying?"

"Women are delicate and fragile, like a flower and need to be complimented twice a day," Jacob blurted.

Tony snapped his fingers. "Right. So you never tell a woman her cooking stinks."

Jacob scrunched his nose. "But what if it does?"

"You deal with it until you can find a solution."

"Nope daddy, I'm not eating nasty food. My stomach sensitive."

Tony felt he was going nowhere fast on the food topic so he switched gears.

"My mother taught me how to cook. It was important that I knew how to take care of myself in the event something happened to her. See, the men in my family depended on their wives to do everything. Count money, iron clothes, cook food, take care of the kids, *everything*."

"They did nothing for themselves but make money and watch their wives spend it. In fact, some of the men in my family didn't know how to make money at all..." He stopped his lecture again, feeling himself derailing from the point he was trying to make.

"What I'm trying to say is my mother wanted me to be different. She wanted me to be self sufficient."

"Self suff-who?"

"Self sufficient. It means being able to take care of yourself without help from others. You need to learn how to survive in this world, alone."

Jacob rubbed his chin like a little man. "So, don't tell Mommy her Mickey pancakes stink, *and* tell her she's pretty twice a day, *and* learn to be self-sufficient in this world because I might be alone one day *and* need to know how to take care of myself, in this world, *alone*."

"Smart kid," Tony said slapping fives with his son.

The telephone interrupted their father-son meeting of the minds.

"I'll get it," Jacob hopped up from the dining room table, bolted to-wards the kitchen, and grabbed the wall mounted phone with his sticky hands.

Spending alone time with Jacob made Tony see how much he'd missed his own father. There were things his mother couldn't teach him. Not that his sweet mother didn't do her best while she was on this earth, but fathers guidance is vital to the development of a young man.

"Daddy, Aunty Lou-Lou on the phone," Jacob shouted.

Tony made a face, quickly stood and hustled towards the kitchen. *Aunty Lou-Lou? Who gave her the right? What does she want?* He grabbed the phone, placed the receiver to his chest. "Go wash your face and hands."

Jacob jetted off towards the bathroom to be self sufficient.

"Who is this?"

"Nigga *please*, stop acting "brand-new". What's good?"

He arched a brow, leaned against the sink, smiled. Same old Lou-Lou.

"Catching up with life. What-up with you?" he asked.

"*Maintaining*. Heard you got out and immediately got on some dad-dy shit."

"This is true."

"That's a good look. He's a great kid."

"This is true."

"You and Jazz back together?"

"Not even," he said dryly.

"She got the cooch on lock huh?" Lou-Lou laughed.

He didn't answer.

"You back on that grind?"

"What do you mean?"

"Stop playing. You know what I'm talking about. You getting money again?"

"Nope. Flying straight."

"That nickel upstate sat that ass down huh?"

His jaw hardened. "Jazzman's not here."

"Tell me something I don't."

"Bye, Lou-Lou."

"*No*. Wait, she's in Houston. Been trying her cell but she's not answering. You got a room number?"

He looked at the receiver crazy. "If I did, why would I give it to you?"

"*C'mon* Tony I need it."

The urgency in her voice made him suspicious. "What you need it for?"

"It's a confidential matter."

"Sorry, can't help you."

He was just about to pry his hand from the sticky receiver when she blurted, "Jazzman know you fucking that rat Champagne?"

"Who I fuck is none of Jazzman's business," he shot back in a nasty tone.

She paused. "Okay, I guess you wouldn't mind me telling her you brought Jacob to Brooklyn when she clearly told you not to," she snickered, "Remember what happened the last time you brought him to Brooklyn?"

Tony's last trip to Brooklyn changed his life. Routine traffic stop turned deadly. Rookie officer caught a few to the chest, died on the scene. His man J-Rock let off without warning, putting Jacob's life in jeopardy. Child Services wanted to take Jacob for the actions of his father. Even though Tony didn't pull the trigger, he pulled the trigger.

Her laughter broke through his grim thoughts. "Jazzman is bound to go ape-shit if she found out her precious baby boy was sitting amongst Wayne's pedophile ass."

"Wait. Don't do that."

And just like that Tony gave up the math. He stood in the kitchen mulling over his conversation with Lou-Lou. The last time he'd heard Lou-Lou's name all sorts of bitches and Ho's followed it. Jazzman wasn't exactly a fan but he didn't know why. However, Jacob seemed mighty comfortable with calling her Aunty.

"Jacob."

"Yes."

"Come in here."

Jacob skipped his way towards the kitchen; Wii remote wrapped his tiny wrist. He was breathing hard. His computerized tennis opponent was giving him a run for his money. "Yes daddy."

"When's the last time you saw your Aunty Lou-Lou?"

Jacob sensed something was wrong. His daddy's eyes were piercing green, with shades of brown, gold, and *anger*, that was the leading agent.

"*Hum*... Mommy told me not to say."

Tony knelt down, grabbed his elbow, and pulled them close to his tiny frame. He forced a smile for Jacob's sake. "Remember, the truth will set you free."

Jacob squirmed until his daddy released him. "I can't. Mommy said it was our secret."

"I won't tell anyone."

"But I'll be breaking our oath."

Tony chuckled. He respected his son's loyalty to his mother.

"Son, I won't tell her you told me. It'll be our little secret."

"But me and Mommy already have a secret. If I tell you then I'll be breaking that secret, and then you and me will have us a secret and Mommy can't know. But when she asks me, I can't lie, so I'll tell her and the whole thing would be messed up because of me." Jacob stared at his daddy, ready to cry.

Tony broke down, got on both knees, and hugged his son.

"Okay. Okay. I'm sorry."

Jacob could tell that this information was extremely important to his daddy, but he was more concerned with what his mother would think. She would be disappointed in him, but his daddy would leave and never speak to him again. There were too many secrets under one roof and Jacob didn't know which parent to confide in. He loved them both.

Jacob's eyes watered. "You promise?"

"I promise son."

Jacob unraveled the Wii remote, sat it on the counter and took a seat. He hesitated, and Tony could tell he was yet again on the fence. He spoke softly, rubbed his sons head.

"It's okay son. You can tell me."

"Aunty Lou-Lou surprised me with twenty dollars one night," Jacob murmured.

"When?"

He shrugged his tiny shoulders in slow motion. "She said it was for all the teeth I'd lost. I was asleep, and thought I was dreaming but then she kissed me, and when I woke up I saw shiny brown gloss on my cheek. And the twenty dollars was underneath my pillow. I could still smell her perfume. Smelled like berries."

"When was this?"

"I don't know."

"Think."

He brought his shoulders up to his ears again. "There was a man with her too."

"A man? What man?"

"He was real tall, had a baseball cap on and he smiled at me. Mommy called him Roy, and then she called him Raymond. The man looked at Mommy weird." Jacob recalled.

Tony stood, straightened his spine. "Roy? Impossible."

"That's what Mommy called him."

"This tall man name Roy, what did he look like?"

"I didn't see his face because his hat was pulled down low over his eyes."

"Do you remember what kind of hat he wore?"

Jacob nodded his head vigorously. "Same cap Lil-Dave and his brother always wear during ball practice. *Yankees*... Daddy, can you buy me one like that?"

Tony felt his body go cold. "Are you sure it was a Yankees cap?"

Jacob stood up, traced the air with his finger. "The big NY."

Roy's trademark. Low fitted cap with a New York Yankees logo stamping the front. But Roy was dead. *Everyone* knew that. Or was he?

"Can I go now?" Jacob asked.

"Go ahead. Don't forget the remote."

Tony headed towards the garage, popped the trunk to the Mercedes. He lifted the wool carpet, pulled the latch, yanked open the small compartment. He grabbed the crowbar and headed back inside the house. He slid past Jacob, who was too busy serving his opponent with a *mean-one* to notice his daddy.

Tony leaped up the steps, four at a time. He stopped at *her* door, breathing like a maniac on steroids. The muscles in his neck twitched, his jaw stiffened. He got into a steady position; feet spread apart shoulder width, both knees slightly bent. He jammed the straight end into the wedge where the lock was. A small amount of pressure he applied. As he increased the pressure dosage the lock made a loud snap.

Open sesame.

He headed straight for the closet, stuck his hand into the furthest coat in the back. He latched onto a garment bag. Inside the bag was a beautiful mink. He shook the fur, checked its pockets. *Empty.* He checked a few more coat inserts and they were all empty. Thoughts of Roy, in this house, smiling at his son ignited his anger.

The top rack held her winter sweaters. He yanked cashmere, angora, yarn, cotton, fleece, and a range of other fabrics ranging from soft and buttery, to hard and scratchy. He noticed something sandwiched between an eggplant colored crewneck, and periwinkle knitted poncho. He cleared the top shelf with one good swoop of the arm. The manila envelope dropped to his feet. Tony bent over, grabbed the huge folder.

"Ooooooooh daddy."

Tony jerked his body around, noticed Jacob standing wide-eyed, shaking his head.

"Go back downstairs."

Jacob stepped over the scattered debris, entered the Queen's domain. "What are you looking for?"

"I don't know yet. Now go back downstairs."

"What's that?"

Tony hid the envelope behind his back. "Nothing."

"Ooooooooh Daddy," was all Jacob could muster. He wanted no part in his father's obvious mess so he skipped his way back down the steps.

Tony had no clue what he was looking for, but he knew if he dug deep he would find something, *anything* to calm his mind about Roy. With his feet he cleared a path towards the bed. He climbed into the sack, noticing it felt a bit lumpy, squeaky. Her perfect boyfriend Rick was probably responsible for wearing down the springs. Or maybe it was Roy? He'd always had a "thing" for Jazzman. He was practically obsessed, so obsessed that he'd threatened to dead Tony for her love.

"Let's take a look."

The envelope was sealed with a gummed flap and metal clasp fastened the lift. He thought of steaming it open, but then said, *fuck it*. He tore into the package, looked inside. Papers stapled together, important lines highlighted, signatures scribbled. *What the fuck!* Gripped by a new kind of anger, Tony hopped off the bed and continued searching.

CHAPTER 37

Canceled flights, stranded buses and vehicles buried along major highways. A monster storm hammered the city, blanketing most, if not all of the East coast. Tony returned Wayne's call from the night before. He needed to get his mind off Jazzman, and the disturbing documents found hid at the back of her closet.

"Yeah man, just heard a tractor-trailer skidded off a road and smashed into a house, killing everybody but the dog," Wayne said.

The news anchor's voice blared in the background giving an account of the blizzards wrath. The city was shut-down, a complete ghost town.

"What channel?" Tony asked.

"Fox5"

"This storm is a beast," Tony said as he watched the same reporter shiver with each word.

"This kind of weather is bad for business," Wayne huffed.

"*Yo'* you know I got you on the damages. Soon as I find me a job, I'll pay you for the car," Tony said.

"I told you it was cool. Don't worry about it."

"That crazy bitch just ran into me, *with her kids in the car.*"

"Welcome home, nigga. Welcome home!"

Tony made himself comfortable on the Queen's bed, eating roasted peanuts, wasting shells. The information that lined the inside of the envelope road his thoughts. Each time he glanced at the fine print, it tightened the restraints on his heart.

"What up with that young chic from the restaurant? Is she your new baby mom's or what?"

"Fuck outta here!"

Tony chuckled. "One day these bitches will be the death of you. One way or another, watch and see."

"I stay strapped up. What I look like sexing these bitches raw? I got a wife at the crib for that."

Wayne had a wife, two teenage daughters, and a son who was Jacob's age at home. In addition, he had a steady girlfriend, and a few bust-it-babies lined up to pleasure him on command.

"She said she missed her bloody-show," Tony cracked up.

"I'm glad you find this shit funny."

Tony laughed so hard his stomach hurt. "Man, you better prove otherwise because her mother is ready to take your head off."

"Tell me something I don't know."

"And you better do it quick before your wife catch wind."

"Fuck!" Wayne released his anger. "She'll leave me for good this time."

"I'm surprised she stuck by your cheating ass this long," Tony admitted.

"Trust me, she's had one foot out the door for years, but stayed because of the girls. And now that the twins are in their last year of high school there would be nothing holding her back."

"What about your son?"

"He's a Momma's Boy. *Lil nigga* got sugar in his tank if you ask me. He goes where she goes. Says what she says. Does whatever she does. He shadows her every move."

"Nothing wrong with loving your momma," Tony professed.

"He got that different kind of love. He gay, word life. That *lil nigga* gay."

Tony busted out laughing. "Stop playing."

"Dead serious. I caught him playing with Barbie and Ken. I fucked his ass up."

"That don't mean he's gay."

"Getting dirty is not an option. Don't let a little mud splash his kicks; he goes into a bitch frenzy."

"He's meticulous. I am too."

Wayne sucked his teeth. "I know gay, and that Lil Nigga gay as the rainbow that represent them homo's. If she leaves, she's putting my ass on paper for sure."

"The infamous child support drama."

"And Alimony. And the house. And the whips, might come for the Subway's too." Something told Tony he regretted mentioning that last part. Wayne had a restaurant in Brooklyn. This he knew. Nothing spectacular, but it generated revenue. The hood supported it. Now Wayne was claiming his wife would snatch the Subways in their divorce settlement.

"Damn son, how many Subway's you got?"

"A few."

"Where at?"

"All over. I bought into the franchise a few years ago."

"Oh."

"Would you believe all of this drama is over twenty five hundred dollars?" Wayne said, paused and continued. "This stupid bitch Raven wanted me to front her trip to LA for an audition."

"What audition?"

"Some stupid reality show. She's trying to break into the business and heard about auditions. Twenty five hundred would have paid her airfare, hotel stay, and fed her greedy ass."

"Why didn't you give it to her?"

"Because she's not wifey," Wayne hissed.

"You had two stacks to toss her way. The girl was trying to do something positive. At least you could have loaned her a whip, and some gas money. Told her she needed to come up with the rest on her own, met her half way or something."

"Meeting that chick half way would mean I would have to support the rest of these hoes dreams. I got college tuition, for *two* I need to pay. I ain't her daddy."

"But you about to be her baby's daddy," Tony said, cracking up some more.

"Fuck you. That ain't my baby."

"Yeah whatever, tell it to Judge. I've been meaning to ask you something."

"Something like what?"

"When's the last time you talked to Lou-Lou?"

Wayne whistled. "Years, why?"

His answer seemed more firm, more real. When asked the same question pertaining to Jazzman, Wayne hesitated.

"She called the crib looking for Jazzman this morning."

"Sounds like trouble to me."

"Yeah, my exact same thoughts," Tony said, with both arms folded across his chest.

"She mentioned Champagne. How would she know about that?" Tony asked.

"How should I know? The streets talk."

Wayne was right. The streets did talk. There were a number of people at the restaurant who could have made the report. Champagne could have mentioned it to someone, and that someone mentioned it to someone else, and before you knew it the story probably changed a hundred times before it reached Lou-Lou's ears.

"Your begging ass cousin came into the restaurant yesterday."

"Yvette? When?"

"Right before closing. She was asking for food and beer. I fed her a sandwich and gave her some water."

"How she look?"

"Like death. She's smoking her life away."

"The next time you see her, give her my number."

"Tried to, she didn't want it. Told me, to tell you, to stay the fuck outta Brooklyn."

Their conversation ended on that note. Tony headed downstairs to check on Jacob. The living room was empty. As he neared the kitchen he heard whispers. Jacob was crouched inside the pantry, near the bottled water and powdered protein shake. The cordless stuck between his shoulder and his chin. Jacob's eyes enlarged when he saw his daddy.

"Who are you talking to?" Tony asked, snatching the phone before Jacob could respond.

"Who is this?"

"What's up, Tony. This is Rick." His voice was professional, corn-ball-*ish.*

"Rick who?" Tony snarled.

"I'm sure you've heard my name at least once before." Rick chuck-led.

"Don't be so sure."

"Right. Okay... *hum* can I speak to Jazzman?"

"What?" Tony snapped.

"Look, I was just wondering if she made it in from Houston before the storm hit. I've been out of town myself and haven't had much time to speak with her." He lied. He'd spoken to her last night, and his last words were *Fuck off!* But of course he wouldn't divulge that infor-mation to the live-in ex-man, who was trying desperately to become her new man, *again.* But truthfully, Rick was genuinely concerned about her wellbeing. Jazzman wasn't answering her cell, nor was she answer-ing her room phone.

Tony's jaw tightened. Jacob knew that look all too well, so he scur-ried off. The sound of the Wii console chimed-on.

"Weren't you seated next to her on the flight there?"

"*What?* Is that what she told you?" Rick suddenly sounded angry, less professional.

"Thought you flew out to Houston to keep her company," Tony said.

"Not me."

"Oh, well she's not here. So..."

"Hold on for a second."

Tony heard a few clicks and beeps, and then Rick's voice came through. There was ringing, like a third party interception. A pleasant voice said, "Hilton Hotel, this is Suzanne."

"Hello Suzanne, I've been trying to reach my *wife*, Jazzman Bridges since this morning. She's in room..."

"*Oh.* Mr. Bridges your wife checked out hours ago," the woman said, cutting Rick off.

"Hours ago?"

"Yes sir."

Silence.

"Anything else I can help you with?"

"No. Thank you so kindly," Rick said deflated.

A few clicks and beeps later, he heard only Ricks voice. Tony could tell the man was just as distraught as he was. Jazzman had checked out without informing either of them.

"*Aight*, if and when I speak with her, I'll let her know you called," Tony said in a voice that indicated he could care less. But beneath his harsh tone was fear, uncertainty, rage.

"Thanks man. Please tell her to call me. Anytime is good."

Tony stood in the kitchen feeling somewhat triumphant. Now that Rick was in the same boat as he, there was some promise for his family after all. But he couldn't help but worry. Lou-Lou's grimy ass was back in the mix, Roy's ghost had mysteriously resurrected and Jazzman was M.I.A.

CHAPTER 38

C onvincing Sonny *not* to call in sick for the second time in one week was no easy task. She insisted on spooning for the rest of the day, sipping champagne to celebrate their intended nuptials. *They were engaged!*

"Let's stay in bed all night and make babies," she recommended.

He loved how enthusiastic she was about the idea of becoming his Misses, and carrying his babies, but for argument sake he needed her to go to work. Lou-Lou sent him a text, stating tonight was the night. The Bradley deal was officially a go. Roy knew Sonny would never allow him to leave, especially not after the morning they've had. He'd pumped her full of seed from the music room, to the kitchen, to the living room, back to the bedroom, where she craved for more of his sperm.

"I think I'm pregnant."

He laughed. "Already?"

"I know my body. I feel different."

He pulled her in, kissed her stomach. "Boy or girl?"

"Maybe both. Twins run in my family."

He watched her twist and turn, taking in side profiles. She even went as far as stuffing her nighty with a round throw pillow. Full frontal image almost brought her to tears.

"My mother will be so proud. She will finally be called Grandma."

Vibrations came from his back pocket. Roy was pretty sure Sonny hadn't heard them for she was talking non-stop about bearing his children, raising a family, and being his wife. She went on about turning the spare room into a nursery.

"We should paint the walls orange. It stimulates creativity and enthusiasm. I want my children to be optimistic, sociable, and successful. Maybe throw in pops of red to evoke love and passion into their beings. Layer the curtains with white sheers for purity, and hardwood blinds to represent the color of earth's abundance."

He took a quick peek at his cell. It was Kema calling him for the tenth time. She was a loose cannon, high risk, but he needed her. Tonight's plan called for her hand, and from the messages left he could tell she needed the loot.

"What do you think about the color scheme?"

"Sounds like you're trying to give my baby a migraine. Look, go to work, please."

She huffed. "Okay, but only because I need to start saving for our kids college tuition. I figure if we start now…"

"Sonny, go to work."

He watched his soon to be wife back out the driveway, glowing from her new found purpose in life. She was ecstatic about the possibilities, so was he, but wallowing in that delight had to come later. Right now he had to refocus. Roy toned down the intense emotions he felt for his Queen and transformed back into that nigga you love to hate.

***

Roy watched Kema closely from the street. Checking her body gestures and movements was imperative to his survival. Lou-Lou warned Roy he was playing with fire, but they needed Kema to score big. She had what it took to make the Bradley deal go down smooth as butter. Without her, their plan would be a bust.

Inside he could see her pacing, chewing her nails down to a bloody nub. He was late. So, she thought. His eyes set on her petite frame since a quarter past seven. He sat low, behind the wheel of an old school Vette, watching her lose it. His inconspicuous cover up kept them jack boys guessing. Coming through the block all shiny and new was a recipe for disaster. Roy possessed finesse and was way too sharp for the average *Taker.*

Kema was a frantic mess, and that told Roy he needed to thread wisely. From a distance she looked to be in mourning, but up close he couldn't exactly decipher what she knew. One thing was for certain, her brother Ace was in the morgue with six to the chest.

His phone trilled. Not shocked to see her number glowing from the screen. Roy was always punctual; his sudden tardiness had her on pins. The buzzing ended and another call followed shortly after. And another, another trailed that until he decided to answer.

"I'm not too far away. Be easy."

"Be easy? Really? I've been waiting for over an hour and..."

"Kill the noise. I said I'm not too far."

She inhaled one long frustrated breath and disappeared from his view.

"Kema."

"What." She was sobbing.

"Look, calm down."

"Calm down? My brother is dead and you're telling me to calm down?"

Roy could have crushed her feelings but he chose to remain somewhat sympathetic to her situation. Unscheduled deaths were always hard to process, and not for nothing her brother was her everything. Just them two against the world.

"I don't know how to be calm... It's just that..."

"What?"

"I need you right now. Shit it hectic and I don't know what to do."

She reappeared back in his view. Fat one rolled tight, kissed her lips. A plume of smoked escaped her lungs, covered her face, and then dissipated into the air. She insisted they meet up at her house. Run down bungalow which anchored the corner sat ghostly, almost demonic in a sense. The street light, busted. Suspicion ran through his veins, so naturally he was on his guard. Sweeping glances took in the block. Every house, parked vehicle, tree, limb, branch could and would catch a slug if it moved wrong.

"Roy."

"What up?"

"They killed my family." Hysteria coated the back of the throat.

"They?"

"*They*. That's all I fucking know, all I have. I need you. Please hurry."

Roy moved towards the bungalow. Pistol tucked at his waist, another jammed in the small of his back. Beneath his bubble coat, a vest guarded his heart. New York fitted pulled down over his lids as he moved towards uncertainty.

Backdoor entrance led him into the kitchen where he'd been watching her. Inside, she sat at the small oval table rolling up another blunt. A baggy full of *Kush* sat on the counter, stems and seeds scattered about on the linoleum floor. Bottle of Hennessey unopened, untouched awaited his arrival. She jumped to her feet and fell into his chest, knocking him back against the pantry door. He gave her sixty seconds to sob, hold and feel him before he broke away from the unwanted embrace.

"No, hold me. Please."

Every fiber within told him not to, but he couldn't help but be humane towards her situation. He held her, looking on from all angles, registering his surroundings. She appeared to be alone, but one could never be too sure. She finally peeled herself away and looked up at him.

"You're wearing a vest?"

"Your brother just got merked, and you don't know who did it. Police have no clue. Damn right I'm rocking the vest."

She sniveled. "Makes sense."

Kema collapsed into the chair, and sparked her blunt. As tears streaked her mocha skin, Roy took a tour of the quarters. Seeing that there wasn't much area to cover, he quickly began to relax.

Her eyes swept all over him, assessing him from head to toe. He seemed different. Besides from being his usual direct, focused, serious self, he also owned a sense of paranoia she'd never witnessed before. She quickly shrugged it off. *Like he said, my brother just got merked. Who wouldn't be a little paranoid?*

"You're limping. What happened?"

"Minor sprain while shooting hoops," he lied, feeling the pain come alive like a fire breathing dragon. Roy refused to pop another *Vicodin*; it had him feeling doped up. Sonny recommended he try *Percocet* as an alternative, but he refused. Popping pills was never his forte, and the last thing he wanted to do was create a habit. He turned towards the *All Purpose* bottle of Hennessey, grabbed it.

"I need stacks. Moms need this new treatment, and I got a funeral to pay for. I'm hurting right now. And since I'm not the type of bitch to ask for no loan, I was wondering if you could point me in the right direction."

Direction: A route to the money bags. She needed the golden path, the precise obstacle course that would lead her to a name, address to where the loot was stashed, and perhaps he'll give her the green light to murder everything moving.

Roy rubbed his chin, looked deep into her eyes. "There is this one thing."

She sat erect, posture straight as a board. She outted her smoke, cleared the fog from in front of her face. Mocha skin still wet, but now attentive, alert, and ready to pump a hole in somebody for the loot. "Where da cash at?"

"Be easy. There's this party. High rollers, big wigs, big money, in one room, at one time. I can use the extra muscle to make sure shit runs according to schedule."

"When?"

"Now."

"Let's go."

"Chill. First and foremost, there are rules."

"Point. Shoot. Kill. What other rules are there?"

"Just be sure to shoot the right motherfucker."

"I'll be sure to keep my aim away from you." She giggled, but Roy didn't see a damn thing funny. Maybe Lou-Lou was right. Maybe she wasn't the chick to trust, especially now that her family was sitting on ice. He noticed that bugged-out-look in her eyes. Same look her brother Ace wore as he stood over Lou-Lou pointing the barrel to her head.

"Damn. I'm joking. Can't you take a joke?"

He rubbed his head. "Fuck the jokes. Listen, and listen carefully. This score belong to Lou-Lou. Her connect, her operation, her rules."

As Roy filled Kema in on the specifics, her eyes grew to the size of dinner plates. He was granting her an opportunity to line her pockets with some fresh Benjamin's. She would have enough to pay off her mother's treatment, and lay her brother to rest honorably. She looked around the small kitchen, finding all sorts of wrong, on all sorts of levels. She needed to reinvest in her grandparents house, fix it up, and make it look like new.

"I'm cool with that," Kema assured.

"I hope so. Make no mistake about it; Lou-Lou's a fucking beast about her bread. Don't ask any questions; just do as I say, when I say."

***

Marijuana smoke billowed from the Vette. As much as Roy despised the fact, he allowed her to distress the best way she knew how. He had no problems with her puffing, but Kema had turned into a straight up pot-head. Her sudden addiction to the *Kush* made her unattractive. He preferred his woman to puff joints, not blunts. He preferred they smoked *regular* weed, not *Kush*. The fact that Kema stayed with a freshly rolled *Dutchy* made her unsexy. She faced forward, in complete silence. Her only act of movement was when she extended hand to and from her mouth to pull vigorously on her medicine.

"Where we headed?" she asked, blowing circles.

"Up north. Alpharetta."

"*Alpha.Retta.* That's big money talk."

"Big money, walk with big protection up in those parts. Don't let that weed cloud your vision. Be on point."

She looked at her burning bush, chuckled as if the mind altering drug didn't faze her.

"My trigger finger flexible."

You should have told me, Roy thought to himself as he eyed Kema from his peripheral. Lou-Lou's hidden agenda's had him in a crunch, a messed up predicament. It felt like déjà Vu all over again. He'd been here before. Having to lay one of his people's kin folk down wasn't the best feeling, but shit had to be done.

Kema was his young pit-bull, a great companion, his watch dog who kept her nose to the ground, and her eyes on them jack boys. She would bite a motherfucker quick fast and in a hurry. No questions asked. Roy loved that about her. Now, their future together was bleak.

"There's a .38 in the glove compartment. Don't hesitate to use it."

She opened the compartment, grabbed the tool, closed and locked the latch. She held the heat in such a way that told him she was about to murder everything in sight.

"Have... my... fucking... back." His words were spaced deliberately.

She turned to look at him. "Always."

Dark circles covered her eyes. They were drained of all emotions, except hate. She made no attempt to shield, cover, and mask what would happen to such individuals who played a part in her brother's murder.

They would all pay.

CHAPTER 39

The required sit down fee was a quarter of a million. Two hundred and fifty thousand a head just to step foot inside a Pokers Paradise. Bradley came through as promised. He'd managed to pull together a circle of high rollers in less than three days. The white boy was a genius. The more Lou-Lou watched Bradley shake hands with the wealthy, the more she respected him. He still had it. He was still the man.

At the center of the Atrium was a fountain. Large naked sculpture spit water, moving colorful lights, and Koi fish swam. Surrounding that were poker tables, a bar, and true die hard gamblers. Lou-Lou sauntered from table to table, flashing her Colgate smile, air smooching the small elite crowd. Dressed in a short black cocktail dress, and sexy studded stilettos, hair swept back into a diamond clip made her look less like the cold hearted bitch she really was.

Across the room she spotted Bunny hugged up with her new catch of the week. She and Double Chin Charlie from Wichita seemed closer than closed. Lou-Lou tossed her a head gesture, smiled. Bunny winked her fake lash, knowing she just came up on a big time baller.

"Hello, I'm Lou-Lou."

"I'm Janet, this is Mary, guess where outnumbered by all the testosterone."

Janet was from Aspens. She had a big nose, thin lips, and sparkly grey eyes with dirty brown hair. She was born into wealth. Her daddy's daddy had old money, and her biggest dilemma of the day was which designer purse to drape her shoulder. She knew nothing about making money, but specialized in how to spend it.

Mary was from Denver, a self made millionaire. A woman of poise, class, and one not afraid to get a little dirt beneath the nails. Everything she got, she earned. She was slender, athletically built, chiseled somewhat like a man. She was a bit more seasoned, humble, and didn't hesitate to speak her mind.

"We met in Vegas some years back. At the Venetian. You were Bradley's new thing." Mary said, glancing Lou-Lou from head to toe.

Lou-Lou flashed a grin. How young and naive she was back then. Before she came along there's was no telling how many "new" things Bradley had glued to his hip.

"I'm solo these days. Bradley and I are just..."

"Just what?"

He kissed the nap of her neck, made her shudder. Lou-Lou side stepped Bradley, providing enough space between them. He gently grabbed her arm, jerking her back where she belonged. *Ass to dick.*

"Now *Bradley*, I know you didn't let this one get away?" Mary asked, now looking at Lou-Lou with a set of promiscuous eyes. Her pupils shamelessly roamed her frame until Bradley cleared his throat.

"We're working out the kinks, right baby?"

"Sure." Lou-Lou smiled.

"If you ladies would excuse us for just a second."

Bradley grabbed Lou-Lou's hand and he led the way. Off the atrium was a room wrapped in intricate gold swirly wall paper. Heavy wood desk, high back leather swivel chair, oversized chaise lounger with fudge colored throws, and a fully stock bar. Authentic Persian rugs, elegant crown molding and high baseboards created an ambiance of sophistication.

"Step inside."

"Why, what for?"

"Because I asked you to," he said, holding the door open with one hand. He looked serious. Too damn serious.

She stepped in. "We got money on the table. What's so important?"

"I know what you're up to, and I'm here to tell you the shit ain't going down."

She kept her game face, but controlling the heart was a different story. It beat like a symphony full of African children playing for their next meal.

"What do you mean?"

"What do you mean?" he mocked.

"You know exactly what the fuck I mean."

Silence passed between them. Her .22, latched at her thigh. She didn't want to, but she would let one off, rattle his brain just to secure the pot of gold. The pot, behind that door, in the atrium, was full of investors. She would send one to his melon with no hesitations. Bradley took a seat, crossed his leg, awaiting her confession.

Fuck! The jig was up. He knew, but how? She thought of putting one in his wig right then and there, but the noise would travel, create chaos. She had to keep his mouth shut, just until she gave Roy the green light to move in.

"You think I'm so fucking dumb. I knew what you were up to the moment we walked through the door. I saw the way you were eye-balling..."

She grabbed the collar of his shirt, brought his face inches away from hers. He could smell the vapors from her cool mint bubble gum. Her cold stare made him snap into attention. Just hours ago she'd been covered in blood, dirt, and twigs, packing heat. Now, she was just as vicious, in a dress, with her knee jammed against his nuts.

"Keep your damn mouth shut and you walk outta here the way you came."

"Is it that important to you?"

She released him. "You have no idea how important this is to me. I need this."

He blinked twice, laughed. "Damn, I wish I would have known you were that passionate about girls. I would have brought one home a long time ago."

"What?"

"*Ah C'mon*, I saw the way you were looking at Mary. She likes you, and you like her. All I'm saying is the shit ain't going down without me."

She collapsed onto the chaise, released a sigh of relief and laughed. *He thinks I'm Bi-Curious. Now that's some funny shit.*

"You want to try it, I understand, but don't forget about me. I'll play my part, and make sure everyone is satisfied."

She laughed so hard her stomach hurt. His mind was made up; she was interested in women, this he was sure of. It made no sense explaining otherwise, so she went along with his absurd assumption.

"I wouldn't dream of experiencing my first time with a woman without you."

"Good."

Back inside the atrium, all tables were full. Money was in full rotation. Drinks were flowing generously. Music was at a comfortable level. Player's concentration zeroed in on each other. The Takumi Brothers had everyone shitting their pants. Lester Patel from Tulsa and Sterling Malone from Palm Beach kept betting for the come-up.

Joey and his brother Antonio were beginning to get a bit too rowdy at the bar. The hired barmaid was obviously under a lot of pressure dealing with those two Guido's from the Bronx.

"Fellahs, how are we enjoying the festivities?" Lou-Lou asked in her sexy voice.

"Doing better now that you're here," said Antonio, turning his attention towards the center of her chest. A considerable amount of cleavage poked out the top of her dress.

"Yo' Antonio."

"Ye."

"Don't catch a fucking Barzotto you meat head," said Joey, slapping his brother across the back playfully.

Joey and Antonio were Bronx style millionaires, born into organized crime. Since their pops got charged with the RICO Act, they've been spending most of their inheritance in Vegas. Betting high, and wining just the same. Since no one was foolish enough to challenge their authority, they *always* made a killing. Joey was the brain, Antonio, the muscle.

"Yo' Joey."

"Ye."

"You think the lady would care for a drink?"

Joey looked over Antonio shoulder, eyes now pointed in the same direction. Lou-Lou held her pose, placing her hand on her hip and smiled. Her cleavage was definitely the conversation piece of the evening.

"I fucking hope so."

Lou-Lou turned her attention towards the bartender. The young girl was obviously intimidated. "Vodka and Cranberry," said Lou-Lou.

She hoped to God the girl had enough sense to hit the floor when shit hit the fan. *Maybe I should relieve her of her duties now. Pay her to get the fuck out and run for her life.* She watched the girl pour liquor over ice, mix juice and stir. *She reminds me of Kosha.* Young, ambitious, and determined to make it. Pouring drinks for a couple of scum bags just to earn a couple of bucks for school beats sliding down a pole any day. But the girl had chosen the wrong gig, at the wrong time.

"You smoke cigarettes?" Lou-Lou asked, just to make small talk with the girl.

"Yes. I'm trying to quit," the girl said shamefully.

"Wanna take a smoke break?"

Tender eyes shifted towards the two Bronx style bullies and back. "Yes, ma'am. More than ever."

"Take twenty. Out back near the pool house, that way no one will spot you puffing."

"Yes, of course. Thank you so much."

With one good deed done for the day, it was now time to pop off like the Fourth of July. As Lou-Lou quickly turned, she accidently bumped into Antonio, spilling her drink all over his shoes.

"*Ah*, see you messed up my Ferragamos," he complained. Antonio was taller, more muscular looking then his brother Joey.

"I'm sorry about that."

Lou-Lou grabbed a stack of napkins from the bar, dropped them at his feet. As she proceeded to walk away, he grabbed her arm. More of her drink spilled over the rim. From across the room she saw Bradley stand in her honor. She shook her head, gave him a look which told him she had everything under control.

"Clean my shoe bitch."

Her mouth curved seductively. *We need to lay this big motherfucker down first*, she thought, glancing up towards the balcony of the atrium.

Roy was in position. She felt his heat pointing down on them. It was settled; the two lasagna niggas would catch it in the Cannoli.

"Let me make my rounds sweet heart. I'll be back over shortly with a nice warm rag." Antonio kissed her hand, and then slapped her on the ass. "I'm holding you to it."

She swayed her hips away from the bar; cell phone in hand. When Roy answered on the first ring, she said, *"One minute."*

Bradley sat regally in the hot seat. He had the wining hand, and everyone knew it. White button down opened at the neck, sleeves rolled up, stopping at his pink elbow. A slow burning Cuban and an untouched glass of brown fluid sat at his right. In front of him, red chips stacked high. He was on fire, in his zone, doing what he set out to do, *rape them for all they're worth.*

Bradley grabbed Lou-Lou's hand as she passed, pulling her into his lap. *No, I don't have time for this.* Her eyes connected with his cards. His hand was unbelievable. She smiled. The boy genius was back. Right hand palmed and squeezed her ass. They both turned a death ear to the loud and boisterous laughter. The sound of money rattled between them. The Art of Seduction working it's number. Bradley slapped his cards down against the table. Pandemonium erupted, but Bradley heard nothing but the music of love. He noticed nothing but her eyes, her nose, her lips. She pressed her mouth against his, for the last time. She pulled away.

"Where you going?" he asked, as she stood and straightened her dress.

"Off to the ladies room."

She stepped away, and proceeded towards the laboratory as planned. She looked up towards the balcony once again. It was dimly lit, but the Devil himself lie dormant like the virus, awaiting the right time to awaken, wreak havoc, and inflict pain. Death. She was in Roy's scope, shielding his intended target.

Don't look back. Don't look back. Don't look back. Against her better judgment, she glanced over her shoulder to see Bradley watching. Her heart clenched hard. She finger waved farewell. As much as she loved the jittery white boy with the periodic coke habit, who loved sipping Crown, he had to perish.

CHAPTER 40

A single shot cracked the air. Bradley caught it in the noodle. Slumped over the poker table, exposing his hand along with his brains. Blood pooling from the wound sent everyone into a frenzy. Chaos erupted, and then all froze as a steady round chopped through the commotion. Sparks flickered as bullets discharged and chewed through drywall. Everyone hit the deck.

North, south, east, and west corners of the atrium were secure. Roy had a wide lens scope on everything moving. Jazzman came from the Butlers Pantry holding two Ninas. Black hoodie pulled tightly around her face, her lips covered in rebellious black lipstick.

"Stay low or die bitch."

Mary froze. Jazzman's boot pressed against her neck, face kissing the marble floors. Janet whimpered and called Jesus. Jazzman's aim shifted across the room, saw movement from her peripheral. As predicted Antonio stood up, rose to the occasion. Bad ass Guido needed to prove himself, uphold his daddy's name as a Billy Badass.

Kema slipped from behind a wall, brandishing a .38 special. Fully loaded, cocked, and ready to rock. She put the burner to his temple, pulled the hammer back. Two hundred and fifty pounds fell in slow motion. Joey's face mirrored pain, but he didn't budge. He stood statue still knowing he would be next.

At the bar, Bunny screamed. She was hysterical in every form of the word. Antonio's blood splashed her creamy white skin. Kema redirected her aim, pointed it at her noggin. Before she would mute Bunny's world, Lou-Lou approached.

"Let her be."

Kema glanced over her shoulder, lip quivering. She watched as Lou-Lou moved about the quarters like the Queen-B. Elegantly dressed, hair flawless, her feet now covered in boots laced to the rim. In her hand was a gleaming AR15. There was no mistaking who was in charge. There were no misunderstandings about who ran shit. This was Lou-Lou's score.

Lou-Lou tossed Kema a Hefty bag, and Jazzman received the oversized duffle. She then ordered everyone to stand and form a single file line. "Empty your pockets. That would include cell phones, wallets, quarters, nickels, dimes and pennies. No funny business or my man will put one in your head." Lou-Lou promised. She gave Kema a once over. *That includes you bitch.*

Roy was her eye in the sky, her overseer, her conflict control. With him looking down on her, she felt invincible, untouchable, she was God.

As Kema collected cell phones and chump change, she watched Lou-Lou and Jazzman handle the real dough. Yet again, she was stuck with the menial task as being servant.

"Now, everyone if you would kindly open your briefcase; dump the cash in the bag."

Each high roller did as they were told. All except Joey, who looked to be contemplating his own suicide mission. He stood tall and unflinching. His hands gripped the handle to the metal briefcase, obviously unwilling to part with his cash. He squared his shoulders and grimaced.

"Open the briefcase Joey," Lou-Lou warned.

"Fuck you, you fucking Mulli." He spat in her direction. Saliva landed on the toe of her boot.

She laughed, and brought the tool to his face. "Joey, don't make me split your head."

His eyes were stern, sharp. A cocky smile formed against his lips. He challenged her with his presence. She was impressed with his will to stay a man, and not squirm. She backed away, and signaled for Jazzman to approach. She whispered something against Jazzman's ear.

"Remember what happened the last time you stopped to play games."

Before Lou-Lou could offer up a justifiable reason to toy with Joey before blacking his world, Kema stepped up to the plate, put the .38 to Joey's head and lullibied his ass. Lou-Lou turned the heat on Kema, pointed it right between her eyes, just the way her brother Ace had done her back at the cabin. A muscle in her jaw spasmed, but she bit back her wrath, smiled.

"Let's go."

***

Outside the mansion on the cemented swivel driveway, the hired barmaid puffed and danced her way in circles. iPOD on full blast. Beats jerked her body all sorts of ways. *The Cupid Shuffle* combined with *Stanky Leg* moves, topped off with *Pop-Lock-and-Drop-It* technique made her wish she was in the club with the rest of her friends.

The pool house was too creepy, and seeing that the party was in full swing, she took her chances with taking her smoke break out front. Besides, everyone had a full drink in hand, and the gaming was intense. No one was coming in or going out for what she assumed to be hours from now. On top of that, she wanted to look at all the expensive foreign cars, and call claim to her favorite ones.

She flicked it up, snapping shots of herself in front of fancy emblems, showing casing her dream cars on FB, Tweeting all her friends, adding fire to all those hating bitches in her Social Network. *"Look at me now."*

Her twenty minute alarm vibrated. "Dang. Times up."

As she took the last puff of her nicotine stick, she saw a group of four moving hastily towards her. She spotted the lady in the pretty dress. The one who relieved her of her workstation for a well needed twenty minute break was no longer smiling. And her Stilettos were replaced with grungy old boots. And the foursome all looked intently at her, but one girl in particular rose her arm, pointing something chrome and shiny in her direction. But the lady in the nice dress, barked some sort of command, but the music was too loud for her to hear. As she yanked the plugs away from her ear, she heard, *"Get down."*

And then a Tahoe pulled up, jerked into an abrupt stop. Three masked men jumped out. The lady with the nice dress, and grungy boots lurched in the young girl's direction, becoming her shield.

Reality rushed through Kema as she felt a slug tear through her side. Down on the cold pavement she heard war echo. Land soldiers eradicating the mission she designed. It was her duty to destroy. An obligation shoved in her lap, which required her to see the demise of all involved.

After Kema left Morrow from visiting her cousin Mike-Mike, she drove in circles. Looping Highway 285, thinking of ways to cope with her sudden despair. She tried calling *LD* again, but no one ever answered. The mysterious *LD* could very well have been the last person to speak with her brother.

Something told Kema to call Mr. Peterson, tell him the news of Ace's recent demise, and to hopefully see if he'd heard or seen any strange activity across the hall. Mr. Peterson's voice replayed in her head. He was certain that Ace left the house accompanied with a young lady, whom introduced herself as Lou-Lou.

"What did you say her name was?"

"Lou-Lou, short for Lou-Ann. It was my mother's name. God rest her soul."

"Are you *sure* she said 'Lou-Lou'?"

"I most certainly am. The police came knocking; I told them the same thing. Gave a description the best I could."

"Thank you Mr. Peterson. Thank you so much."

It was now clear to Kema who *LD* was. Roy had yet to return her call which only confirmed his involvement. Homicidal thoughts were lurking in the back of her mind. She wanted to ruin them all. Make them pay for killing Ace, which is why she had Mike-Mike on standby awaiting further instructions.

***

Guns went off. Bullets whizzed past Jazzman's head. Roy shoved her to the ground as he returned fire. The AR chopped through the air. His intended target: *Anything moving.*

As Jazzman took cover behind a now riddled Maybach, all she could do was pray that nothing touched her. When prayers went up, she hoped that blessings came down.

Roy wasn't about to lie down so easily. Heavy guns boomed and cracked the air. The AR pumped big holes into the Tahoe, surgically tearing into the metal frame, altering its appearance. Three men lay dead on the stone. No mistakes allowed. He had to get home to Sonny, and their soon to be baby. Jazzman had to get home to Jacob and *Lou-Lou*... He whipped his head around, saw Lou-Lou sprawled on top of the girl. His heart stopped. A pool of blood surrounded them. Jazzman released a wail from the pit of her gut that pained his heart.

"*Lou-Lou,*" she screamed, running across the stone, falling to her knees.

"*Lou-Lou,*" Jazzman wept at her side, begging for her to wake up, move.

Sirens were heard blaring from a distance. The Law was definitely closing in. He gripped Jazzman's arm, forced her to her feet. "Get the money bag. We have to go."

"We can't leave her here," she moaned painfully.

"Pull yourself together. We have to go," he said through clenched teeth.

Suddenly, there was movement.

"Not without me."

Relief escaped their lungs.

Lou-Lou was breathing, alive, but they couldn't say the same for the other girl.

***

Lights. Cameras. Action. Helicopters circled above. News reporters were already pushing through yellow tape for the horrendous scoop that would soon rock the Peach State. Police patrolled the city limits like *Saddam Hussein* himself was camped out in some hidden cave.

Roy handled the wheel like a NASCAR Driver.

Lou-Lou and Jazzman stripped down to their bare bottoms, changing clothes, stuffing their old garments into trash bags. Lou-Lou scrubbed splattered blood from her cheek; finger combed her messy hair into a single braid. Both ladies double checked each other for any obvious signs of struggle. A simple nod of approval transferred between the two. Fear in their eyes, and uncertainty on their backs.

The chopper was in the sky scouring Georgia's red clay in search of the threesome. *Breaking News* hit the radio. Every station blared with information concerning the Alpharetta shoot-out. Those presumably dead hadn't yet been identified. Those who were alive were transported to a safe haven for intense questioning. A sketchy description of Lou-Lou came over the wire. Everyone in the car stopped breathing.

"This just in. Fulton County Authorities have released a description on the intended suspect in the Alpharetta shooting that took place just moments ago."

They had height and weight measurements. They had skin tone, hair length, and first name details. And that intricate tattoo that stained her back finally found its way onto a public easel.

"Authorities say that the woman, who goes by the name of Lou-Lou, is considered armed and dangerous. If spotted, do not approach."

Roy turned off the main road, dipped down a lonely residential street. The houses on that block were older, smaller in scale, less glamorous, which was an indication they were almost out of Snootyville. The expressway was across the bridge, *almost home free*, but they wouldn't get far in the getaway van.

They pulled into a small recreation area, which had a couple of cemented picnic tables, grounds to dribble a ball, torn hoop, bleachers, and a deep wooded area that outlined the parameters. From a certain angle they had privacy, but they needed to move quickly and quietly.

Roy jumped out from behind the wheel, and grabbed the money bag. They had no time to count their earnings down to the penny. On the cemented picnic table, he doled a helping to each of them, keeping some for himself. Everyone was satisfied, but now the true test of their wits would show. As a unit, they were strong. Bond unbreakable, unmovable, unshakable, but alone they must go. The question never weighed on who would make it across the finish line first, but more or so who wouldn't.

CHAPTER 41

Kema died three different times, followed by a coma. Doctors kept a close watch on her recovery, as did Detective Olive and Detective Marshall. They needed medical officials to salvage what was left of her.

Ace's murder, stolen military guns, Alpharetta heist, three dead hoodlums outside the mansion, one innocent bystander, all linked together. The future of their case depended on the once snappy, sassed mouth Kema, who now looked deflated with tubes running everywhere.

"She's off the ventilator," said Detective Marshall

"That's a good thing. When she comes to, I'll be right here waiting," said Detective Olive with a slight snarl.

"She knew all along, but didn't tell us. Why?"

Detective Olive looked up from her iPhone, laughed. "Revenge is mine, saith the Lord."

Two weeks later, Kema's eyes parted. A hopeful Detective Olive pounced to her feet, and immediately dove in with an arsenal full of questions. Detective Marshall requested that she back off, give Kema a moment to find her voice, adjust her blurred vision. They needed her coherent, fully aware of what she was thinking, saying, doing. Her testimony needed to hold up in a court of law. They needed a concrete confession.

To their surprise Kema clenched her fist. Her eyes partially open. The lights were on, someone was definitely home. She was back!

After a twenty-four hour evaluation, the doctors permitted the detectives to speak with Kema about the night in question. Detective Olive, as usual cut straight to the chase.

"You have the right to remain silent. Anything you say can and will be used against you in a court of law. You have the right to speak to an attorney. If you cannot afford an attorney, one will be appointed for you. Do you understand these rights which have been read to you?"

She nodded.

"Is that a yes or a no, Ms. Anderson?" Detective Olive asked sharply.

"Yes. I understand."

Detective Marshall asked, "How are you feeling?"

"Like shit."

She felt the bag on her hip. Doctors told her she would need to wear an ostomy bag for the rest of her life. Her reservoir bag was put in place to capture her urine and bowel movements. It adhered to her quite easily, and required changing regularly. Watching the nurse change, and properly dispose of her bodily fluids made life not even worth living.

"I shit in a bag."

Neither detective said a word. They couldn't began to assume what that felt like. Life as she knew it was forever changed. Kema stared at the recorder which sat at her bedside. They wanted her to tell a story, drop names, close their case, and make them the hero. They wanted recognition, perhaps a picture on the front cover of the Atlanta Journal Constitution.

They left me to die.

Roy's lethal hand was underestimated. Shots rang out. Screams echoed, followed by more shots. The bang the metal kicked out shook parked vehicles, triggering alarm systems. In the still of the night, sparks lit up the city of Alpharetta from one determined trigger finger. Roy inflicted punishment, demanding respect. Mike-Mike and his goons never stood a chance.

Leafless trees swayed as she looked towards the black sky. The air chilled her skin as blood oozed from her side. Roy stepped over her body without so much as checking her pulse. *You assumed I was dead.*

He didn't care about her, never did. So, why should she care about him? Detectives needed names and faces, and if she didn't answer the question properly she would be their sacrificial offering. They had her at the scene of a crime, hefty bag full of cell phones, wallets, a murder weapon, two bodies inside, four bodies outside, and a gang of folks tied with plastic flexi-cuffs.

"I'll talk, but what can you promise me?"

The detectives looked at each other with a triumphant smirk buried beneath their cheeks. Detective Olive popped the tab to an energy drink, slurped red caffeine, and said,

"What do you want?"

"To go home, no jail time."

Detective Marshall chuckled. Every criminal wanted to go home, walk away from bad decision making. "Impossible request, you will do time, but the deciding factor depends on how much information you tell. If your story is solid, and doesn't fall to pieces in a court of law, then you will see the light of day again. If you give us shit, we give you life, possibly the chair."

She understood the ground rules, and knew what she had to do. Roy, Jazzman, and that bitch Lou-Lou were going down.

Roy, you thought you were so slick. Giving that fat bitch my watch was a mistake.

Kema thought back to that day Sonny entered her world. Her eyes lit up whenever she spoke of her man. Twinkled in delight, mesmerized by his strength, his sexy coolness, hot love making. There was no denying the big girl loved her some Roy. She probably loved him just as much as she loved cake.

That watch was rare, and cost an arm and a leg, so naturally Kema examined the back of the ticker. Her initials were engraved. Putting the burner to Sonny's cheek was her first choice, but then old man Carlson came to mind. *He'll finger my ass in a line up willingly if she doesn't show up for work in the morning.*

Sonny should have heeded the old man's advice, and not allowed Kema inside her car. She did have sticky fingers, and would swipe almost anything if the opportunity presented itself. *Put your mail in a safer place next time you fat bitch.*

Kema possessed Sonny's power bill, which had her physical address printed. A wedding invitation, sat un-opened from a Connecticut address. *Your moms live in Hartford, and she's getting married. How sweet.*

Kema wet her dry lips, wondering where she would begin. All she had on Lou-Lou and Jazzman was a first name, but she did have that cell number locked under *LD*. Maybe the detectives could form a trace, locate them through other channels. *I'm sure you used that burn-out to call Jazzman, and Jazzman called Roy, and the detectives will be able to connect the dots.*

Mr. Peterson would also testify. She was sure of it. And the evidence in her bag, she needed to turn that over. The map, receipts, route schedule, all put away in a safe place. *I knew it would come in handy. Just didn't know when.*

Detectives would need to gain access to the old cabin in Locust Grove, dust for prints, dig for clues. Stolen AR15's didn't just disappear within thin air. There was a buyer, but who? And lastly, there was Flap's murder. Detectives would love to wrap their grimy fingers on that case file.

Roy was the brain. He orchestrated it all. I'll show the detectives where they abandoned the rental. Jazzman was the getaway driver. Lou-Lou canceled Flap for the drugs and money. This should be enough information to set me free, or at best reduce my time to less than five years.

Besides, I'm the victim. Roy made me do it. He threatened my life, and threatened my poor sickly mother. He took advantage of me. I was young, and came from a broken home, and my mother has cancer, and I watched my daddy die from a bad liver, and my brother was a loon, with a bullet that rattled his brain. Because of the war... yes... the US Army ruined my family dynamics, made us all crazy. Yeah, that's it. I'm the victim. That's my story and I'm sticking to it.

Detective Olive pressed the record button, introduced herself, her partner, and the subject who would divulge information concerning criminal activity, *murder.*

CHAPTER 42

The package from FedEx rested between the windshield and dashboard. Inside the medium sized envelope were fake passports, birth certificates, driver's licenses, all with legitimate and officiated seals and stamps. Sonny grabbed it, shook it, and tore the tab across the top.

She held the driver's license to the light, examined the hologram markings; high resolution lines, perfect shade of ink, wave patterns, sharp micro text, encrypted detailing on the front and back, all security features in place. Authentic looking.

"Shit. Roy, I'm nervous. I mean, what am I going to do in Europe?"

"Thought you always wanted to go?"

"Yes. It's a childhood dream of mine, but not like this. Not on the run from US officials. I mean, shit, I have to become this new person. This... this... Camille Simone Laurent."

He smiled. "Sounds so French doesn't it?"

"Roy, I'm serious."

"*Shush*. I'm no longer Roy. Get into habit of calling me Elijah Noel Laurent. This is who I am now; this is who you must address me as. Roy is dead."

"Okay, Elijah, What if I'm pregnant? Will my baby have this *Laurent* as their last name? What if we have to abandon Europe, move to another continent, and become someone else, adopt another last name?"

He pointed towards the package. "There's more. We can drop Laurent if for some reason we feel the heat. Mr. & Mrs. Clarion, Barker, Murphy, Owen. Everything's there. My guy assured me these documents will stand up to the sharpest eye of scrutiny."

She grabbed the package, dumped the remaining four encrypted officiated documents with authentic stamps and seals from other countries onto her lap. Student visa, passport, marriage certificate made her pause. The thought of never becoming his wife, legally made her panic.

"What will happen to my baby's identity, my identity? My music?"

For heaven's sake, my music. What would become of it? Would she be an artist who never got their true time to shine? Would she be discovered fifty years later at the bottom of a crate by some bubbling eighteen year old rifling through his grandparent's belongings on the wake of their funeral? What about her father's saxophone? *I should have at least gone back home for it.* What about her mother? She'll never get a chance to be a grandma. Concern rested on her face, making her haggard, old.

"Stay."

"No. I'm going."

"Sonny, listen. This is all too much. I'm on the run, not you. What kind of life will that be for a baby, for you? I was selfish to even consider this."

"Camille, remember?"

"What?"

"You called me Sonny. My name is Camille Simone Laurent."

One thing was for sure, he needed to leave the country. Having her by his side was just the icing on the cake. But at the end of the day, she would have to become whoever he said she was. He did love her, but staying would only pose more harm than good. He'd done too much, laid too many fuckers down to stay.

"I stand corrected."

Roy made it out of Alpharetta by the hairs on his chinny-chin-chin. The old school Corvette was parked a half a block away from the recreation area. So far all was going according to plan, except there was one thing missing. His heart just didn't beat without her. He needed balance, needed *Ylang Ylang*, needed her soulful voice humming tunes and singing the blues, and loving him to no end.

Roy floored the pedal and headed South on Highway 75.

"But Roy, I can't just leave work. My shift doesn't end for another four hours."

"Listen, you need to leave now. Don't go to the house. Meet me at the Chick-fil-A on the corner of Eagles Landing Parkway in one hour."

"What's this about? Are you hurt? Oh my God, you're hurt. Are you bleeding? Oh my God you're bleeding. Are you..."

"Shut up. Do you love me?"

"Yes, of course. What kind of question is that?"

"If you love me like you say you do, trust me when I tell you, you need to leave work now. Don't go home. Don't stop for anything. Meet me in one hour, at the Chick-fil-A, corner of..."

"Eagles Landing Parkway. I got it."

He snapped out of his train of thought as they approached the ticketing booth at Hartsfield Jackson International Airport. The Delta attendant asked for their passports. She started to sweat profusely, and slightly hyperventilate. She leaned against the counter for support.

"Mrs. Laurent, are you okay?" the lady holding the passports asked.

"I'm... I'm okay. Just a little sick."

Mr. Laurent patted his wife's stomach, kissed her flushed cheeks. "Morning sickness."

The lady clasped both hands together. "Well, congratulations to you both. Here are your boarding passes. Enjoy your stay."

Getting through customs was a breeze. The Laurents slipped through TSA with just the clothes on their back. No luggage to tie them down or hold them up at checkpoints.

"What will we do for money?" Camille whispered, when Elijah returned with Ginger Ale, and salted pretzels to ease her upset stomach. Her concerns were legitimate, and the fact that questions hadn't risen sooner was just a clear indication that she loved him beyond limitations.

Camille wasn't hung up on materials, fabrics, designer bags and scarves. She wasn't a label whore, and didn't require the soles of her feet to click and clack with each step. Her love for Elijah over powered dollars and cents, but every woman needed security right?

He stared intently at her; surveying her eyes, her nose, her mouth. He wondered how their baby would blend their features. A baby girl with her mother's innocence, love for music, desire to stay in harmony and peaceful. Or a boy, who from birth already would know to stare a person in the eye when addressing them. A boy who would always trust his own judgment, and never be taken advantage of. Or one of each, to complete them would be perfect.

"Let's just say we have plenty."

She sipped, belched. "What's plenty?"

"More than you can ever imagine."

Since his abrupt disappearance five years prior, Roy invested, saw return on his investments, and reinvested the invested, tripling and quadrupling his funds. He'd become a cash cow. Everyone wanted to represent him, have their greasy palms on his portfolio. But he trusted only one person. White boy Bradley was a genius. The Einstein on Wall Street. The Master of *Know-How*. He was very savvy, skillful, with the knack for turning small money into big money. Big money became a fortune.

She laughed. "You're saying we're rich?"

"Rich and wealthy, two different worlds."

The smile on her face flattened. "Which of the two categories do we fall in?"

Within five years, Bradley performed miracles. He'd managed to take Roy's drug money and flip it, multiply it, divide it into funds that grew even in the worst economy in US History. Bradley had a trusted face. He represented White America, and played risky with Roy's capital.

But their thriving relationship hit a speed bump when Bradley's obsession for Vegas grew. His coke habit, combined with Lou-Lou's need to have more designer shoes, bags and custom made jewelry, forced him to dip into funds, steal money to support his lifestyle. There was no question that Roy would black his world. It was just a matter of when. Timing was everything. Stopping Bradley's clock meant putting Lou-Lou in a bind, and he refused to trouble her waters. But when Bradley lost his job at the firm, he already knew that his time had come.

"But how?" Camille asked.

"How is not important. Just know money is the last thing you need to worry about."

In the air, Camille nestled closely against Elijah, thinking of what life would bring them. Good fortune, a healthy baby, peace and happiness on earth. Uncertainty rested on Elijah's shoulders, and as a man that kind of pressure came with the territory. Elijah was born to overcome and transcend above the haters. He was made to fly below the radar, maintain a presence of power, and at all costs stay humble. He was crafted to flex his muscles when needed, not when provoked. Only fools jumped off the ledge without assessing all possibilities. But when it came to her, he'd leap head first.

All in the name of love.

CHAPTER 43

After Jazzman returned home from whatever rock she'd crawled out from under, Tony cornered her. He demanded answers. Straight forward answers. He went in on her seconds after she stepped through the door, looking and smelling like *Who did it and ran.*

"Where the fuck have you been, and why didn't you call?"

"Boy, move out my damn way."

"I'm not moving until you answer the damn question."

She shoved him, and without thinking he shoved her back. She slapped his face. He slapped her back. She clenched her fist tightly, so did he, even went as far as squaring his shoulders. She was shocked beyond words. Tony was many things, but abusive, *never.*

"Get your shit, and get out."

"Fuck you. I ain't going nowhere."

She planted both fist against her hip, rolled her neck. "Oh really?"

"Really."

"Stay right there. I got something for that ass."

"If you're looking for the Nina. I've got it."

Jazzman ran up the steps, stopped at her room. A tornado struck. Clothes, shoes, and papers littered the floor. She stepped over her mink, headed towards the closet. She picked through sweaters, and pants, and purses, and hats, and, and, and...where was it? Her chest got tight. She knelt down, found her breath.

"Looking for this?" he asked, taunting her with the manila envelope.

Oh God, he opened it. She gasped and fell to her bottom. He tossed the papers in her face. They fell upon her like confetti.

"You scandalous bitch."

"Tony, wait..."

He stopped, jaw twitching in rage. "Keep your fucking voice down. My son is asleep."

In her house, under her roof, she got checked. On her feet she begged him not to leave, to give her a moment to explain. The last thing she wanted was for him to jump to conclusions and assume awful things. Tony turned a deaf ear to her pleas and receded back down the steps.

She found him inside the kitchen, pacing.

"Yo, don't fucking touch me."

"Tony, just listen to me for a second," she cried with real tears, but he didn't care.

"You hate me?"

"If your ass was on fire, I wouldn't throw water."

Obviously livid, and beyond reasoning, she backed off, gave him some space. Tony never laid a finger on her, even when she probably deserved it. This was a "new" low for him, for her too.

He slammed a closed fist against the broom closet door more times than she could bear witnessing. She covered her ears with her shaky hands, pleaded with him to stop. Blood spread across his knuckles.

"I asked you if something happened between you two and you said..." He swallowed his rage, but a vision of Wayne fucking Jazzman entered his brain and he lost it. He tipped the fridge, and it, along with all its contents went crashing to the floor.

"We never fucked."

He pulled in his bottom lip, clenched his fist. "Keep lying to me and see what happens."

She backed away, afraid of what he might do next.

"*Please*, stop. Listen to me. He was in Atlanta opening a Subway, and he came through, checked up on us like you asked him to. We went to lunch a couple times. Wasn't no harm in it, but he started coming to Atlanta often, on business. The Subway was doing well. He was looking

196

to expand, open up two more restaurants. He was even contemplating a McDonald's at one point."

She stopped talking, noticing his knuckles. She tossed him a dish towel.

"Atlantic Station was a new development. It was booming with pricy condos, restaurants, shops, even a big movie theater. I mean the place was spectacular." She realized that her voice carried a tune of excitement, so like always, she toned down her enthusiasm, made situations seem ordinary for the sake of him.

"We met there, at Atlantic Station. He wanted my opinion on a spot to lease for the Subway, and I thought it would be a wise move."

He grunted.

"He presented me with an opportunity to run it."

He folded his arms. "Go on."

"With him living in New York, and me, already living in Atlanta, he felt that I would be ideal for the job. At first I told him no. I had better things to do than make sandwiches. So, he offered me a deal I couldn't refuse."

"Go on."

She tugged at her sleeve, fidgeting and moving nervously.

"He needed a business partner. Wayne couldn't be in two places at one time. So...I accepted. I mean, I would have been a complete fool not to right?"

"Yeah whatever."

"C'mon, he invested his money. *So did I.* Supervising kept me in the loop of how much money was coming in, and let me tell you we have prime location. Atlantic Station is where it's at. But then I had to leave Atlanta."

"Why'd you leave?"

Damn, what is it with everyone wanting to know why I left? Can't a bitch just decide to leave, come back to her roots? Fuck! She inhaled deeply.

"Never mind why I left, just know Wayne and I are just business partners."

He stared at her long and hard. He wasn't sure what to believe. They both lied about seeing and talking to each other. Had he not ransacked her room and found the documents, he would have never known. Copies of the business license, lease agreement, and insurance papers lined the inside of the envelope.

"And that's another thing. Why the hell are you carrying a million dollars worth of insurance on Wayne?"

"Because we're partners. We're both financially vested in this venture. If he dies tomorrow, I need to be able to keep that place afloat. It's kind of like a marriage."

He chuckled. "I smell a set up."

"What do you mean?"

"You try'na set my man up. Get him merked for the insurance money."

She sucked her teeth. "Boy you watch way too much television."

He narrowed his eyes in on her. "Yeah, maybe but you've thought it. Bet that."

Tony was right. Jazzman had an easy million on Wayne's head, and deleting him from the picture would allow her to retain full ownership, plus have spendable cash. All her money was tied up in her rental properties, and that damn restaurant, which left her no wiggle room for much more. Wayne will always be a target in her eyes, but burying him now would prove to be insanely stupid. They had good chemistry, a variety you don't often find.

"From what I hear he's got trouble brewing on the home front. His wife just might beat you to the punch."

"*Shit*, which one of them rats got his sperm now?"

He shrugged. "That's that man's business."

She stood, feeling better now that the truth was out. But by the looks of things, she could tell he wasn't through.

"I apologize for putting my hands on you. But you've got to be honest with me. Don't let me find out things this way. I'm not your man, I know this, but we have Jacob to think about. Finding those papers put all sorts of thoughts in my head."

"Okay. Fair enough."

"Speaking of your man, he called."

She slapped her forehead. Rick had called her so many times that she'd lost count.

"He never went to Houston with you, which means you've been lying all along."

Busted!

She looked down at her nails. They were dirty. She was dirty.

"Hotel said you checked out."

"Let me deal with Rick, okay." She tried shuffling pass him, but he blocked her way.

"Still running from your past?"

"I don't know what you mean."

"Lou-Lou called the house looking for you."

She looked him dead on. "So."

"And for some reason Jacob swears you're talking to ghost."

"Ghost?"

He looked at her from head to toe. "Jacob said you were talking to Roy."

She rolled her eyes. "You sound ridiculous. Move out my way."

He refused to budge.

"You still haven't answered my question. Where have you been?"

She leaned against the counter. A dizzy spell came over her. She felt nauseated all of a sudden, and the urge to barf had neared.

"Move."

She bulldozed passed him, and headed straight for the bathroom. Both hands gripped the sides of the seat; her face disappeared inside the hole. When she came up for air she noticed him standing in the doorway. Arms folded with a look of disappointment on his face.

"How far along are you?"

She balled into a fetal position on the cold floor. "This can't be happening to me."

It was happening. Jazzman was pregnant, and Tony knew things were about to change. He left, went to the kitchen, fetched a bottled water.

"Drink this."

"Thanks," she mumbled, holding the frigid plastic to her forehead.

"You need to tell him. The sooner the better," Tony recommended.

"I can't."

"Why not?"

"I'm scared to."

"He loves you."

She looked up at him in amazement. He couldn't believe that he'd said those words himself, but he spoke the truth. Rick loved the ground she walked on and for good reasons. Jazzman was a rare jewel, a one of a kind. And Rick, he was her Knight and Shining Armor, the *Safe Choice*.

***

Tony moved out two weeks later. He found an apartment in Hempstead, Long Island, right above a Jewish deli. It was a decent sized one bedroom, with a shabby kitchen. His water almost never turned hot enough, only two burners worked on the stove, and his window wouldn't stay open without wedging something against it for support, but it was affordable.

Jazzman was even nice enough to loan him his first and last month's rent to help him get started. She even gave away her living room furniture, and television to make his transition a comfortable one.

Seeing her happy, made him happy, and that made Jacob even happier. Rick wasn't all that bad once Tony got a chance to talk with him man to man. They weren't best buds, but they were cordial, and kept Jazzman's and Jacob's best interest at heart.

***

Tony had no idea the amount of pussy that was accessible while working as a Professional Trainer. After joining a local gym, he'd noticed that he was in Becky Heaven. The owner, a fine ass redhead by the name of Ginger spotted him lifting, and offered him a job right on the spot.

Within a week Tony had two clients, who he saw on Mondays and Wednesdays. Both he had the privilege of bedding the first session. Word spread like wild fire that the new trainer was Mandingo hung, and before he knew it, it was raining rich white women.

Surrounded by Snowflakes of all shapes and sizes made him feel like a young *Michael Jai White*.

The Becky's threw themselves at him, literally. His buff, athletic build caused quite a ruckus amongst the staff too. The other trainers didn't appreciate his presence, and the sistah's, which by the way were only a handful, didn't appreciate his preference.

Tony was experiencing a new kind of hate. One he'd not been accustomed to, but it beat fighting niggas on the prison yard.

CHAPTER 44

Rick joined Jazzman on the new leather sectional he'd purchased for their home. He insisted that she donated the other sofa, rugs, end tables, lamps and all. They were starting from scratch. With a new lease on life, they had no room for the past to hinder their future. And in Rick's eyes, keeping the furniture her ex man had sat on and ate at, would only serve as a toxic reminder. So, it had to go; all of it.

Rick watched as Jazzman stuffed her face with chocolates, popcorn, and every so often she would reach for her pizza puff and nibble. Her fork hadn't touched the side salad, not even once. She noticed him staring.

"What?"

"You're glowing."

"Am I really?"

"Yes. Can I get you anything else?"

"Nope."

"Which movie do you want to see first?" Rick asked, standing to his feet. He shuffled around the new wood coffee table, and stopped in front of the newly purchased flat screen he'd had professionally mounted.

Jazzman put a fistful of chocolate Reese's Pieces in her mouth. Before she could chew, swallow and respond, Jacob came running down the steps screaming, "Despicable Me!"

"Well, I guess the Prince has spoken," Rick said, easing the shiny DVD from its case.

Jacob nuzzled against his mommy's belly and rubbed it.

"Is he asleep?"

She grabbed his hand, placed it at the center of her protruding stomach. They both sat quietly, without moving an inch. The television boomed as the previews began to roll.

"That sure made him jump."

"It did Mommy. *Wow*. Hi little baby," Jacob said, as he placed his ear to his mommy's belly. He felt life move. The baby's footprints thumped against his ear.

"I bought you new toys today. Soft-ones. Can't wait to see you."

Rick dimmed the lights, and took a seat next to his lady. He draped an arm around her, kissed her forehead.

"Thank you."

She smiled. "No, thank you."

He kissed her ear. "You know, this request of yours is a bit ridiculous."

She looked at him and laughed. Rick refused to leave well enough alone. He was persistent, determined to have his way, *always*.

"Let's fly to Bora-Bora and do it."

"For the millionth time, the answer is no. I'm not about to say my I-DO's looking like a pumpkin. The date is set for next spring. Invitations are already in the mail."

He sighed, "Okay, your wish is my command."

***

Breaking the news to Rick hadn't initially gone so smooth. As anyone could probably imagine, he had some reservations. His scrutiny came like a hail of hollow point bullets. Questions tore into her one after another until she broke.

"Which is it Jazzman, Houston or Atlanta?"

"*Both*. I was in both places. Received a call from the management company I'd hired to oversee my property."

"They said you checked out," he yelled.

"*I was in Houston*, but when the call came in, I left on the next thing smoking."

"What was so damn important that you had to rush to Atlanta on whim like that? Why not fucking call, say something?"

Wait for it.

W-a-i-t –f-o-r- -i-t.

She inhaled deeply, exhaling her fear. She kept eye contact. He needed to see the truth in her, needed to witness her pain. She let one tear fall. "We fought the night before, remember? You told me to *fuck off*, remember?"

He said nothing.

"Investigators suspect arson."

His eyes ballooned. "Tell me you didn't."

"Fuck no. It wasn't me. I believe my tenant did it. She was angry when we last spoke. I threatened to evict her. She threatened to burn the house down. Her words exactly, *I'ma burn this motherfucker down!*" Jazzman demonstrated with pistol arched fingers in the air.

"Yeah, but all black people make that threat. That's a universal threat. People don't really do it, right?"

"Oh please. Your Aunty Binky was arrested for threatening to blow up the Post Office. Who's to say she wouldn't have done it?"

He held back his laughter. "This is true."

"There's nothing left of it. Just a few metal beams and rubbish. My insurance company went out and took pictures."

Part lie. Part truth. That was the makings of a beautiful story. Some truths sounded more dramatic, better woven with little white lies sprinkled here and there. A dash of fib, if proportioned and served at the right moment could shift the dynamics of any story, make it palpable.

The truth was investigators were still digging, poking through charred remains like scientists on a lab rat. A ruling hadn't exactly been made. *Arson, faulty wiring, gas leak.* With the verdict still out, Jazzman could only pray that they ruled quickly, and in her favor.

The lie, the fib, the sham of details that dripped from her lips was applied like a top coat of wax to a vehicle, a fitted sheet against a mattress, a glaze against a donut. It was there to protect, seal the truth, but add a glimmer of hope, comfort, and taste.

"I would love to see those pictures."

She knew that he would. "Yes, of course."

The truth was sour, bitter, likely to place a permanent bad taste in Rick's mouth. *No*, she couldn't tell him that *the ghost of Southside Jamaica, Queens past* came back, and included her in on a heist that rocked Atlanta. *No*, she couldn't tell him she drove the get-away car, where multiple people died in a hail of bullets in College Park. *No*, she couldn't tell him that the ghost who put cheese in her pockets had a thing for her, and she for him. She couldn't mention the Alpharetta hit which almost left her riddled with bullets, but because of her ghost, she'd survived, *yet again*. Roy was the unmentionable. He was dead.

Rick imagined the pile of debris, charred and still smoking. He believed her, besides, Jazzman wasn't capable of pulling something off like arson, or was she? Setting your business, house, and cars on flame wasn't out the ordinary. People did it every day, just to get from under their loan obligation. What made her any different?

He didn't know what to think when it came to her. The woman he'd met on the lawn of Central Park, sitting beneath a tree, with that *really good book* was full of mystery. She intrigued him in a way that no other woman had been able to. She had issues. Baggage. Baby daddy drama. But he still wanted her. *No*, needed her.

"And there's one other thing."

At first Rick just stood in shock. Hands jammed inside pockets, head tilted, eyes at the ceiling. She was pregnant. And he was the father, or was he?

"Is it mine?"

Jazzman bit back her rage. He had all rights to question; even ask for a damn blood test to prove the legitimacy of the child. Who was she to gripe or snap off like some crazy person? She'd allowed Tony, her ex man to come and live in her home. They had close calls, and yes she wanted to feel Tony again, but her love for Rick was undeniably real; strong.

"I assure you, I've been with only one man. And that's you."

"You telling me ya'll never…"

"No. Not even once."

"Marry me then."

***

Despicable Me blared from the surround sound hook-up. Jazzman had her King at her right, and her Prince on her left. And inside of her belly was love, growing, thumping its way into the world.

CHAPTER 45

Lou-Lou left the baby blue Bentley parked on the *South-Economy Parking Deck*. She took a chance with leaving the keys. She'd purchased a nifty *Hide-A-Key-Under-Your-Car-Magnet Case* for just ten bucks at AutoZone. Inside the armrest, *Twenty G's* for her cousin Kosha. She figured a new car, and twenty thousand dollars would be suffice to jump start her college years. She had a free four year ride at Spelman, so tuition would be the least of her worries.

Lou-Lou smirked, knowing her cousin would be the talk of the town. Bitches were definitely going to hate, niggas too, but she knew Kosha was a Dobbs. That alone assured her that her baby cuzz could handle the pressure. She just prayed to God that Kosha followed direct instruction, and changed the color of the Bentley immediately. She had more than enough cash to fade the blue to black, even white; both classic colors.

She moved across the parking lot swiftly. Her leather blazer open, the lapels flapping in the wind. Her blouse, shiny and partially see-through. Her jeans tastefully hugged her hips as she high stepped it across the parking lot in her red bottom Louboutin's. She took purposeful strides as each second counted.

Inside, travelers hustled and bustled to check-in booths, already having an idea of where they were headed. She, on the other hand hadn't given it much thought. She knew Atlanta was no longer an option. The *A*, would be a thing of the past, just as soon as she decided on which way the wind would blow.

Eeny-Meeny-Miny-Moe

The departure board offered a variety of destinations. There were so many places to travel, set roots, become grounded, live a normal life. She laughed to herself. Who was she fooling? She was young, beautiful, paid up the ass, and was looking for her next set of deep pockets.

She lived for adventure. Spontaneity mixed with a little danger would one day find its way onto a page, perhaps she would become a ghost writer. She smiled at the thought of changing names and locations to protect the guilty; fuck the innocent.

Her eyes shifted from one destination to the next. *Arrivals, Departures, Delays*, all glowing and calling her name.

Always wanted to see Fiji.

Life around her was moving.

Time was definitely ticking.

The sun would rise and fall.

And come this time tomorrow –

Lou-Ann Dobbs will be on to the next.

Acknowledgements

Patience. Persistence. Endurance. Staying Power. That's what my loyal readers embody. It's been a long time coming. I've received hundreds of emails, phone calls, text's, social network inquiries regarding the release of this piece of work. With no solid answer to when it would see the light of day, you guys never gave up hope. As life happened around me, but *never* to me, I kept pushing and shoving until "Just One More" was completed.

As I speak to you, my location is my laundry room. HA! I know right, what the heck am I doing here? The energy is lovely, light, and almost aromatic. Could it be the lavender fabric softener? My thoughts seem to flow freely here, and the moment is never taken for granted.

First and foremost I give thanks to God, for without him I'm nothing. Each day offers me a second chance to *live* and not just exist. I refuse to sit on the bleachers and watch the rest play. I'm blessed!!!

My media connects: Big thanks to Editor Tashima Jones (www.tashimajones.com), you're amazingly brilliant. Thanks for touching this project, as well as LM's monthly newsletter. It was a pleasure working with you. Urban Belle, M.U.S.O, and all others, thanks so much for the media write-up! Marion Designs, you did it again. Love this book cover. Marcus, of Nubian Books, you provided a platform for this New Jack to sell-sell-sell. Georgia Public Library's, Thank you. Infinite thanks to all the Book Clubs that selected my debut novel *(The Last One)* as their monthly read (too many to list). Huge thanks to Ms. Tina Hayes of Between-Friends, thanks for being the first.

Those who supported my humble beginnings: I'm grateful for Aunty Earth, and Jamel Howell for placing multiple orders at your day job. How big is that! Dad-In-law you were my first book sale way back when. To my Besty Jo-Diggity, thanks for the video montage on "The Last One", you're super talented. My time traveling friend, Kamilla: We're creatively connected. Connie, because of you Philly is buzzing!

Southside stand up! 40P is always in the building. Big thanks to Carol from C&B. Thanks to Sha-Da God, and the Crew at Hair Cutter's in Jamaica Queens for your purchases. Brenda, thanks for organizing the Bronx book signing. I'm so forever grateful. Harlem World – I see you! Thanks to all the Chi-Town folks who supported my novel.

Mom, your Hustle is so Russell *(In my Jay voice).* Thanks for hitting the pavement with your pulley, *(Inside Joke)* you're a survivor! Dad, you point out the real and the fake. Because of you, I remain authentic. To my Brother Tyrell, thanks for shoving my book in the hands of those none believers. Unconditional love extended to my kids. Mommy loves you like a fat kid loves cake.

To my Super Duper-Wonderful-Sexy-Strong-Gifted-Talented-Patient-Unmovable-Unshakable-Husband: You keep me grounded. You provide an air that's needed to maintain my creativity. When I'm entrenched in my manuscript, and my fingers are banging away at the laptop, you always ask, *which characters life did you ruin today?* LOL... Thanks for being attentive. You understand the kid. This one is for you!

If you haven't already done so, please drop me a note on my Website/Guestbook.

Don't forget to check me out on Facebook!

Best Wishes,
Author LaQuarn Michaels

On to the next...

Website: www.LAQUARNMICHAELS.com
Email: books@LAQUARNMICHAELS.com

About the Author

LaQuarn Michaels is a freelance writer, poet, and author of *The Last One*, and *Just One More*. She was born and raised in Jamaica Queens, New York. Ms. Michaels now resides in Atlanta, Georgia with her husband and children. You can expect more blazing stories from this author.